FEATHERS OF DESTRUCTION

BRITTON BRINKLEY

Feathers of Destruction
Britton Brinkley

Landingham Stanley Press

Author's Note

So as well know, I originally wrote the first book in this series, Feathers of Truth, as part of an anthology. The intent was for it to be a single short book and that was supposed to be the end of it.

Well, obviously you're here, so it wasn't.

First, I'll say thank you for continuing on this journey with me. As many of you know, I love to make my characters go through it. Just hit after hit after gut punch. Feathers of Destruction isn't any different. We might get some more romance in this one and those heartfelt family moments, but we'll get just as much heartbreak, fear, and unrest. The stakes were high in book one, but they're so much higher this time.

The interesting part of this one wasn't the action, but that division between being who you were and who you are now. How to merge those two halves can be a tricky thing. Especially when your past and the things you've done weigh heavy on you. It was fun to explore that for several of the characters this go around.

I likely got a few too many kicks out of writing those twists and turns this time. As an author who claims her characters write their own stories, I was on the edge of my seat, just waiting to see what new shit storm was coming with each new chapter. Our cast grows too. New paranormals we'll all love or hate. Many of them are likely to show up in book three and some secret spin-offs that will be coming down the line.

As a reminder, this is a semi-fictional version of Chicago. Some places are real, some aren't. THIS IS FICTION!

Please don't yell at me for the ending again! Enjoy!

<u>Trigger/Content Warnings:</u>

- Murder

- Guns

- Assault

- Stalking

- Torture

- Death of a Parent

- Crime Scenes

- Blood

- Explicit Sexual Content

- Explicit Language

<u>For the most up-to-date list of content and trigger warnings:</u>

One

Ari

I've died once.

Then I was reborn.

A process that can only be described as an excruciating tearing apart of my insides. Every fiber burnt to ash. The dust barely settled before the grains whipped into a charging vortex. Every microscopic piece welded back together was agonizing torture. What seemed like an endless torment before the bliss of rebirth filled my veins, elevating my being as if I were only the weight of the feathers my phoenix bears.

An experience as terrifying as it was exhilarating. The first test of the limits of my mythological creature.

This death is no match. A growing inferno that never ends. Continuous demolition of my flesh being eaten away by the bullet lodged in the sinew of my chest.

I must be dead. Truly dead. Never to be reborn again. A Purgatory meant for those who have done wrong. Their indiscretions so unforgivable that no right could erase them.

My confinement is payment for every murder. Writhing while screaming out in unimaginable pain, only my ears can hear.

This is my punishment.

This is my curse.

There are no endorphins this time. No sweet release to settle the snaps of my body, breaking apart into the tiniest particles and then rebuilding.

Yet a voice reaches the outer edge of this consciousness. His voice. The deep timbre vibrating in the darkness above me.

Fear smothers each word. Distorting them as the desperation creeps in. Pleas and bargains that will go unanswered.

Adrian Alexander, my pair, would never beg. Just another confirmation death has found me. Just not the peaceful kind others more deserving are graced with.

I'm dead.

I'm dead.

I shouldn't be able to feel his arms around me. Shouldn't be able to curl into the warmth of his breath on my face or the rumble of his growled words through his chest now pressed against my spine.

I'm dead.

The pain is too much. Too intense for me to fight against. The agonizing tearing of my flesh not worth the struggle to stay here with him.

I tried.

I came here to end Salvatore Danarius. An attempt at stopping him before he could dismantle both the human and paranormal worlds beyond repair. Before he can rain down more destruction than we can feasibly recover from.

The goal was to erase the man who used and deceived me. The warlock who put a hit on my parents. My blood.

I tried.

I failed.

Forgive me, Adrian.

In time, my family will freely give that forgiveness. They'll understand I did what I did for all of us. The others will, too. But will Adrian? The man I unknowingly fell for. Will Adrian forgive me for sneaking out in the dead of night to save them all?

Deep down, I know the answer. *No.* He won't. And that knowledge shatters my heart even more painfully than the scorching shredding working its way through me.

I was ready. My finger was already pressing against the trigger when he called my name.

The sole voice capable of diverting my attention in an instant. The baritone voice of the one I realized I couldn't live without. Not in the human world or the paranormal.

My name uttered on his lips is all it took. That single syllable on his lips making me hesitate for a split second. Just enough time for Sal to pull the trigger and put a bullet through my chest.

Murdering me likely meant nothing to Sal. Sure, he'd taken out his prized hitwoman, but I doubt he felt a damn thing as my body collapsed to the floor. Maybe there was even something like relief knowing he'd erased me. It was clear I no longer sat on his side.

I am just a corpse now. Nothing for Sal to worry his pretty little head over anymore.

For me, I linger in this place in between. Each twinge of pain makes me feel like time has stopped. The essence of Adrian keeping me just close enough to feel him. To hear him pleading for me not to leave him. To make it out of this. To come back to him.

My imagination must be stringing the words together in his voice. Or maybe it's this torturous place where I'll remain trapped for eternity, taunting me. Reminding me what I will never have because Ari Luxembohrg once again took matters into her own hands.

I'm sorry, Adrian.

Adrian doesn't need to beg for anything as my parents' second. He is cold. Brutal. Unforgiving. He does not beg, but he is my pair. My other half. A bond between us we didn't choose, but would keep us tethered together even if we never chose one another.

But I choose him with every remaining fiber of my being.

Of course, I would decide such a thing after I'm dead.

Dying.

No, dead.

Whatever I am.

Fuck, it hurts. My insides continuing to burn away against the unique metal nugget that pierced my skin, nestled just above my heart. I can feel it there. Moving with each ever-slowing beat.

Minuscule movements producing disproportionate destruction for such a tiny object.

Until now, I didn't grasp the impact of my bullets on beings like us.

I'm so, so sorry.

My strength weakens. Each pulse of my veins and pump of my heart fading. Slower. Slower. Slower. Weaker. Nearly gone.

My lungs ache. It's impossible to draw breath. To inhale Adrian one last time.

I am losing him.

I am losing my connection to this world.

The surrounding darkness becomes impossibly more inky. Just a blanket of the deepest onyx no matter where I look.

I see nothing.

Hear nothing.

But I feel... everything.

I can't fight anymore. I accepted the risk of coming here tonight. Understood it might be my last and I wouldn't get to say goodbye. I can only hope Adrian won't waste time mourning me. That he'll finish the job I couldn't.

I'm sorry, Adrian.

Two

Adrian

I don't panic. It's not a reaction in my emotional vocabulary, but that's the only term I can use to describe my current state as I cradle Ari's limp form in my arms. Warm blood soaks into my pants and the sleeve of my shirt. A small pool beneath us from the viscous fluid seeping through my fingers.

I should be tearing Salvatore to shreds with my talons. Making him die a slow, torturous death for what he just did. For what he just took from us. From me.

It's not just any bullet nestled in Ari's chest. The dermanium killer eating away at her insides is pulling her further and further from me with every second wasted.

The woman who captured my heart and inspired me to break free from my self-imposed isolation in the dark world of my creation is dying. Sure, a good deal of my time has me at the safe houses, interacting with the leaders of our various species each day, but when I'm not needed I'm home, alone.

It always worked for me. Served me well until this ball-busting woman started following me. Hunting me as she did for so many other targets Salvatore paid her to move out of his path. But I knew the moment I first saw her, she was my pair.

That night I found her huddled in the dark outside my home nearly broke my resolve. It took every bit of control not to sink my teeth into her supple skin the second I dragged her into my kitchen. Fingers wrapped around the column of her throat, those defiant midnight eyes narrowed at me. I wanted to mark her even then.

I shouldn't have desired those things, but not much rivals a pair bond. Little can stop you from yielding to those impulses. Willpower often isn't enough.

That moment I touched her marked a point of no return. An invisible thread inside me linked to her grew taut, glowing brightly with new life. The golds, reds, and oranges of her being swirling with the cobalt and cerulean of mine.

There'd been a change in the way she looked at me after that. It was clear in her eyes she felt something inside her change. But I knew she wasn't raised in our world. She didn't know how these things worked and I called myself being a gentleman by keeping my distance.

I fought it every step of the way. Chopping away ruthlessly at that thread. Determined to block the pull toward her.

She's the daughter of our leader. I'm sworn to protect her. To protect them. Not to mention, she has been mercilessly killing our kind for years with utter disregard.

For that alone, I should hate her, but I can't. In truth, did I ever?

Watching every moment with Ari flash behind my eyes fills me with unimaginable regret. Now I wish I could take that all back. Take back my leash of control. Revisit the moments she'd asked me to take her, to make her mine.

If I could go back, I would. All I want is to erase the lost time and the painful expression on her face that I've been staring at for who knows how long. *No*, I need it.

This courageous, unphased woman changed me. Saved me. Yet, there's nothing I can do for her right now.

Ari has no fear. Never. That's the woman I fell in love with.

My thoughts return to the man who did this to her. My focus should be on bringing him to his knees and then ending his life. But I can't let her go. My hands literally refuse to leave her body. Not until the physician arrives. Not until I know the use of my healing tears will do something productive.

Should she survive, my only gifts for her are the priceless tears of my bloodline and my devotion. There's nothing left for me but her.

Salvatore's laughter pulls my focus from the haunted features of her face for the first time in countless minutes. Hours. Days. I couldn't tell you how much time has passed. The concept of time passing me by as I stew and pray to gods that don't exist, so she lives.

Laughing eyes stare back at me as his thin frame leisurely slouches against the couch cushions. Legs crossed as if he has not a care in the world, he chuckles.

Why would he? I'm playing my role perfectly. Broken pair on the verge of making an irreversible decision while Ari dies in my arms. Maybe she's already dead. The blood flow is so slow now, I'm sure it means that the heart of hers — the one I adore so much — has stopped.

For a moment I wonder if she possesses a similar magic to her father Lanham James, the warlock who rules alongside her mother Syriah James — a phoenix, like us — that will freeze her in time. Preserve what bit of life force still exists within her. A chance at saving her.

My tears can mend, but they have limits. Limits I refuse to consider.

"How does it feel?" Salvatore's taunt is like a punch to the gut. Like flaying my skin from my body. The loss is unimaginable. He must know that.

"I. Will. Kill. You." The words spewed past my lips in a rabid snarl.

I mean each one. With all my being.

If Ari weren't in my arms, I'd be on him, tearing his flesh from his bones with my talons and teeth. I'd do a lot more than engage in this fucking staring match, but I can't let her go. If I release her from my grasp, she'll slip away. I'll never see her again. Even my tears and prayers cannot bring her back with that bullet burrowing deeper and deeper inside her if the doctor can't get it out.

Shouts drift from the stairwell behind me. Voices I recognize. Those I trust calling out to, but the words won't come. Each one lodged in my throat since voicing my threat.

"We'll see about that." Salvatore's cheeky grin is the trigger for my lips to curl back forcing me to bare my teeth. Each one elongating in a split second, the tips biting into my lower lip. The normal smooth curves now the pointed daggers of my phoenix. "Such a pity. That one…" His hand flitting in Ari's direction. My jaw flexing with enough tension to burst a vessel. "She was such a promising study. It's no matter. Another time, then, Firebird."

Our species voiced as nothing more than a curse on his lips.

Just as Tucker James, Ari's younger brother, and Willam Gruchio, our "on-call" physician, angle themselves through the doorframe behind me, Salvatore stands. Those long thin fingers straightening the lapels of his gaudy metallic gray suit jacket, as if he didn't just murder one of the most important beings of the paranormal world.

Willam already has his bag wide open, hands guiding the scissors through Ari's clothing, pulling my gaze away from Salvatore. Each slice stripping away the dress she'd looked so tempting in. A fitted number I would have loved to peel off her body tonight.

As her bare skin hits my palms, its slight warmth allows me to inhale. That sucked in breath burning my expanding lungs.

She's not dead. Not yet. My pair is still here.

"Keep fighting. Please, Ari," I whisper before finally releasing her to Willam.

I need her phoenix to survive this. To be reborn.
If she doesn't... neither will I.

Three

ADRIAN

Chaos erupts as one of Salvatore's cronies charges Tucker from behind, spearing him to the ground. His roaring shaking the walls as he twists in the hulking werewolf's grasp. The man may be in his human form now, but there's no missing the telltale wet dog scent werewolves often carry.

The snapping of bone and tissue vibrates through the space. The thunk of flesh and bodies pounding on one another thunderous in our ears.

Yet none of it distracts Willam from his task. He's been doing this for hundreds of years. A creature accustomed to frontline action, performing miracles without dying in the process.

Tearing my eyes away from Ari's still form, my gaze locks on Salvatore once more. His frame slightly angles away from us, looking down over the edge of the railing before slowly swiveling his head in my direction.

His eyes, once brimming with confidence, now hold something else. The haze fleeting as his mask slips back into place.

A slow, devious grin spreads. His thin lips stretching unnaturally wide. Those long fingers curling just a fragment tighter around the metal bar.

Just as he adjusts his footing, ready to launch himself over the edge, a glimmer of the witch's shield ripples. *Fuck,* it should have been easy to spot, but I'd been distracted.

Below, a sleek wall displays moving lights. Yet inside this room, there's nothing but open air and Salvatore is fitting to jump. Hand braced against the shimmering black metal rail, his eyes narrow as Tuck throws the guard off him, chest heaving, eyes alight with the internal flame of an apex predator.

It's my only chance. My one shot to avenge that woman who was willing to risk it all for us.

I charge Salvatore, fingers fisting in the fabric of his jacket to pull him closer before my free hand squeezes around the column of his slender neck. Feet dangling several inches above the ground, I snarl in his face.

Still, he smiles down at me. No visible sign of discomfort in his expression. He should be terrified of the rage inside me. The hurt roars to the surface at what he's done. An outcome that may be irreversible.

There will be unruly retaliation in response to Ari's death. With the murder of the offspring of the most influential leader of all paranormals, it's inevitable. The probability of others going after that power is now higher in response to the expected mourning that will come.

This is about so much more than my broken heart.

Salvatore's wicked grin spreads wider, his child-sized teeth revealing themselves to me. "Until next time..."

Then he's gone. Nothing but air where my hands held him in place by his clothing and throat. Tuck and I lean over the rail, sweat streaming down our temples, while Salvatore reappears below, smirking and waving before vanishing into the crowd.

"Did you —" Tuck's question dies on his tongue. The answer is *no*.

Teleportation is a rare gift. More likely Salvatore is using another's power or some sort of spell.

Television depicts the act as nothing more than simple relocation. It's so much more. Just as our bodies break and rebuild themselves with our deaths, teleportation is very much a similar concept.

The body's molecules disassemble and seemingly vanish into thin air before swiftly reassembling elsewhere, too fast for the brain to comprehend. The image of a full person is the smallest breakdown our weak eyes can process.

"If you're done, I need you over here," Willam calls, his hands drenched in dark congealing blood. *Ari's blood.* It's soaked into her dress, and his shirt, staining her paling skin.

We both kneel beside her, me cradling her lolling head in my hands. I can't get this wrong. I can't mess up. Just as her life depends on Willam, it depends on me, too.

Phoenix tears are a peculiar thing. The power to heal is as much a gift as it is a curse. The healing potency is greater, the stronger the bloodline. I am what they would call pure. The blood flowing through my veins, ancient. Untainted. No one can heal others with their tears like my family can.

Too much of a good thing, as with anything in life, can be just as harmful as the bullet that was lodged in her chest. Should I give too much, I could kill her just the same.

"You've done this before?" Willam questions, eyeing me over thick-rimmed glasses. His preference in public. He doesn't need them. They hold no prescription but fit his style. An intellectual born in the late eighteen hundreds. He's never left his time behind — not entirely. I doubt he ever will.

"Yes," I breathe. I don't tell him it's only been once, and I messed it up.

I can't fuck up this time.

"Cry for her."

His words are like a prayer. A command my phoenix immediately responds to. The aqua-blue liquid seeping from the corner of my eye, my head tilting toward Ari's wound just in time for it to strike the now exposed and blackened tissues from the bullet doing its damage.

"One more," Willam coaches.

My body trembles. This pivotal moment is make-or-break. His words are enough to coax that last tear from me. Rounder and bigger than the last. Fear seizes my heart. It's pumping faltering. Was it too much?

With a pat on the back, Willam shoves his tools back into his bag. "Good work, Adrian. Very good." Then he's gone.

There's nothing left for him to do tonight. All we can do is wait.

"Come on." Tuck slips his hands beneath Ari's back and legs, ready to lift her from the floor, only to lock eyes with me. My glare so dark and menacing that he immediately releases her. "I'm just trying to help," he sighs, backing away from the two of us.

Logically, I know that's the truth. Ari is his long-lost sister, but the pair in me can't stand the sight of another man touching her when she's in such a fragile state. Any man touching her at all under any circumstance would equate to them signing their own death certificate.

Most would fear my sudden rage, but not him. Tuck is his own brand of Jekyll and Hyde. A coin with two opposing sides. The sinister half more demented than the Joker himself.

Understanding flashes behind his eyes as he continues to watch my face. He respects the bond. He respects what it means to me to pick my woman up off the ground. To cradle her hopefully healing body to my chest. To protect her.

The bond is sacred. He has witnessed a part of us that remains unbreakable.

A bond he has yet to experience himself. He and Talia, partners for years, understand they have no future together. One day their pairs will appear. On that day, they'll need to make a choice.

Until then, they enjoy each other's company. Pretending that the inevitable day won't come.

He may understand the agony of watching a pair want to wither and die with their other half, but he certainly can't empathize.

Tuck doesn't know what this bond feels like. I hope someday he does. Despite the difficulties, the connection with Ari is one I value above all else. A gift I won't take for granted should she make it through this.

With a shuddering breath, I slip my hands beneath her body. She seems to weigh nothing but everything all at once as I carry her down the stairs. A silent descent between the Tuck and me while the club-goers still rage around us.

Not a single one seems to know about the shit show that happened upstairs. Their eyes appear glazed, bodies sweaty with drinks sloshing in their hands. Every crack of laughter only fanning the flame of my irrational anger.

Don't they even care that someone got shot here tonight?

The man they worship did it.

They don't. Never bite the hand that feeds you. They'll continue on with their escapades, either oblivious or uncaring. Anything to remain in Salvatore's good graces and be welcome in his places of debauchery.

The already-open elevator doors are like a beacon of relief. Our escape route from this bullshit. The swift ascent only leaving me enough time to adjust Ari's rag-doll body in my arms once before striding straight out of the building.

Our unmarked SUV idles at the curb, Bronson Carrion, our most trusted warlock, behind the wheel, waiting for us. If you're ever in a dangerous situation, he's the one you want at your back. He's seen more war and fighting than any of us here, born in the Middle East where he's fought for and against the Americans.

It doesn't matter what weapon you place in his hand. He excels with it, eliminating any obstacle with unheard of efficiency. And that's before he even bothers to use any of his given gifts.

He understands loyalty and duty in a way most people don't. Yet, he has only ever used his magical gifts for good. For the betterment of this world he was born into.

Tuck slides into the front seat with a sigh, his skull smacking into the glass window the moment he has the door closed. It's awkward climbing into the back, still cradling Ari in my arms, but I refuse to let her go.

"Where to?" Bronson grunts, pulling out onto the street.

"My family home." The safest place I can keep her. A home my grandparents left for me. A bit of my history, I didn't tell her.

Prior to taking Ari there — a necessary evil after my house was ransacked — only her parents knew I owned it. The only good thing my parents ever left me. My lip curling just thinking about those bastards. Their cruelty is a brand I never want to encounter again. Though, as long as they breathe, someday I will. Yet another inevitability I can't control.

With a heavy sigh, I give Bronson the address. Secrets only remain hidden for so long.

Four

Ari

The burn is back. A sensation I can only equate to being incinerated with the hottest flame.

The fire that lives within me was always a warm blanket, but this is different. These are coal-heated knives repeatedly stabbing, tearing, and scorching my flesh. Over and over and over. Unrelenting. Their forceful jabs only increasing in intensity and speed.

Only brief moments exist for me to breathe between bursts of torture. If breathing is what I am doing. The struggle for those air sacs to inflate seems near impossible. The stretching of the tissues adding to the pain coursing through me.

Voices drift in and out of my consciousness. My ears straining to put together the strings of words that jumble together into nonsense language.

The only word processed with unmatched clarity is Salvatore's name. The vitriol behind the voice spitting it disorienting.

Adrian's voice.

He's here.

He can't be dead too. Stuck in this in between. Adrian isn't supposed to be here with me. Despite my absence, he deserves a fulfilling life. We never sealed our bond. He can move on, right?

It doesn't stop me from reaching for him. A leaden limb cutting through the ocean's crashing waves. I can't reach him. His voice drifting further and further away. The other voices leaving with his.

Don't leave.

Come back.

Once more, I'm draped in darkness. Silence. The dread of loneliness.

The pain shifts. A smooth segue into an ache, then nothing at all.

I'm dead.

I. Am. Dead.

I can't say how long I've been here. Trapped in this in between. There's no time here. Only the pain. Just the voices of individuals fading in and out randomly.

Adrian's voice is the one I can always pinpoint. Always the closest to me. So close I convince myself I can reach out and touch him, but I can't move.

My body won't do what I want it to. It won't move toward him. Each finger refusing to extend straight in search of his solid form. All I want is to hold him close. Just until the pain fades again.

Adrian shouldn't be here. He can't be dead. He needs to kill Sal. Sal needs to die.

"Hey." Adrian's voice is softer than I've ever heard. The volume is loud enough he seems to be right next to my ear. The warmth of his breath easing the pain slightly. My vision so vivid I swear I can smell the pine of his aftershave.

I swallow repeatedly, trying to form words. Wanting to apologize. Needing to convince him to live. To get out of here.

He needs to protect us. To keep us safe.

"Adrian," my throat sore. His name croaked, instead of the no-nonsense monotone I usually carry with everyone except my mom.

Where is Mom?

Warmth engulfs my hand. My stiff fingers curled inward toward my palm. It hurts. But not like my chest. A stark contrast to the hole of dead tissue left by the bullet. A bullet like the ones I keep in the gun Sal gave me to murder those who stood in his way.

"Open your eyes."

A weight comes down against my head. Not heavy. But a brush of my hair back from my forehead. A warm rough palm I'd know anywhere.

I feel him.

I am imagining him.

Regret over my shoulda, woulda, couldas washes over me. I wish I had told him how I felt before I left. I should have conveyed how much I'd come to need him. We both just needed a little time.

He's everywhere, but I can't see him. Only the darkness of an abyss surrounds me. My other senses heightened, enveloping me in his scent, his voice, and his touch. Each one guiding me back to him. Or rather, this fantasy of him.

He's here. He can't be here.

"Please, Ari." A plea against my forehead, where invisible lips brush my heated skin. "Open your eyes."

They press shut against the dark. Light shimmering behind my heavy eyelids. I want to open them again. They're so heavy. It's more energy than I have to spend.

I'm trapped here. There is no escape.

My chest burns, the muscles trying to find their way back together.

Wait. If that's what I'm really feeling, am I dead?

Yes.

I must be dead. Phoenixes can't survive those bullets. They take away our ability to be reborn.

I'm dead.

"Open." One more plea for me to follow his words.

This time, they do. The lids peel back as if moving for the first time. I'm panting when the bright lights of the room hit me. The blinding nature of it scaring me more than the darkness did.

A blur distorts my vision. Slowly clearing with each flutter of my lashes. Nothing around me is distinct, but somehow familiar. Perhaps death will return us to our safe havens. I can't pinpoint where I am, but I know it's somewhere I would never have to fear being. It's somewhere I could close my eyes and know nothing bad will happen to me.

"Syriah. Get Syriah." Adrian's voice booms in my ear, making my head pound.

But I feel him still. Then I see him. That hulking form of his leaning over me. Lines of worry etched into his forehead.

"Ad —" I try.

"Shhh, it's okay."

He shifts the hair back from my forehead again. The tender touch of a lover. A protector. Someone who thought they had lost the person who meant everything to them.

Footsteps sound just beyond us. More than one set tramping into the room before the bed shifts underneath me. The added weight moving me just enough to spike the pain anew.

Several blinks later, and my vision finally clears. The sharpness brings clarity to the memory of where I am. *Adrian's room.* The same one he'd let me curl up beside him in bed when I didn't want to be alone.

His bed.

Mom.

Tears stream down my cheeks into the pillow beneath my head. Hers streaked in lines to match mine. She bends to hug me, keeping her touch light.

It does nothing to stop the searing pain. To keep the scream from launching itself from my mouth as she slowly releases me.

"I'm sorry, sweetheart. I didn't mean —" She chokes on her words, a hand clasping across her mouth to hide her sob.

With my last bit of strength, I reach for her.

"S'kay." The slurred combination of words all I can manage.

"We weren't sure you'd make it. The bullet caused significant tissue damage, despite Willam's best efforts to clear the debris. Your body has been healing itself slowly for weeks now."

I stop listening.

Weeks. Weeks?

I've been asleep or in a coma, whatever that was, for weeks.

"How —" A cough followed by a swallow. "How man —" It's impossible to finish the sentence as the pain tears down my back, shooting into my glutes and thighs.

"Shh, sweetheart. You don't have to talk. It doesn't matter." My mother brushes a hand across my cheek, the same way she does to all of us she considers her children. "You have a lot more healing to do. We're going to keep you here at Adrian's until you're ready to get up and move around on your own. When you're up to it, I'll tell you about your rebirth. I've never seen anything like it."

I give her a weak smile, my eyes drifting closed.

There's no fight left. With each blink, my eyelids grow heavier. The tiny weights attached to the ends finally anchoring them shut. It's barely a minute before I'm draped in darkness once more.

This time, I know the darkness won't consume me. It's not Purgatory. It's not permanent. The next time I open my eyes, the people I love will be right here waiting for me.

I'm alive.

The next time I recall my eyes opening, I'm draped in dark blue light. The large TV against the far wall, flickering with images from a movie I don't recognize. Adrian is propped against the headboard next to me, his fingers twined with mine. His neck is oddly notched at what must be an uncomfortable angle.

Where I'm tucked under the comforter, he's atop it. Those long legs crossed in front of him, a curt snore sneaking out of him every few minutes. It's the type that wakes you from your own sleep. An alarming noise I don't recall from the night we slept together.

A short beard has grown across the lower half of his face. The golden brown wiry strands sticking straight above his lip, but slightly curving under his chin. I've never seen him with facial hair. His appearance transformed into something a bit more rugged than I am used to with it. More dangerous than his attitude usually portrays him as.

Slowly slipping my fingers from his, I grit my teeth, shoving my legs to bend over the edge of the bed. Those same panting breaths find me. The energy I just had to expend for such a simple action is absurd.

This rebirth differs significantly from my last.

When the death was clean.

When I woke up rejuvenated and new.

"Where are you going?" he grumbles, rolling toward where I sit, so his body curves behind me. His warmth is enough for me to sink into him with exhaustion. A large palm holding me steady at my waist.

"Pee."

I figured shorter words will serve me better. This time it hurts less to speak, but I still sound like I smoke ten packs a day. *Gross.*

I've only started to attempt to put weight on my feet when the bed shifts behind me. The sudden dip throwing my balance sending shooting pain down the left side of my body. My hiss long and pronounced.

"I'm sorry," he whispers, tucking an arm under my thighs and behind my back before lifting me with ease.

The shuffle of his jeans on the hardwood floor is louder than it should be in my ears. A side effect I recall from my last rebirth. Your senses remain heightened for weeks until your new form recalibrates. It was annoying as hell, but this time I'm grateful. It means I'm still here. Alive!

"Can walk," I croak, followed by another cough and sigh.

"I've got you."

With a kick of his foot against the toilet seat, he lifts the lid before lowering me to sit. I hadn't even thought to check what I was wearing. Only now realizing I'm draped in one of his shirts with no undergarments to speak of. Everyone has been coming and going with me dressed like this. *Shit.*

He turns his back to give me privacy. Just enough time for me to sniff my pit. I assume they've been bathing me, but just in case I needed to make sure I don't smell like ass next to this Adonis. The thought enough to make the corner of my mouth tilt up.

It's clear he's not leaving, so I do my business. The flush of the toilet his signal to face me again. The reach behind me sending new bolts of pain through me so suddenly I nearly topple off the seat. Yet Adrian is there to catch me.

Each panting breath comes with a new trickle of sweat at my temple as he just holds me there. There's no energy left. Wiping myself and flushing took it all.

"This... sucks," I huff.

Fuck! Why is this so damn hard this time?

"I know." His voice is low, laced with sadness. Those gorgeous green eyes likely filled with the same.

Lifting me again, he deposits me on the bathroom counter, closer to his Jack sink versus the Jill. The neatly lined products along the far edge indicate which side he always uses. He lets the water warm as he lathers my hands in soap. The coarse texture of his palms against my skin more uncomfortable than it should be.

Somehow peeing with him in the room didn't seem weird, but this does. It's too intimate. Too caring an action for me to accept or understand from him regardless of how much I may want it.

"Can do it..." I inhale a deep breath. "...myself."

"I know," he sighs, dragging my hands forward to rinse them.

Once they're dry, we stay there. My legs spread just enough for him to step between them. His hips snugly wedged against my inner thighs.

"I want to hold you."

"Is okay," I breathe, sucking in a deep breath to combat the pain before he wraps his arms around my middle.

Opting for sliding my hands up his chest to loop them around his neck seems like the most energy-efficient way to hold him back. His deep inhale at my neck the moment they settle in place, tightening the muscles of my lower belly. His breath warming my skin.

My back aches and my chest burns as he holds us there. Our bodies melded to one another. Wanting to be close to someone isn't supposed to hurt so badly, but wanting Adrian only seems to bring unimaginable pain to me now.

"I'm sorry," he mumbles before pulling back, eyes searching mine.

"You didn't do 'nythin." I take another shallow breath. "You sav — saved... me."

Once more, my hand meets his chest, the muscles stiff from weeks of immobility.

"I thought I lost you." He buries his face in my neck again. The tip of his nose rubbing back and forth against my over-sensitive skin.

I've seen the sweet sides of Adrian before all this happened. There were even some silly moments when I realized he was far more than he seemed. The brief glimpses told me he could be someone I could actually grow to enjoy versus loathe.

My movements are jerky, nearly stopped by the pain radiating down my sternum as I pull him close, my lips pressing against his. This isn't like the kisses we shared before I ran off. This one is soft. Tender. Cautious. He's being careful with me.

I need to know if his feelings for me match the ones that I developed for him before the shooting. The sexual attraction was there. We both accepted that, however, that's not the reassurance I need now. I want to know if he'll give his heart to me.

He answers my question with fingers slipping into my hair. The tips curling into the roots of the longer strands that now rest against my back, just below my blades. Our mouths slant together, exploring one another with anticipation and trepidation. It feels like years have separated us and now there is a risk of our connection breaking once more.

Our moment is short-lived. The parting of his lips from mine leaving me cold. His movements slow, as if terrified he'll hurt me. It's there in the shift of his eyes. In the light hold of his fingers against my torso. The pads lifting every few seconds as if ensuring he's not leaving a mark.

"I'm like a cockroach," I laugh. "Can't get rid of me so fast."

It hurt like hell to get all the words out. My voice is deep and raspy, but it's worth it to witness the light return to his eyes. His laugh vibrating through the bathroom before scooping me back into his arms, then depositing me in bed the same way you would a newborn in their crib. This time, positioning me on the opposite side of my wound before curling up behind me.

Sleep finds me quickly, wrapped in the arms of the person who makes me feel safest in the world.

If only this could last this time.

Five

ADRIAN

My temper is raging today. It's as if a viper is digging through me when I have to be away from home, even if just for a few minutes. Hell, taking out the trash while Ari's fast asleep has me sprinting through the place like my ass is on fire.

It's the first time in the past six weeks I've left her alone.

I'm fucking pissed. But Tuck called with business we needed to tend to. Code for him needing me to keep him in check should his dark side threaten to consume him.

Ari nearly shoved me out of the house.

"Adrian, I promise I will be right here when you get back, but only if you go handle what needs to be done now. I'll be fine."

The lighthearted glimmer that sometimes finds its way into her eyes was enough that I could trust her words. With a gentle push, she forced me to step through the doorway and into the garage.

There's been no sign of Salvatore since he waltzed out of his club. No one mentioned him or his activities. That overly expensive penthouse remains furnished as if he and his wife,

Genevieve, will be home anytime. Everything set as if any moment now they'll continue to live their lives within its walls. Reports of their hired staff still bustling about ping to my inbox every fucking day.

A decoy if I've ever seen one. When he disappeared, his family did too.

It's smart of Salvatore to want to keep his wife hidden away — either with him or without. I'm not above revenge. In my head, I keep repeating the mantra of an eye for an eye. He tried to take my pair from me, so I would damn sure take his wife from him.

It's the ruthless part of me I wish I'd left behind a hundred years ago. Remnants of a cruel upbringing courtesy of my family. Reminders of them that won't leave me.

They were urges I could lock into the dark recesses of my being. Then Ari got shot, and every cruel tendency came racing back to the surface. I allowed myself to believe nothing could save her. Not me or her phoenix or Willam. Torturous moments I was certain that the one soulmate I was destined to meet in this life wouldn't get to live hers.

Genevieve's life means as much to me as it does to Salvatore. A woman he doesn't even show a modicum of respect for. Constantly sleeping around with others, all too willing to spread their legs or ass cheeks for him while ignoring her existence. Salvatore has no preference for partners. If they've got a hole to fuck or a mouth to get him off, he's game. *Fucking pig.* It almost makes me feel bad for Genevieve — his chosen companion for at least two hundred years.

I'm not entirely sure how old he is. I'm not sure anyone does. It's not uncommon to guess at ages in the paranormal world. After a while, you stop counting. The years tick forward, and we barely change. Our features aging so slowly that it's barely noticeable to us. Depending on the species, we age at different rates and have varying life spans. Warlocks and witches tend to wither away around the five-hundred-year mark. I can only hope that bastard gets what's coming to him soon.

Only photos capture the subtle changes. They are a visual walk through time, capturing the minuscule the eyes miss. As I merge onto the highway, my mind wanders, wondering how different I look through the years. In truth, I haven't paid attention since I ran from my family.

Traffic is a bitch as I swerve through the lanes to the address Tuck texted me a few hours ago. Our argument driving the grinding of my molars now. My plea for him to recruit someone else to be there for his sick shit falling on deaf ears. He's in the mood to torture someone. Anyone. An uncontrollable response to what Salvatore did to his big sister. It's kind of cute how protective he is with her. However, I know that the man I will find at the warehouse will not be him.

His dark side will have taken over already. Sweet Tuck locked away until his monster is satisfied. That sometimes meek version of my only friend buried in a grave he dug for himself.

That demented calm will greet me. His blue eyes darkening to pits of depravity.

When Tuck loses himself to that dark half, it's best to stay out of his way. Unless you're willing to join him in his torment. Not my thing. Not after having been raised with my family.

But above it all is the loving brother. The one who will fight to make sure his sister is happy. Even with me.

The "talks" he's given me about breaking her heart have been far more intense than necessary. His warnings against knocking her up or leading her on have become a broken record. Each pointed threat describing the many ways he'd dismember me for so much as looking at another paranormal or human send shivers down my spine. I'm always the one here to witness his brand of torture, so it's easy to picture his promises.

If only he knew I hadn't noticed another woman since the first time I caught sight of his sister. The moment that pair thread glowed to life in her presence, I knew I was done.

I barely notice anyone else at all, period.

I fought like hell to ignore the pull to her. That tether snapping into place so fucking quick I couldn't breathe. I was a dick to her. Pushing her buttons at first because I needed to keep away. An attempt at making her hate me. My baser animal instincts fighting me every step of the way.

Back then, my taunts were in place because I had to convince myself I couldn't trust her. She was stalking me to kill me. Slowly, it shifted. The barbs meant to grab her attention. To make her look at me or interact with me, whether positive or negative. I would do anything to hear her voice or have her hands on me, even if it meant being pushed away.

I've zoned out, nearly crashing into a muscle car in front of me when he slams on his brakes. Scrubbing a hand down my face, the beard that's been growing out scratches my palm. It's been decades since I allowed my facial hair to grow. Taking care of Ari was my top priority, so shaving was the least of my worries.

I was going to get my shit together a week ago, but Ari had played with it that morning. Running her fingers in the lengthening strands at my chin and cheek with something like awe in her eyes. She never said if she liked it or not, but I wouldn't deprive her of touching me. Never. So it still grows. Thick and lightening several shades, as it dwarfs my face.

I'm about two days from looking like a fucking lumberjack.

The traffic loosens as I take my exit onto Division. The ramp takes me uphill before curving back down. It's an area where old warehouses still stand. Some in use. Others abandoned.

It only takes another five minutes to find my destination. The parking lot empty except for a few other cars. There's no stealth needed for this mission, so I park my car right out front. A few growled breaths forced out to calm my temper.

Hand on the door handle, one more calming deep breath fills my lungs. My eyes pressing shut for several brief moments to picture something good. Ari's sparkling navy blue eyes coming to mind before I peel my eyelids open again. The only preparation I get before walking in on Tuck's shit show.

Sauntering inside, I'm greeted with a scene no amount of breathing could have prepared me for.

Tuck paces back and forth. A few of our guys standing tall behind him, legs spread wide, arms crossed over their barrel chests. A mix of phoenixes and wolf shifters. Our typical guards.

Four men and one woman hang from chains finagled into the ceiling several stories up. All except for one have chins resting against their chests. Sweat and blood dripping down any of their exposed skin before eventually finding the cement under their feet. The claw and teeth marks marring their marked bodies just the beginning of what Tuck will likely do to them.

Their faces, etched with gaunt lines, hint at how long they've been here. A week at least. That's a considerable duration of time to endure what Tuck likes to do to his victims. How he plays with them like little mice caught in a trap until they squeal and beg for it to stop.

Tuck has that Joker grin. His face lighting up as he smears speckles of blood across his brown skin. The knife cradled in his dominant hand, glinting in the soft yellow lights, while the crowbar in the other only appears darker than the painted ebony.

Seems he's in the mood to make a mess today. I can't blame him either. If any of these fuckers know where Salvatore is, Tuck will get the answers out of them. He'll make them bleed while screaming from the pain into the empty warehouse. A repeated cycle until Tuck gets what he wants.

No one will come to their rescue. Their survival chances are slim. Daylight is the last thing they will see again. And my boy will never give the false hope that they might.

Paranormals know if Tucker James takes you hostage, it'll be the last time your loved ones see you.

Secretly, I hope he can garner some additional information I want for myself.

How could he, though?

Those are the deepest parts of me I've kept hidden away. If anyone knew what I had done. What I let happen, they'd kill me. They'd kill them too.

Shaking myself out of my own thoughts, my chin cocks in Tuck's direction.

"Not yet," he breathes.

They haven't talked yet. Each keeping their words buried inside. The James family is not the only one who has earned unbreakable loyalty. Powerful paranormals, such as Salvatore, have built similar followings. Their pledge to him born out of perceived injustices against them. Simple-minded creatures who don't understand the purpose of the hierarchy. Traitors who are better off dead anyhow.

The power lies in the wrong hands, according to them. They live and breathe off Salvatore's empty promises of a world where phoenixes don't rule. Where a single bloodline doesn't hold domain over us all. What he hides from them is his desire to acquire gifts and magic that aren't his, so the world — human and paranormal — will bow to his every wish.

It's never been a secret that Salvatore is ambitious. He covets everything he can't have. A hunger for power so strong he'll destroy anyone who gets in the way of him reaching for it. He's been vocal about it through the centuries. An ongoing saga we've been able to keep at bay until he hired Ari. She was the key to his success. A silent killer to eliminate his obstacles. Looking back, we knew he had an assassin he favored, but none of us could get close enough to know who. Maybe it was fate that he sent her after me. Fate that chose me to lead her to her actual family.

The list Salvatore had constructed for Ari was impressive. Each kill was nothing more than another tied-up loose end for the murdering warlock. One after the other, Ari disposed of her targets like trash.

It took me weeks to piece together what Salvatore was doing with some of the paranormals he had murdered. The truth should have been glaringly obvious when he teleported inside the club that night. That's not a common power amongst the warlocks and witches. One bloodline exclusively possessed the ability — that I know of.

A single name rings through my head. Janelle Sanhuez. One of Ari's earlier targets. I knew her many years ago — in more ways than one. Janelle was nearly pure-blooded Lanae — those with the gift of moving from one place to another with as little as a flicker of a thought.

Seeing her face in that photo, I felt pity for her family. Her parents had long since disappeared, leaving her husband and children behind without the wonderful woman she was. That woman embodied both angelic sweetness and a wild, tiger-like spirit, unlike Ari's fiery nature. She spent her days caring about everyone else, doing what she could for others. She dedicated every other spare second to her family. No matter what it cost her, she'd be there.

Her gifts were unusual and strong. I can only imagine Salvatore took the opportunity to steal her power once her parents disappeared. The Lanae line ended with her. His possible connection to her parents' disappearance crosses my mind. A thought I hadn't considered before now.

"Adrian!" Tucker barks my name, pulling me back to the present.

"Nothing on Salvatore, but they know where his children are hiding." A salacious grin spreads on Tuck's face. His boyish good looks transformed into something straight out of nightmares. Those vibrant eyes, so unusual for his family line, glowing brightly.

There are only two times we present like this. The pheromones are flying between you and your pair, and it's T-Minus five seconds before you're fucking on the floor, wall, table — really whatever surface is closest — or your bird's killing instinct is fighting its way through.

History books paint us as docile creatures. Peacekeepers shown as symbols of rebirth. Our bodies going up in flames to recreate us after our sacrifices. But that's not entirely true.

They never show how violent we can be. How our rage can simmer to the point that the shift isn't something we can control and the carnivorous nature of our Firebirds breaks through. Razor-sharp teeth and talons ready to tear our enemies to shreds. Only ribbons of a corpse and chunks of meat will remain.

Bottom line, we're not so peaceful when pushed to the edge.

Another hidden gem of our kind is our human forms. We may occupy mortal-like bodies ninety percent of the time, but we are a phoenix first. The human body is just the storage unit to keep us from walking around like giant balls of feathers twenty-four-seven. The phoenix rules, and if we can't control it, nasty shit happens.

It's not even worth watching as Tuck shifts into his bird. The feathers are an exact match for Ari's. An ache growing in my chest for her. My mind and my heart hating being away from her for this shit. It's been less than two hours; that's all. Watching the small ticking hand on my watch, I count the minutes until I can be with her again. Until I can curl my body around her and inhale her scent.

Tuck's shift continues. The parts he chooses morph and change. Ari is large for a phoenix. Something innate in her heritage, but her brother is almost double the size, a single wing nearly fifteen feet long. His talons extend from the spot his fingernails had just been. Each one dark like the night as they lengthen into position.

The two individuals at the end shudder, barely conscious to observe the transformation themselves. Sniffing the air, the scent fills my nostrils. They're warlocks. But that's not all there is. Uncontrollable fear fills the air, too.

The woman vomits, sickness overtaking her, accepting that her death is near. She's a shifter, too. I can sense it on her, but I'm not sure what creature she is. Not a wolf. Not quite. The scent doesn't match. Some sort of rare hybrid.

The whole debacle is over in minutes. Tuck eviscerates the three men one by one. Their heads lolling forward with a single swipe of those sharp claws. The tension that held their bodies taut while they hung there, completely relaxed. The metal clinking loudly in the open cavern of a room. He positions himself in front of the woman, head cocked, before shifting back into his human form. He'd shredded his clothes in the process but stands before her bare. Again, his head tilts to the side.

Why he is so fascinated by her remains to be seen.

"You'll come with me. Since you seem willing to give me the information I need, we can have another chat."

She whimpers loudly before our guys unhook her from the chains, throwing her over one of their shoulders. The clap of their footsteps out the back entrance echoing through the nearly empty space.

The fourth man groans. His string of saliva mixed with blood landing at Tuck's bare feet. He nonchalantly stops before the man. Tuck's grin only widening as he stands in the hanging man's shadow.

Only ten more seconds before the snap comes. Tuck's hands leave the man's head as fast as they arrived. The man's neck broken with barely any force. The spinal cord severed with no chance of repair. This one is a vampire. His need to hide from daylight no longer an issue.

A clean-up crew will be along shortly. It's imperative we keep the dark things hidden. As paranormals, we may have our hands in every bit of society, but we don't rule humankind.

Within the hour, it'll be as if nothing happened here.

Six

ADRIAN

"Leave it," Tuck growls, sliding into the backseat of a non-descript SUV.

With a heavy sigh, my palm runs over my face again. I just want to get home to my girl. Ari texted a picture showing she was still alive, but it's not the same as being there holding her.

"Now, Adrian."

"Yeah. Okay." Slipping in beside Tuck, the metal tang of blood hangs in the air. The scents of every species that had been inside with us seemingly clinging to our clothes or my nostrils. Despite Tuck removing every trace of blood and piece of flesh from his skin, the smell lingers. A reminder of the ruthlessness that took place here. A reminder of my upbringing churning my stomach.

You can wash away the physical evidence, but is it ever really gone? Do we ever really feel clean again?

I've killed before. More times than I would ever care to count. For a future my parents desired more than anything else, I took risks with my life and others. I am not proud of what I've done for them.

Any kills since then were to protect what the James family stands for. I regret none of them. There's not a single death I would take back in their name. I did what was needed to maintain the balance. To keep peace in our world.

My life growing up with my parents and brothers is the number one reason I act the way I do. Why I walk around like even the invisible dust in the air has personally offended me. If you're an asshole, no one fucks with you.

Along the way, I actually became that man. My priority was safeguarding everyone, without caring about who I pissed off in the process. I alienated myself from everyone except Syriah — my surrogate mother — and Tucker. The brother I wish I had, despite his violent tendencies.

"We find his son and daughter, we find him," Tuck sniffs, flicking a crumb of dried blood from beneath his fingernails with disgust.

It's mind-blowing how quickly he can shift from psycho to regular Joe. He no longer has that manic look in his eyes when he is in the mood to torture information out of his captive. I've stuck to questioning as much as I can, but not Tuck. It's frequently why he's kept out of the inner workings of what goes on behind closed doors. That switch of his can flip at the tiniest detail.

"Did she say where?"

"No," he shrugs, sliding sunglasses onto his face. "But she will."

I nod, turning my gaze out the tinted window.

"Don't tell Ari." His tone shifts. The confidence gone, shame pushing his bushy brows together.

I hadn't planned on it. The last thing she needs to know is what Tuck does behind closed doors. That's for him to share if and when he chooses to. I'm also slightly terrified that Ari might be angry enough to join Tuck occasionally.

I wish with everything that I am that I could protect her from this war she's unknowingly walked into. Anything to shield her from the politics and the death that comes with battling bloodlines greedy for power. That I come from one of those families only makes it worse.

My bloodline — the Alexanders, originating from eastern Europe — is second only to the James line. The ability to channel a wider array of phoenix gifts putting them ahead of our healing tears. The one thing we are best at besides eradicating those that stand in our way.

"I won't say anything. She has enough going on."

His turn to nod. His thoughts race, searching for the right words to express his true feelings. It's one of his many tells. His eye twitches at the corner when he's trying to make a point or ask a question sure to flare tempers.

"Are you two..." His words trail off.

"No."

A simple answer. The truth. Nothing has changed. I won't have sex with Ari until she chooses *me*. Chooses *us*. If that's what she wants.

That bond, once formed, becomes nearly unbreakable. The agony she'd go through if she ever decided she regretted it and didn't want me would haunt me. A reason many phoenixes choose death over immortality.

I sure as hell want her. I've waited lifetimes for someone like her.

In my younger years, I never wanted a pair. Prayed I would never find my own. Determination not to continue the Alexander bloodline through me kept me from forming anything beyond casual relationships. I was certain that having children would mean passing my family's ruthless cruelty on.

Then I met Ari. A strong, confident woman who doesn't give a fuck about the world's opinions of her. One who has led as much of a lonely life as I have. The woman who frustrates me like nobody else also makes me feel more alive than any rebirth I've ever had.

The one who will take the hit for the rest of us. That's a woman you keep. A woman you breed with.

The thought sends a shiver down my spine. My head actively shaking away the thought. Bringing children into this fucked up world is the last thing I need. Not with the way it spins now.

Still, I need her to choose me. A choice that I won't allow my desires or manipulation to influence.

"Okay. Yeah. Good," Tuck sniffs.

"I wouldn't do that to her. It has to be her choice."

A stretch of silence fills the space between us. My friend's features shifting back to the sweet boy we all love. "Thank you."

The gratitude of a brother to his sibling. To me, for respecting those boundaries. Being protective of his big sister is his only option in situations like this. The blood he's only known for four months. I envy the love he feels for her. That same love I have never felt for my four brothers. Except, maybe...

No, not even him.

Four men I hope I never see again.

Our car ride continues in contemplative silence, both of us lost in our thoughts. The childhood memories flashing through my mind, churning my stomach. Years better forgotten than dwelled on. Moments not worth carrying with me, but yet they stay like an infection that never quite leaves.

Ezra, Orson, Finlay, and Kenji; then me. I'm the youngest of five.

Five boys.

Five chances for my parents to build ruthless killing machines. A success they will always be proud of.

It's unusual for a phoenix to have so many offspring. Even more uncommon for all of us to share the same sex. A coincidence, Lanham questioned once. His suspicions witchcraft was used to make that happen have yet to be confirmed.

To our knowledge, none exists to make it true.

As I grew bolder and wiser with age, I recall asking my mother once if there had been girls at one point, and she killed them off to keep the line male. The sting of her slap still vibrates my teeth with the memory. The only confirmation I needed. Her reaction taken to mean there was some truth in my question.

"You think I'm so cruel, Adrian? Continue with these lies, and you'll see just how cruel I would prefer to be."

She'd walked away from me then, ignoring me for weeks while we lived under the same roof, and I still did my parent's bidding.

My thoughts come to a screeching halt as we near Tuck's house. A typical single-family home from the outside. The top two floors embody exactly that, but he lives here alone. Concrete containment rooms outfit the basement. Walls so thick no one can hear the inhabitants scream while he tortures the answers out of his captives. Rooms I've had to spend too much time in as of late.

"Do you need me?" I ask.

I may be a brutal asshole myself, but I rarely have the stomach for Tuck's brand of it. It was more than enough witnessing what he'd done in the warehouse. The strike of his claws through flesh is always a reminder of what my father had often been like.

They often beat us — mostly me — as children for our impertinence. Ezra was always next to be punished just as violently for defending me.

My father preferred the tips of his claws drawn across our skin to leave an impression. Only for me to sit in my room, harvesting my own tears for hours to heal myself. Our gift was something

I resented all these years until they became what Ari needed to live.

"Why did you come if you weren't going to participate?" he scoffs.

It'll do me no good to remind him he practically dragged me here with him. While he was still in his dark place, my protest never quite sways him to do anything he hasn't already decided on. "I'd prefer to get back to Ari if you've got it handled. I can send Cooper to be here to... assist."

Despite their usual friction, Tuck and Cooper Ermstrong share a common, twisted outlook on punishment. It's also why they are never on assignment together. Allowing those two loose canons to wander off by themselves is certain to result in a lot of trouble. We don't have time to handle damage control after the fact.

"You really care about her, don't you?" His door swings wide, one leg poised to exit the idling vehicle.

A heavy sigh leaves me as I sink back into the seat. "You don't want me to answer that."

"I do, actually."

Grinding the heels of my hands into my eyes. I give him as half a truth as I can afford. "Care doesn't even begin to describe it. Let's just get this over with."

Seven

ARI

Adrian's barely been here for the past week. There have been too many supposed sightings and additional murders for him to keep sitting here babysitting me.

This house has become my cage. I'm tired of being laid up and treated like a newborn chick. I'm tired of the endless pain that accompanies the healing process. Just done with not being me.

It's been weeks since Dr. G was last here. His work is done. There's nothing more he can do to accelerate the process. Time is the ultimate healer here. His recommendation: drink a few of Adrian's tears each day.

Adrian, happy to do whatever I need to get better, leaves me a generous amount every day. Those tension-filled shoulders disappearing into a room at the rear of the house to collect them alone each morning. Only to return with the three-inch vile of glowing blue liquid he places on the dresser without meeting my eye.

I don't question the doctor's orders or Adrian's care. I just follow the instructions given to me. Anything to get me back on the streets, solving murders, and protecting my family.

"Well, well," Gomez chirps as he answers my call.

"Ha. Ha." My tone anything but amused.

"How are you healing up?" That fatherly concern he's always shown me laces into his tone. A protectiveness I used to think was over the top, but now I understand it's because we were the same.

"Everything still hurts, but I'm coming along. I emailed the chief about coming back next week."

Gomez goes so silent I pull the phone away from my ear, expecting that we got disconnected. "Hello?"

"I didn't hang up," he scoffs. "I think it's too soon."

I know he's right. There's no way my body is ready to be back in the field, but spending my days locked away here isn't doing it for me, either. There are only so many movies I can watch.

The shutting of a downstairs door makes me freeze. I deliberately waited until Adrian left before calling my partner. Neither is going to like what I have to say, but at least Raphael Gomez isn't here in person to glare at me.

"Hey! Hey!" Gomez calls. "You okay?"

"Uh, yeah. Adrian's home. I'll call you back."

I'm quick to end the call, sauntering out of the bedroom, my phone left abandoned in his unmade bed. A bed that feels like it's become *ours* over the past few months.

"Adrian," I call as I bounce down the stairs, his t-shirt brushing across my thighs with each step. "Adrian," I call again.

There's no answer.

I round the bottom of the stairs, but there's no sign of him. Raking my eyes over the open floor plan, I notice the front door is unlocked. *That's... unusual.*

One: Adrian doesn't use the front door. Not once since we've been here.

Two: he always made sure the door was locked. Adrian damn-near stomps through the entire house, checking every window and door before he curls up beside me.

My bare feet pad along the hardwood floors, knees bent as I creep toward the kitchen where one of my Glocks lies nestled in the drawer.

The house remains spine-tingling silent. No breathing or footsteps. The pull of the drawer thunderous against the quiet.

It's the first time I've held a gun since being shot. It feels strange to carry the weight after being laid up for so long. I wish I had the one from Sal, but it vanished after the debacle in the club. My safety net lost to the chaos that ensued. More than likely taken by one of Sal's guys to hide what he'd given me.

My arm hangs at my side, finger poised on the trigger. The muscle memory is not gone, just not quite right. I take two backward steps out of the kitchen. The creeping dark creating shadows that may or may not be whoever is in the house with me. It's not Adrian. I know it's not him. The moment he gets home, he practically tackles me as if we've spent thousands of years apart.

A chuckle sends a chill down my spine. The sound drifting from the exact spot I just retrieved the gun. A scent carrying my way that's unfamiliar, but not all at once.

"And what are you going to do with that?"

A man. In this house with me. A voice so deep and husky it sends my pulse into a frantic race. A voice I don't recognize in the slightest. An accent I can't quite place but know I've heard before.

Spinning toward the voice, arm outstretched, I flick on the light.

A fucking GQ model sits propped on the counter. Legs spread wide, upper back casually leaning against the cabinetry, he oozes danger. His face identical to Adrian's except pitted with storm gray eyes and hair so blonde I question if it's natural.

"You are?"

I don't raise the gun. It won't kill another phoenix. This Glock won't do a thing but slow him down — if I'm lucky.

Long legs dangle over the edge. Feet swinging through the air in the most carefree manner.

"Ah, so he hasn't told you about us? Pity." Sarcasm and humor mix with his words. That hint of accent slipping through once more.

Who the hell is this bastard?

"Get. Out of this. House." Venom coats my words. I don't know who the fuck this guy is, and frankly, I don't care. But he has sixty seconds to get out before I shoot.

My trigger finger twitches. That smooth surface just beneath the pad so familiar. The killer in me ready to do it again, my kind or not.

"In due time." Everything about his posture, to his tone, is non-bothered by the threat in mine.

"Now."

"After I leave a message." A dark grin spreads across his face as his feet clap to the floor. The dress shoes and slacks are too formal for a first meeting. A tactic I assume is meant to intimidate me. Scare me even.

His form stalks toward me, fear gripping my insides. I can't recall the last time I feared anything other than my feelings for Adrian. Getting shot by Sal has left something in me. Apprehension I didn't even have when I was ten years old and jumped off the edge of that cliff for the first time.

My chest rises and falls in the most exaggerated way. My steps retreating as he closes in on me. The icy surface of the fridge halting me in my tracks. The flat surface keeping my back in a rigid straight line.

A long finger trails down my cheek. Yet, I can only stare at the face in front of me. A face alarmingly familiar. So similar to...

"Mmm, I like how you respond to me," he purrs. "I like them scared." His nose trails up the curve of my throat. "I like them even better when they belong to someone else."

"You've got ten seconds to get that finger off my face before I break it off."

"Cute." He backs away a step, hands in his pockets. "Time to go."

Without a care in the world, he stalks out through the front door. The garage door closing the moment the front clicks shut. I didn't notice the garage opening because I was caught up in the moment and the feeling of another man's hands on me. Hands that weren't Adrian's. Disgust and fear twisting in my gut at his touch.

Leaning against the fridge, I remain frozen until Adrian approaches me. Panic etched into my every feature.

"What's wrong? Didn't you hear me calling your name?"

I hadn't. That fear now living within trapped me. Yet one more thing holding me captive. My finger trembling against the trigger of the gun still in my hand. The weapon finally clanging to the ground, capturing Adrian's attention.

"Ari, why do you have your gun?"

"There was someone here." My words are a distant drone. Eyes trained ahead where the blonde Adrian disappeared. "He had your face." The words sound moronic on my tongue, but all I can muster. It's a truth. The best one I can structure into a coherent thought at the moment.

His posture immediately goes stiff as he looks behind him. Although the front door is out of sight from where he stands, he clearly followed my gaze.

"Ari?" He shakes me, my mind starting to clear. The coiling inside me finally beginning to loosen. "Ari, look at me."

His gorgeous face comes into focus. Those jade emeralds shining bright against the kitchen lights. This is the face I know. The one I...

My hands draw to his cheeks. Petting him once. Twice. Fingers twining into his hair to pull his face down to mine. Our mouths crash together in a torrent of emotion. My body burning from the mix of the heat he fills me with and the healing still taking place.

His body presses into mine, his length already hard inside his jeans. Our fingers weaving together as he raises our joined limbs overhead. A hiss snakes out past my lips at the bite of pain.

"I'm sorry, baby," he swallows but doesn't lower our arms. His mouth trailing across the curve of my cheek and down to my jaw, leaving a heated trail in his wake. "I want to take you upstairs."

"Do it."

A taunt.

A challenge.

A plea.

Anything for this man to finally sleep with me. I'm tired of asking. We've had the conversation in a roundabout way for weeks now, and the only answer I ever get is *"When you are ready."*

His mouth pulls away from my skin, dropping one hand and dragging me behind him with the other. Our mouths collide the moment he tosses us onto his bed, hips grinding between my spread legs. The tiny seamless panties barely a barrier against the fiction of the denim holding his cock captive.

Shoving my hands down between us, I undo his button; the zipper requiring a shuffling of my shoulder to slide it down. Another sharp hiss seeping into his mouth as his tongue wars with mine. Digging my toes into the thick fabric, I pedal my legs, shoving his jeans down his thighs. His chuckle a vibration against my chest as he lets me.

"Eager?"

"Adrian, please. Stop fucking around. I want this."

Anticipation flutters through my insides. My need to feel his throbbing cock inside me like needing to breathe air. Thank you phoenix gods above.

A rough tear of fabric leaves my pussy exposed to the soft cotton of his boxer briefs. This man has torn way too many pairs of my underwear for my liking. It'll have to be the first thing I purchase in bulk when I return to my apartment.

"Dammit, Ari. You're always so wet."

A hum is my only response I can muster as I work to free him. To make it so we're skin-to-skin. An inevitable moment I've been waiting for.

The moment his length touches my swollen flesh, he jumps back. His movements so quick I would think he's part vampire.

His features contort, those lips parted with an apology as he runs a hand through his hair.

"You've got to be fucking kidding me!" I groan.

"Ari, please." The emotion in his voice isn't enough. Not this time. Not anymore.

Yet again Adrian rejected me.

It's the same shit every time. We are both on the brink, about to step over the invisible line, and then he declines.

When am I going to learn? When will I stop hoping that this man truly desires me and is ready to give me what we both clearly want?

"Adrian, I'm done. I won't keep doing this with you."

"Baby, you don't understand."

I hate when he calls me that. As if a pet name will make me melt for whatever bullshit excuse he feeds me next. It's related to the pair bond, I know that. The reason he keeps me at arm's length until he wants to eat my pussy or tell me what to do.

"Then explain it to me."

He runs a hand through his hair again. A deep sigh leaving him as his mouth turns down into a deep frown.

"I can't..."

Standing from the bed hands up before smacking into my thighs, I lose all hope I've been blindly clinging to. I've never felt so stupid. So similar to those women who chase after men but fail to see what they're doing wrong. I swore to never be one. "Okay, then this is done."

"I'll give you anything else." He takes two steps forward, reaching for me. Just far enough away, I can slip away from his grasping fingers.

"If I wanted a dry-humping buddy, that would be fabulous. Just leave me be." I wave him off. "I'm going home tomorrow."

With a growl, he stalks from the room. The slam of the door rattling it on its hinges behind him.

It's hours before he comes to bed. He doesn't reach for me. Doesn't apologize the way he always does. Rolling to his side, his back to me, he says nothing at all. For the first night in weeks, our bodies don't touch. Our limbs aren't tangled beneath the sheets, and his hair isn't slipping through my fingertips.

For the first night since I've been here, I miss him.

But I won't be kept at arm's distance. For this pairing to work, he needs to let me in. He's going to have to choose to be with me or be without me.

I'm not staying in this in-between for another minute.

Not anymore.

Eight
ADRIAN

I don't sleep as I roll to my back, Ari's breathing long since having evened out. My fingers itch to touch her. My body craving folding around hers as we sleep soundlessly through the night.

I waited outside her door for hours, resisting the urge to climb into bed with her. If I hadn't been in the hallway, I wouldn't have known she was still in our bed. I certainly wouldn't have expected her to be.

Knowing she's done knots my stomach. The truth was there in every word and the resolve in her eyes. A look that damn near destroyed me.

I should have told her. For months, I've been cautious about the implications of her sleeping with me because of our bond. I'd begged Syriah or Talia, anyone else, to explain it all to her. And even then, it wouldn't be the whole truth. It's about so much more than Ari binding her existence to mine; it's my surname and bloodline too.

Still, I was desperate for anyone to take some of that burden. Anything to not have to look her in the eye and tell her why I needed her to choose. The shame of being part of my bloodline and the things I've done are topics I would rather leave dead and buried.

Choosing that bond means choosing life with me. She would be choosing a future clouded by my past. Agreeing means she truly wants all of me. I doubt she saw marrying an "old man" as her future, despite the jokes. Because if she says yes, I won't be able to let her go.

The moment I enter her, the bond locks into place. That thread thickening with each stroke inside her. There will be no skirting around our feelings. The possessiveness that lives within bonded mates is ten times more deadly than what she has seen from me so far. My personality likely to border on becoming as demented as Tuck's Mr. Hyde side.

Not to mention my brother Kenji was here today. The next oldest above me, our births separated by seventy years. He was the one I always butted heads with the most growing up. My arrival ruined the life of mayhem my parents allowed him to get away with. He often became my keeper and resented me for it.

Dad would beat me senseless. Kenji would then beat me worse. Not just with his fists and talons but his words and obvious hatred of my existence.

The man responsible for five of the times I've been reborn. The bastard was determined to get rid of me in my teenage years.

And did my parents blink an eye? No. They congratulated him for succeeding.

Why he was here is beyond me. I haven't spoken to him since my family disappeared over a hundred years ago. Time and distance almost made it easy to forget about the family I had before creating one with the Jameses.

Rustling leaves draw me from bed. I shouldn't think they are anything more than Illinois winds. Sounds I've heard a million times. Sounds that were innocuous before Kenji showed up here today, likely aware I wasn't home. Every single sound will, until I know why he's here and if he's alone.

I do my best to convince myself I'm nothing more than paranoid. He's been here once. Message received. He wouldn't chance coming back. To the Jameses my family is nothing more than fugitives against paranormal law.

Slipping into a pair of joggers, Ari stirs next to me. A small groan sneaking past her parted lips. Thankfully, her eyes remain closed as I hover over her, placing the softest kiss on her temple, whispering my apology. One she'll never actually hear.

I'm out the door in minutes.

It's a quiet night. When you're far from the city, it's always like this. The neighborhood filled with an older population that prefers to sleep at early hours. A place as residential as it gets. A sanctuary of sorts.

The same rustle of leaves pulls my attention to the house's far side. Kenji leaning propped against a tree at the edge of the lawn.

Hands deep in his pockets, his stance is a match for the one I always hold while watching Ari from doorways. Ankles crossed, head cocked to the side. A one-sided smirk.

When Ari told me our intruder had my face, I knew it was Kenji. None of my brothers look as much like me as he does. Yet another fact that made it easier for him to resent me.

I've always hated how identical our faces appeared. His lighter hair was the starkest difference between us. Oftentimes, once I hit human adulthood, many thought we were twins. Kenji always quickly told them they were wrong, adding that he wished he wasn't my relative at all. The feeling has been mutual for over a hundred years.

Back then, it hurt. I was just coming into the fold with my family, and even though I didn't agree with their ways, I wanted to belong. I had to because the only thing I ever heard while growing up was that I would be nobody and unloved if I didn't have power. If I couldn't reach out and seize that power, my position in the world would be meaningless. A fate that would leave me crushed under its boot, and that wasn't acceptable.

"Why were you in my house?"

"She's a pretty thing," he grins. His stance not so much as shifting an inch.

"Don't."

Boisterous laughter bursts from him. His eyes twinkling in the moonlight. "Fuck me. She's your pair."

My hands curl into fists. A fire raging inside me. I never wanted a pair; this is why. I never wanted that vulnerability when it came to my blood.

"Tell me, baby brother, does it excite or piss you off knowing I had my hands on her?"

Kenji takes several steps toward me, the tips of our matching straight noses nearly touching. I won't give in to his jab, despite wanting to tear his head from his shoulders for so much as looking at her. This will only be worse should she decide to bond with me.

I'll be absolutely uncontrollable then.

"What are you doing here, Kenji?"

He returns to his stance, leaning against the tree. Hands tucked into the pockets of his perfectly pressed slacks, the corner of his mouth quirks high. His style changed to keep with the times, but not his overall presentation of self.

"Mom and Dad asked that I pay you a visit. Word is you've had a run-in with Salvatore. That he shot that pretty little thing in there with one of his special guns, and now you've kidnapped his people."

The paranormal world mirrors high school. Everyone knows your business all the time. There are no secrets. No places to hide for long.

"So, you all came here just to collect gossip from wherever you have been for years?"

There's no hiding the snark in my words. I hate that Kenji's here. That he put his hands on what's mine.

He stays silent, my insides stirring as I stare at my brother. It's unsettling to see a slightly altered destructive version of my face reflected back at me.

His gaze suddenly tracks up to my bedroom window. Mine following. The sheer curtains are still. The room as dark as I left it. I can only assume he's doing his best to get a rise out of me by using Ari. The number one arguing chip anyone will ever have against me — whether we bond or not.

"No, baby brother." He takes a step closer, his inch of height on me putting his nose just a fraction higher. "I came to warn you... for Ezra's sake. He always had such a soft spot for you."

My eyes beat closed for a moment. My family treated me poorly, except for Ezra. The eldest was the only one who'd ever shown me some decency or respect. He taught me how to use my phoenix to my advantage. How to fight and do math equations. There were no regrets about leaving my family. Only an ounce of remorse to be found for leaving Ezra without so much as a backward glance.

Though my eldest brother was never cruel to me, he could be the worst of us. A swift killer who took action first and asked zero questions later.

Just the same, I haven't heard a peep from Ezra since I left. I made no secret of where I landed. My brother never checked in, even though they all knew.

"Ezra is a big boy. He'll be fine."

"You don't get it, do you, baby brother? Keep your nose out of this. Or the next one with a bullet in their chest will be you."

With that, Kenji turns his back on me, sauntering off into the night. I watch him go. Wait for him to turn back. He never does, climbing into a sedan several blocks down the road.

A chill runs through me, replaying that interaction with my brother. I'd hoped I would never see my family again. I never want to experience the mental anguish I had to unravel from spending the initial sixty-seven years of my life with them. Then, for the next ninety, they beat me less, but forced me to torture and kill far more.

Ominous tension pulls my body taut as I slide back into bed. Not caring if Ari doesn't want me, I curl in behind her. An audible sigh escaping us both as I rest my cheek atop hers.

If her rejection is real, tonight might be the last time I hold her like this. I'm going to take advantage. I'm going to savor her scent, and her smile while she sleeps, and the way she breathes.

Memories of her time recovering here play through my mind as I hold my woman. Moments I will cling to because, without them, I can't live this life. Without her, there's no point in existing.

Hours later, I'm still wide awake. Ari rotated in my arms shortly after I cuddled up to her. Her face nestled against my neck, the warmth of her breath keeping the chill away.

Those dark thoughts slowly surged to the surface, blocking out the peace I'd found thinking of Ari. My phoenix alert after being disturbed from his slumber. My family is at the forefront of my mind. There's no settling down for me. Just a blanket of deadly energy hanging over me.

Something is coming. A storm so much worse than what we thought we were battling.

Nine

ARI

Walking out of Adrian's grandparent's house two days ago was one of the hardest things I've ever had to do. The pull of our bond wanted to root me to his side. My resolve shoving me through the door.

I couldn't stay. Not anymore. I'd made it abundantly clear how I felt about him, yet he couldn't be straight with me. Women like me won't put up with shit like that. It's just this fucking bond. This inescapable intangible thing between Adrian and me that keeps me on the hook like a helpless fish.

I knew I wanted him before the shooting. I'd become more drawn to him and was lucky enough to see there was more than a brooding asshole beneath the surface.

Then he took care of me.

Adrian selflessly tended to everything I needed for months while I recovered. He's held me. He's soothed me. Cried for me. Held me. Anything I needed, he was there. But what I cherished most were the countless hours curled up next to him where we just talked. Sometimes about the most mundane things like animals in the zoo and other times about the future and our hopes and dreams. I didn't expect him to be funny, charming, or so damn smart. I didn't expect my heart — Ari's, not my Firebird's — to need him so much.

And that's why I couldn't stay and continue to be jerked around as if I'm some child who doesn't understand I am choosing life with him. A messy one, perhaps, but fuck, why are men so dense and stubborn sometimes?

Adrian refused to take me home, leaving me to call Tucker, who stormed in there raising hell. His fury pointed straight at Adrian. Roaring anger, I wouldn't have thought him capable of consumed him as spittle flew into Adrian's face with every shouted word. Not once did he raise his voice or battle my brother. His sparkling eyes narrowed as he took every slander Tucker threw his way.

The onslaught continued even when I attempted to pull Tucker back, explaining Adrian hadn't done anything wrong. He hadn't hurt me, not the way my overprotective brother was thinking. Only made it clear whatever it was we had wasn't progressing forward.

"You're a fucking idiot if you think my sister isn't good enough for you," he'd roared, slamming the door behind us.

Once I'd gotten Tucker into the car, he'd calmed back into the softy I've come to know. He understood when I explained how Adrian made me feel less like myself around him. Before Adrian, I was a woman who became a cop on a whim and turned into one of the best homicide detectives Chicago has ever known. The opposite of the assassin Salvatore molded me into. But did he really?

In truth, that was all me. Salvatore put the gun in my hand and gave me targets, but I took my ruthless nature out on them. He never taught me how to do that.

Another reason it seems better to distance myself from Adrian as much as possible, despite my heart saying not to. The guilt that settles in my stomach when I'm around him is too much to take. The number of paranormals I've killed because I was told to weighs heavier on me each passing day.

And for what? Nothing more than the fun and a stack of cash I'll never spend in my lifetime.

Every time Adrian updated me on the outside world, my intestines twisted into knots. My mind wondering how long it would have been before Salvatore handed me their information had I not found my family.

Not wanting to stew alone in my apartment, I decided today was the day to return to the job. The department hasn't given me clearance yet, but maybe if Captain Barlow sees I'm doing just fine — sort of — he'll sign off on the paperwork. To survive, I need to return to the aspects of my life that I am proud of.

A round of cheers sounds as I enter our home base. The desk and chairs and cluttered folders of paperwork on each one, a reminder of the piece of me I've been missing the past few months. Three months without the Ari I built.

"Welcome back, Luxembohrg," Garrett laughs as he pulls me into a tight hug. The pain that still lives within ratcheting a little higher, but I hold my closed-lipped smile, determined not to show any weakness.

My relationship with the guys has always been solid, but we don't hug. We clap hands like men do and crack inappropriate jokes, but that's where it ends.

His thick arms finally release me, his body keeping close before addressing the room. "Drinks on me tonight."

"Yeah, sure," I laugh, driving a fake punch into his shoulder before he scuttles back to his desk.

I turn to find Gomez perched on the edge of mine with his arms crossed. Relief shines in his brown eyes, but he wears a scowl. "You're so hard-headed."

"I missed you too," I lean an elbow on his shoulder as the captain shuffles in from his office.

"Ari, what are you doing back? I didn't clear you."

"Sir, I know, but I'm ready to get back."

"Did you re-qualify?"

"I'll go now."

Captain Barlow only pats me on the shoulder before giving a small nod. My cue to do as I said. The dark glare in his eyes was a warning that I better pass, or I'm not getting cleared anytime soon.

I dart from the room, ignoring whatever warning Gomez was trying to give. His words of wisdom aren't what I need right now.

It's the release of the trigger and the high of our murder cases that will cure me.

Unsure if I can just walk in, do my test, and then walk out, I debate putting into a call to the training unit. While searching for the number, Gomez appears at my side, the both of us waiting for the elevators to come. "Ari, you need to go home."

I ignore his comment. These men in my life need to stop acting as if they have any say over what I do. As if they can dictate how a woman like me should live and what she should do. It's not their choice. It's not their business. I am my own person. Have been for the longest time.

"Did you get anywhere with that lead for my..." The words stall in my throat. Gomez knows Syriah and Lanham are my parents, but my tongue won't seem to assist me in saying the words aloud. Outside of the safe houses and my apartment, I haven't voiced it once.

"No, I didn't touch that one. You're not going to either."

Spinning to face him, my mouth stretches into a tight line. "Gomez, you are not my father. I'm tired of all of you thinking you know what's best for me."

"Lux —"

"My last name is James."

Stalking into the elevator, I nestle in the farthest corner. Maintaining physical distance from my long-time partner, who has always looked out for me, is challenging within the confined space of the small cube. It's not fair to take my frustrations out on Gomez, but right now, he's only adding to them. Fueling a fire within, attached to the anger I carry around for everything Salvatore has done.

The moment the elevator doors whoosh open, I'm stalking out. It's a short walk to the onsite shooting range. A perk of our precinct also serving as one of the major police training academies in Chicago.

The sign for the shooting range comes into focus ahead. One of the few places I'm happiest. Countless days and nights spent there, firing away at invisible targets down the range.

"Eh, Joe," I call as I waltz in like I own the place.

"Luxembohrg, whatcha need?"

"To re-qualify."

He quirks a brow at me before eyeing the computer on his desk. Tapping at the keys, his brow furrows, eyes narrowing on the screen in front of him. No doubt searching for a request from the captain confirming my approval to be here.

He won't find it.

"Jerry, come on. I wouldn't be here if I wasn't ready."

Though I tried to hide it, there's a whining quality to my words. The difference in attitude between a child not getting their way and a woman eager to resume work.

Cocking my chin higher, I shove that usual Ari confidence to the surface. An attempt at blocking the fear that now lingers like a slithering dark tendril lurking in dangerous corners inside me.

I've never feared dying. Sometimes I even longed for it. A chance to relive my rebirth until that single bullet pierced my chest, almost stealing that opportunity from me. The healing process was long and arduous, both physically and mentally. An immeasurable number of minutes spent wishing death would take me because I couldn't fight the dark and the pain anymore. Then Adrian's voice would pull me back. He kept me here. And suddenly, I feel guilty for walking out on him.

In the end Adrian proved I'll have to move forward without him.

The doctor warned me that healing tears and his expertise could only take me so far. It will take my body almost a year to eat away every bit of that bullet. Until I am nothing but the soft tissues of Ari again, the pain will linger.

"You know I've gotta call the captain."

He gives me an apologetic smile as he dials Captain Barlow. Uninterested in any more men dictating what I will and won't do today, my hand flicks out to the side, waving him off. I wander away from the desk and gaze at the weapons displayed on the wall. There are countless options depending on what type of poison you choose. The Glock right in front of me a replica of the one I carry and the weapon Sal gifted me.

"Luxembohrg!" Jerry barks behind me, flagging me toward him. "I just took an ass chewing for you. You better pass."

With a nod, he leads me to the range. Itching to hold an issued gun again, I can't stop fisting my hands, only to extend my fingers once more. The ones I've held lately are my personal collection or Adrian's.

I miss the weight of the one Sal gifted me. The extra catch to the trigger before that deadly bullet fired. I should hate that weapon. Despise the damage it's done. The damage I've done, but I can't help but feel like a part of me is missing. After being a hit woman for so long, unknowingly fighting for the opposite team, I find it hard to simply be Ari, the phoenix. The cop. The solver of impossible crimes.

Jerry drops a department-issued weapon into my hands before leaving me to apply the noise-canceling ear protection.

My feet spread to their stance. The heels of my boots *thudding* against the floor as I settle into position. The target comes into focus, my arms rising in preparation. Sweat trickles down my temple as the tingle that works its way up my arm intensifies. The added weight from the gun was enough to disrupt my still-healing tissues. Still, I grit my teeth, holding my arms at shoulder height, both hands wrapped around the firearm.

I don't care about the pain. I don't care about Gomez and Jerry behind me, their eyes boring into the back of my skull. If it kills me — which it might — I am passing this requalification today.

My left arm quivers as my finger curls around the trigger, the initial pop enough to make me wince against the pain. Despite this, the bullet pierces the paper target, ripping a perfectly centered hole through the chest.

Ignoring the intense pain, I shoot again. This bullet a headshot that would end any life. A shot I've taken so many times. The faces of every paranormal flashing through my mind as I empty the clip. My focus never leaving that paper filled with holes as I switch the clip only to continuing firing.

With every pull of the trigger, new tears build behind my eyes. Tears no one will ever see me shed. I'm horrible for what I've done, but now I have a chance to fix it. An opportunity to unleash destruction on our adversaries.

"Okay. Enough, Luxembohrg," Jerry groans behind me. "Always trying to make us all look bad." He snatches the empty gun from my hands. "You passed. Get your gun and badge back from the captain."

With a single nod, I turn on my heel, strutting right past Gomez. Every blink needed to keep those tears at bay.

Tears of joy.

Tears of relief.

Tears of pain.

Tears of loss.

With a single sniffle, I step into the elevator, leaving it all behind me.

Ten

ADRIAN

Blind fury rages through me. Every thought or image of Ari playing in my head only rocketing it higher. Every grunt is more forceful and louder than the last.

The bench press bar, loaded with an extra three hundred pounds, is not enough to even damper the anger rolling through me. Not only did she demand to leave my house, calling Tuck to come get her a week ago, but she's back at work. She can barely hold her gun with two hands, and she's avoiding my calls.

When I went to find her two nights ago, she was back in her spot at the bar, nestled close to one of the guys she works with. The epitome of tall, dark, and handsome. With his light eyes, he appears to be as otherworldly as we are.

I nearly burned the place to the ground, watching her laugh with him. The crack of the wood beneath my fingers pulling me back to the present. A necessity before I burned myself alive from the inside out.

It wasn't until a series of drunk women tried to stumble out the door that I left. I should have gone home. Stewed in private.

Drank or tortured another witness alongside Tuck — also not speaking to me outside of official business — but no. I sat outside her apartment building for hours. Enough time for my anger to become unmanageable.

Somehow, I ended up finding my way to Tuck's front door.

He almost didn't let me in when I showed up. His bare torso and fitted boxer briefs indicative of what was going on before I arrived. The scent of sex thick in the air.

Still, he put aside his own anger when he looked into my eyes. Instead of mutilating another body, we sat out on the patio draped in the blanket of darkness the covered area provides.

"Why isn't she good enough for you?" he'd whispered, and my heart all but stopped.

I sat in silence so long I thought he'd abandon me out there. The words scrambling in my mind, attempting to structure themselves into a specific order meant to convey how much Ari means to me. A way to explain it without digging up my horrid past, so it didn't sound like an excuse. Unlike many, Tuck knows most of what I endured living with my family, but like everyone else except Syriah, he doesn't know everything.

The words never came, but he sat there with me until the pinks and peaches of the rising sun filled our vision.

"Tell her," he urged, as he patted my shoulder before venturing back into his house, returning to the woman he loves with every ounce of his being. The phoenix, who isn't his pair, but is willing to tether herself to him until the inevitable happens and they find

their mates. Their relationship will end no matter what they may feel when that time comes.

Then there's me. My pair is standing right in front of me, begging me to take her, but I've done nothing but keep her at arm's length.

I've told myself it's for her benefit, but it's for mine. Our hatred and attraction were equally strong before Salvatore shot her. The first night we spent together in my grandparent's home shifted the pieces into place for both of us. For the first time, we both recognized and felt a connection that was not filled with conflicted emotions and unspoken truths.

When that bullet drove into her flesh, a part of me died with the tissues touched by that metal. Every piece of me that wanted her to reject me as her pair slithered away. I knew I needed her then, but I needed her to need me, too. To want me. To understand what it will mean if we sleep together. The baggage that comes with choosing me.

The moment I slide into her wet depths, the bond anchors itself into place. So reinforced that even death doesn't break it. A dead mate dooms a surviving partner to a lifetime of heartbreak.

The door to the gym creaks open as I shove the weight away from me again. The sharp exhale of breath sending droplets of sweat flying.

Many of us do our workouts at the safe houses. A way to keep us concentrated should we need to quickly organize or to maximize time between meetings.

"Hey." Her voice sings behind me. The short clip is not harsh but possesses a tenderness that makes me close my eyes.

I allow the weight to sink back to my chest before shoving it upward three more times. Anything to put her voice and scent out of my mind. To ignore that she's suddenly right beside me.

"Adrian," she snaps.

"What!" The bar thrown aside before launching myself up from the bench. My face angled down to hers as my chest pumps so wildly it hits her with every panting breath. To her credit, she doesn't back down. Doesn't flinch. Just stares back at me with her face completely blank.

"You're training me today. Oliver had to go on patrol."

"The hell I am."

I slip around her, reaching for my towel and roughly rubbing it across my face.

There's nothing more I want than to be in her company. To watch her shift into her bird without abandon. To sit beside her as she strength-trains her body to be whole again.

But I can't. To be alone with her means the leash holding my desires in place will snap. I will have what she's offered so many times. Explanation or not.

Her hand curves around my sweat-soaked biceps, preventing my fantasies from taking center stage in my mind. My insides settling at her willing touch.

"Please."

A word I'm not sure she's ever said. My insides come alive at her touch. It's been a week without her sleeping beside me. That should have been the worst, but now, as she clasps my bare skin with her pleading navy blue eyes locked onto mine, I realize this is worse. Her standing right here looking for nothing more than platonic help damn near kills me.

"I need to get back into shape. We both know Sal and whoever he's recruited aren't done."

She's right. I know she is.

My chin drops to my chest, a long exhale snaking past my parted lips.

"Okay. Let's get this over with."

Determination gleams in her eyes. Despite a stoic glare, her jaw works visibly with each movement. Watching her daily, I could tell she was experiencing more pain than she let on, and it seems that hasn't changed.

She progresses through every exercise I give her without question. Despite the pain almost tearing us apart, she pushes on. Fat tears falling down her flushed cheeks with every rep. Droplets of moisture, I wish I had the right to wipe away.

Not once does she try to hide them from me. Every bit of emotion shines through her eyes with pride.

"That's enough for today," I grunt.

A relieved sigh escapes her as she slouches forward onto the machine we were just working her upper back on.

Sitting on the bench next to her, I wipe my face again. "Come here."

She shuffles over to me, standing just close enough my knee brushes her leg. Instinctually, I grab her wrist, then behind one thigh, shifting her to straddle my thighs. But I let her stand there. The barest sliver of space between us, so I can honor what she asked of me. The choice has to be hers.

When her hands find my shoulders, my gaze drifts up to meet hers. That same burning desire that's always been there for me is radiant as ever.

"Ari…"

"Adrian, please don't. You don't want this. That's fine. Just let me know whatever the procedure is here."

A dark sadness coats her words. Those eyes shifting to what-ever emotion is now drowning her by my lack of answer.

"Ari, listen to me." I pull her toward me, forcing her to sit on my lap. Her core kept away from my aching dick as she settles further down my thighs. Disappointment lances through me. A week ago, she snuggled so closely into me in bed you couldn't see where my body began and she ended. It was normal for her to sit in my lap or shower with me.

Not now, though. Not anymore.

"Adrian, you listen to me. I won't be jerked around by you anymore…"

Dragging her forward, I slam her straight into my throbbing cock. Her body arching against my arm looped around her back.

Her eyes drifting down to where the essence of what will solidify our pairing sits nestled together.

"I want you. I think that's clear. But I needed you to understand what it means to fuck me."

Her eyes dart up to mine. Her brow crinkling low. "I know what it means to have sex with you, Adrian. Did you think I would keep asking for it if I didn't, knowing you were my pair?"

"How?" The single word a breathy gasp.

"Talia told me everything. Initially, I was clueless, but I've understood for a while. If you'd had the balls to ask me earlier, we wouldn't be in this situation. I wouldn't be here hating you again." The last part barely above a whisper.

Her forehead drops to mine, eyes pressing shut on a deep inhale.

"You don't hate me."

"Yes, I do." Her words hushed.

Ari has unlocked the door she shut on me a week ago and left it cracked. Slamming it wide open, I take my shot. An opportunity to go back to the place we were at prior to her leaving.

"Prove it."

Her eyes search mine for seconds before she kisses me. The rock of her hips into my throbbing dick, making me groan loudly. Warm fingers drift under the hem of my shirt, shuffling the sweaty fabric up my body. Our kiss only breaking long enough for her to rip it over my head.

"That's my girl," I growl into the hollow of her throat.

"I'm not yours."

"Yet..." My promise to her.

She swallows her sharp intake of breath as her lips meet mine again. Her hands in my hair, mine snaking under her fitting crop top and into the band of her leggings. Right now, what I need most is the heat of her skin against mine.

My finger curls into her top, my nail shifting to a sharp enough point to shred the thing in two. The heat of her mouth at my throat drawing out another rumbling growl from my chest.

Then a familiar click pierces through our heavy breathing. The door to the gym creaking open seconds later.

I've barely processed that someone has entered the room with us when Ari all but falls off my lap, stumbling to a stop several feet away from me.

The moment is over. The mood broken.

The distance in her eyes upon entering has returned. The door she'd allowed to crack open isn't anymore.

"Hi, Mom," she waves.

Fuck.

Eleven

ADRIAN

My heart hammers in my chest seeing Mrs. James, the woman who is like a mother to me, stationed in the doorway, shoulder leaning against the doorframe. A position I often find myself in. Even her smirk is a match for mine. *Did I get it from her?*

Heat runs from my gut up my throat. My skin on fire for a whole new reason.

She only stares at us. Ari appearing completely unaffected. I'm doing my best not to writhe in agony from blue balls and crippling embarrassment.

"Sorry to cut your time short. I need you both upstairs."

Ari heads for the exit, grabbing her water bottle with more force than necessary.

"You two might want to shower first."

Ari's gone in an instant, likely disappearing to the room her mother has now deemed as hers upstairs. Her bedroom door is directly next to mine. Our en suite bathrooms wall to wall.

By the time I make my way to mine, her shower is already running. Loud singing emanates through the wall. Selena today, I think. It's a quirk of hers I love most. Always singing when she thinks no one can hear her or is watching. The number of mornings I pretended to still be asleep listening to the screech of her voice seems ridiculous now. Despite her inability to carry a tune, I love everything about that woman.

An admission I can make freely in my head.

I'm quick to hop under the warm spray. The suds washing my body clean, my cock still painfully hard. Her singing continues, serving as the beat I use to pump my fist against my sensitive flesh. The pulsing of that thick vein harsh against my grip. My opposite palm lies flat against the shower wall, my torso curving, abs convulsing as my release draws closer.

Images of her naked body flash through my mind. A body I've gotten to know the past few months of her living with me. One she's let me touch, lick and suck as much as I've watched and cared for her. The memory of her pussy on my tongue flashes through my mind. Nothing or no one has ever tasted as good as her. My fingers and tongue were the only two parts of me lucky enough to enter her. Her core always squeezing me tight.

I miss her.

I need her.

I've had enough of this shit. Tonight, after whatever Syriah needs to talk to us about, I'm settling this.

She wanted me as bad as I wanted her down there. I felt it. Felt us. The bond itching to lock into place.

Hair still wet, I make my way downstairs. Myself, Syriah, Oliver, Talia, Tuck, Bronson, and a few others crowd around the kitchen island. Multiple pairs of hands quickly moving in and out of what must be twenty pizza boxes.

"Great. We're all here now," Syriah chirps, her tiny hands clasping together. "We have an idea where Salvatore might be hiding."

"Where?" Bronson quirks a brow. His meat-lover's slice of pizza, poised at his mouth then dropped to his plate.

"There have been a series of murders in Indiana, Wisconsin, and other Chicago suburbs. Each location has been close enough that they could be Salvatore and his followers."

"How many?" I growl.

It's not that I need to hear the number. There's no need to confirm that our own kind has been gunned down like worthless animals, but the question spewed past my grinding teeth anyhow.

Ari flinches next to her mother. Her shoulders scrunched up around her ears before Syriah drapes a motherly arm around her.

"All but two. So forty-seven total."

The room goes silent. Every breath held. Chewing stopped. Our eyes trained on Syriah, praying she didn't speak the truth.

"How is that possible without PD or the FBI getting involved?" Ari booms.

"Sweetheart." Syriah runs a hand along her cheek, much like she used to do to Tuck and me when we fucked up. "Are you not a detective yourself? We are everywhere and Salvatore has many allies."

Matt — short for Mateo — a young phoenix from Talia's bloodline, scoffs. "You should know. You're one of them."

As if I have no control over my body, I launch myself across the island. His small throat engulfed by my hand. Our faces are a finger-width apart as I heave panting breaths into his face. No one stops me from squeezing tighter, Matt's eyes bulging as his hands claw at my forearm. He's about to find out what happens to those who disrespect my pair. I won't have it.

Matt has never been reborn, but tonight he might get the chance.

"I would suggest you apologize and then proceed to never address my pair directly again."

He forcefully swallows beneath my tightening grip. His light brown lips beginning to go blue.

"Am I understood?"

He gives the slightest nod. One more squeeze of my palm before I throw him to the ground.

My chest heaves as I turn back to face the room. "If anyone ever brings that shit up again, I will fucking kill you. Do you all understand me?"

Nods flow from around the room as I stalk to Ari, grabbing her chin between my fingers and slamming my mouth to hers.

She immediately opens up for me. The scent of her arousal overwhelming the aroma of the pizza. Each inhale fueling my lungs with the sweet air I need to breathe.

Our display goes indecently long. Her fingers tangling in my damp hair, pulling me closer. I only pull away when I know I'm seconds away from fucking her on top of these pizza boxes covering the island.

No one will be there to witness my first time with her.

"That's settled then," Syriah breaks up the silence of the room, shifting aside so I can position myself next to Ari.

Her body immediately sinks into mine. Her back to my front, my chin resting atop her head, our fingers linked as our tangled arms fold across her stomach.

"As I was saying, these murders have drawn attention. The World Council is sending... assistance."

The pause is unusual for Syriah.

This woman commands us. Even though they are the ruling family of every paranormal entity, this situation has still managed to shake her. Enough that her news has left her less than the fearless leader we all follow.

"Just tell us what to do, Mom," Ari chimes in. Her voice sure and steady. My warrior is coming back to life.

I've missed her.

"For now, we operate as usual. Draw no unnecessary attention to yourselves." Syriah's eyes drift to Tuck. His nonchalant shrug acknowledgment of exactly what kind of attention she's referring to. "The representative will be here sometime within the week from Manchester. You'll show her respect. You'll do as she asks."

A chorus of *yes* fills the room.

"Great. Make sure you all clean up after you're done."

"Yes, ma'am," every voice sounds except Ari's.

"Adrian, Ari. With me, please."

Refusing to allow Ari to unravel her body from mine, we move as one. My legs straddling the sides of hers as we waddle into Lanham's office. The strike of my heel shutting the door behind us, causing her to flinch in my arms. I only tighten my grip on her, realizing it must be a response to that traumatic night. Something we'll talk about later.

"Sit." Syriah gestures us to a loveseat across the room from the desk.

I do, pulling Ari down into my lap. This time she resists, shifting to sit beside me. My jaw works, pissed she's chosen to sit next to me instead of on me. Our bodies no longer touch at all. Enough space between us for Syriah to fit comfortably.

A frown draws down the corners of her petite mouth. Cop Ari is back. The focused assassin blocking out or attraction understanding there's business that needs to be handled now.

We sit in silence. Syriah's eyes on us, ours on her. Our breathing a matched even pace as if lounging poolside.

"What is happening here?" Syriah gestures between the two of us.

Neither of us jumps to answer.

"I'm waiting." That no-nonsense tone forcing me to shift in my seat. It's not that I'm uncomfortable answering, but I want it to come from Ari. I want to hear her say just one more time she wants this bond with me.

"Well, if you want to know, Adrian won't sleep with me because he's scared that I don't know what it means for the bond. He thinks whatever shit he has going on internally will trap me somehow." Her gaze drifts toward me. "Did that cover it?"

"And do you?" Syriah's eyes settle solely on Ari. The press of her mouth meant to intimidate instead of comfort her daughter.

"I do. It would mean the bond can't be undone. It would mean choosing all of him for life."

Syriah nods, as if accepting her daughter's answer. Her brow rising as Ari continues.

"I understand perfectly fine what the bond means. I've told Adrian what I wanted. He has refused me over and over. My only conclusion is he doesn't want me as his pair. But I won't renounce us. That's on him."

Ari stands from the couch, a whimper escaping as she digs her fists into the plush leather to push herself up. She gives Syriah a one-armed hug and leaves, not once looking back at me.

"Fix. This. You're better than this, Adrian," Syriah growls before following her daughter from the room.

Defeated, my head falls to my hands.

My only chance is convincing Ari that I want this. That I want her.

If only she'd take five minutes to listen to me. If only I had taken the initiative to explain everything sooner.

The anger surges once more. Stomping from the room, the door slamming against the wall behind it, there's only one available cure for my piss-poor mood.

Hopefully, the gym is empty.

Twelve

Ari

"And we're going where?" Gomez asks, his words muffled by the Boston cream donut he's shoveling into his mouth.

He only eats them with me, in the privacy of our cars. Far away from the guys who chastise him for his dad bod and his kids who crave sugar like no tomorrow.

"To see Rolan, of course." My voice is as sweet as the doughy pastry squished between Gomez's fingers.

"Excuse me?" His eyes go wide.

"You heard me. You may have told me to drop it, but I won't. Sal is out there, and he had someone try to kill my parents."

I know Gomez knows the orders my mother gave. The whole keep a low profile thing ringing through my head, but she also said to continue as we normally would. And before Sal shot me, I was already ready to hunt Rolan. Determined to find that motherfucker and tear his heart out with my bare hands. Normal... for me, at least.

"Ari..." Gomez groans.

There's no escaping the daddy-knows-best speech Gomez is about to give me. From the moment I learned about him and his family being wolf-shifters, he's been so much worse. Hovering so close, he's suffocating. The orders come from Adrian. I know they do.

"Look, just let's check it out. Okay? I owe that much to them."

"Fuck," he barks, fingers pinching the bridge of his nose. "I can't believe I stayed on late with you for this shit."

"Yes, you can," I grin. Earning a side-eye from him. "And you will not call Adrian."

"Too late."

Shit.

The bar isn't where I would expect to find one of Salvatore's men lurking. That is until I spot the young women nestled around the bar top and corners toward the back. The outfits that barely cover their coochies and tits hanging so far out, I'm pretty sure I'm seeing areola. Fucking disgusting.

Trust I have no problem with a woman expressing her sexuality. Dress provocatively, if that's what she chooses. It's no different from me in my leather jackets and booties. Everyone is free to express themselves as they choose, but there's a difference between dressing for yourself and wearing a costume for someone else.

There's a cheapness to what these women wear. Desperation in their eyes begging these men to take them home. Payment for their services either to support their families or bad habits. My conscience growling at me for casting any sort of judgement when I'm a fucking murderer.

Gomez drifts away from me a few steps past the entrance. Just a split second of me catching him slide on the bar stool before a large body hides him from view. With a crowd this dense, it's easy to lose sight of anyone not within arm's reach.

I changed clothes before we arrived, but my partner remains in his slacks and button-down shirt. To look weary after a long workday, he loosened his tie. A sign he needs to take a load off for the night. Just a few drinks. A little ass. He's playing his role well.

The strips of fabric that streak across the back of my dress pull my posture tall. My hemline is extremely conservative compared to the other women in here, despite two-thirds of my thigh being exposed.

Slithering through the bodies that seem to ooze booze out of their pores, I go in search of Rolan. Identifying him was easy using our access to paranormal databases, so I know my target.

Big, burly. A scowling face, as if every inhabitant of the earth scorned him.

I've neared the rear of the bar, Gomez still out of view, when I find him tucked into a booth. There's a woman on his lap — just thin enough to fit between his thick body and the table — and two more flanking him.

"Mind if I sit?" My voice a sultry purr. The quirk at the corner of my mouth matches the cockiness I feel at approaching the bastard who may have murdered my family.

The man I'll murder if I find out he did.

"Go!" he orders the three women. Each one scampering off in heels too high and with darting, confused eyes. I don't give a fuck about them. I'm here for him.

"So great to finally meet you." My words are a faked drawl of excitement.

"Ahh, so Sal's former pet thinks she can walk in here and scare me?"

"Rolan, I'm not here to scare you. I'm here for you to answer a few questions, and then we can go our separate ways."

A thin brow rises. His equally thin lips pressing into a line so straight it's as if he doesn't have any. Hands steepled beneath his chin, we keep eye contact. Neither of us willing to break first.

He knows my name. He knows what I've done to so many others like him.

"Well, ask away." Rolan leans back into the booth. An arm draped across the back, something clear in his glass. Definitely liquor. Who cares what kind? Only bitches drink anything clear.

"Did you murder Syriah and Lanham James?"

His smirk replaces that straight glare. A loud gulp of his drink before signaling a waitress for another.

"You got me." Laughter bursts from him. His ego getting in the way, allowing him to believe I'm not a threat since I'm no longer under Sal's thumb.

"Just one more question…"

"Not like I have a choice. You're going to sit here chasing away my pussy until I do." Another audible gulp. The glass now empty.

"Did they scream?"

His eyes go wide, unprepared for my question. Realization settling in for why I asked it.

By the end of the night, he'll be the one screaming. Loudly. Agony will course through his body as I tear him apart.

"No." The simple answer meant to hide the sweat trickling down his brow. Or the uncomfortable shift in his seat.

"Good… But you will."

Thirteen

ADRIAN

Traffic hates me. Literally holds a fucking grudge against me if I'm trying to get to her.

There's no getting to Ari fast enough.

Raphael's text didn't come soon enough.

She did this on purpose. Waiting to tell him where they were going so he couldn't object. I bet she drove, too. The only way to guarantee she controls the situation. With my pair behind the wheel, Raphael has no choice but to follow.

I've been scouring the bar for a solid twenty minutes. Raphael cannot tell me a damn thing about where she is. They separated when they arrived, and that's the end of it. Unless she left, the only places I haven't checked are the storerooms and a small office in the back of the bar.

Grunts greet me as I turn the last corner to the final storeroom. The door locked when I yank at the handle.

"Occupied!" Ari shouts from the other side. The edge to her voice ratcheting my pulse that much higher.

My patience is gone. How can I protect this woman if she insists on acting out constantly? Her mean streak is hot as fuck. The number one quality to drive my dick into a stiff rod. But fuck, she might be the death of me, and I hate the rebirth process.

"Ari, open this motherfucking door! Now!" Each word, a rumbling growl, my fist poised to pound against the surface.

Her chuckle greets me. Muffled words just clear enough. "Oh man, if you thought I was bad, wait until you meet my betrothed."

Who the fuck says that? Yet something like hope swells in my chest. She still wants me. Still wants our futures tied together indefinitely.

Two distinct clicks sound. My pulse bounding unsure what will greet me on the other side. A laborious creak sounds as the door slips open a fraction. Just wide enough that the storage shelves along the far wall are within view.

The sharp tang of blood wafts up my nostrils.

Rolan Damistikoff's body slumps against the wall, but his legs still keep him standing. Blood oozes from countless knife wounds along his abdomen and palms. But that wolfish grin still stretches across his rugged face.

"Rolan, meet Adrian. Adrian, baby, this is Rolan. He tried to kill my parents."

Rolan laughs. A gurgle of bubbling blood dripping over his lips and down his front.

"Fuck you, you dumb cunt."

Anger roars through me. No one speaks to Ari like that. This man certainly had a death wish if he thought he'd get away with calling her anything but the queen she is.

"Ari, give me the knife."

A wicked grin pulls at her wine-painted lips.

"Only if you make him scream," she purrs. Her mouth finds mine in an instant. My already semi-hard cock swelling to attention. I don't care if we're in a filthy storage room with a man bleeding out behind us. I would fuck her regardless. Still might. Just take the plunge and make her mine.

I yank my mouth from hers, fingers tangled in her long waves. So much more hair to knot around my fist that wasn't there when we met. I like the length but secretly hope she cuts it again, too.

"By the end of the night, we'll all be screaming." My gaze shifts from her face to the piece of shit in front of me. "But you..." I cock my head toward Rolan. "...you'll be screaming for an entirely different reason."

For the first time since the day she left my grandparent's house, she smiles at me. A genuine, wide smile that pushes at the corners of her eyes, displaying her pearly white teeth.

Reaching down, I pull the knife from her hand. One specially commissioned for times like this against our own kind. She releases it to me without a fight. Driving to the tips of her toes to plant another kiss on my cheek before I position myself in front of Rolan.

Unlike us, when I slaughter him, he won't be reborn. Werewolves heal fast, but they can't come back to life.

"You attempted to murder the only good parents I've ever had." Throwing my arm back, it crashes down, the blade cutting through flesh and tissue before lodging in his sternum. Anyone nearby heard his howl, no doubt about that. "You called my pair a cunt." I drive into him again, dragging the blade down.

Flesh and cartilage and tendon and bone are shredded by the metal embedded in this man's chest.

"Fuck. You," he spits in my face. "They're dead. They're not fit to rule." He coughs, like so many of the victims from Tuck's torture rooms. Blood spatters across my face and clothing, but I don't care. No one will disrespect the James family in my presence.

"Wrong," I whisper close to his ear. "You failed."

His eyes go wide, his screams ringing in our ears as I drag the knife all the way down to his groin, fileting his body wide open.

Rolan's body crumples to the floor as I yank the knife free. Only a few more gurgling breaths from his direction as I drape my arm around Ari's shoulders, leaving the battered corpse on the floor.

Those blue eyes find mine, a look I've never witnessed splashed across her face. "Take me home."

I'd do anything she asked of me.

Blood-soaked, riding the high of removing one more piece of filth from this world, we fold ourselves into my SUV. She doesn't say a word as I navigate the streets of Chicago. I'd already texted

Raphael as we left the bar, so he should be home with his family by now.

It shouldn't bother me that Ari's focus stays strained outside her window. Her body seems relaxed enough, but the silence between us is alarming. No banter. No arguments. Nothing at all.

Ari has killed before, so it can't be witnessing a death. She's slaughtered plenty and with no remorse.

But that was before. A time when she didn't know those targets were like us. Like her. Before she felt guilt for killing the "others" in our world.

A time before she found her family and me.

However, there was a distinct difference in what occurred in that storeroom.

"You okay?"

"Peachy." Her sarcasm adding to the tension that is seemingly leaking back into the space between us.

The woman in that closet was totally different from the one beside me now. A mirror image of the one from the kitchen a few days ago and then in Lanham's office.

I don't get it. I can't figure out what it is I'm doing wrong to make her so hot and cold with me. We've barely interacted since the day she walked out my front door, so it shouldn't be this wild swing every time we're in the same room.

I've never felt this strongly about a woman, but I've never had a pair either. With my family's reputation, there was never an opportunity to latch onto any sort of genuine relationship.

Women couldn't stand the cruelty or wouldn't so much as come near me for more than a few fucks.

This overwhelming tornado of emotions and primal instinct is all new. It never stops. Never slows. Their force so much worse than the brutal winter Chicago winds.

"Right." My teeth audibly grinding.

I'd convinced myself tonight would be the night. I would finally make her mine, but now doubt creeps in. Part of me convinced what she said back in the storeroom was part of the tough girl act she was putting on for an already dying Rolan.

Perhaps that fire that crackled between us in the kitchen and storage closet were nothing more than her being in the moment. A show for the others around us to prevent additional commentary or questions. Regardless, the gym lacked an audience. There was no one to perform for. We'd been there together, ready to tumble over the edge.

We both felt it. There's no denying that moment.

I pull up to the curb, throwing the car in park.

"Want me to walk you up?"

She shifts to look at me. Her brow lowered as she stares at me as if I spoke another language. "You're not coming in?"

I hadn't expected that. Thought for sure the quiet of our car ride meant she wanted me gone.

Without a word, I speed into the public garage across the street, parking the car in the first available spot. My movements are clumsy and rushed, eager to get out as quickly as possible before she changes her mind.

She takes my hand as we dart across the street. Our fingers tightly linked, speed-walking through the lobby and all but throwing ourselves into the elevator. Our connection refusing to break even when she has me open the door for her — her other arm too sore after her stab fest — or when we enter the bathroom and she starts the shower.

Only then does she release my hand. Stripping her leather jacket from her shoulders and tossing it on the floor, her eyes never leave mine.

"I'll be out here." I point beyond the door, turning on my heel before she even speaks.

A tight grip wrapping around my forearm stops me in my tracks. Her breaths are loud behind me. Pressing my eyes shut, the racing thump of her heart fills the silence. It's pace a match for mine. The throb in my swelling dick also keeping time.

"You're covered in blood. You should shower, too."

Her olive branch. A way to keep me close, even if she's not quite herself right now. With a nod, I yank my shirt over my head, keeping my eyes on her while she struggles to remove the dress that fits her like a glove.

I've watched her wince and fight enough before I gently spin her around. Curling my fingers over the edges of the back, I make eye contact with her in the mirror. A check to ensure she actually wants me to ruin such a delicious piece of clothing. With a nod,

I tear it in two. The electric blue pieces fluttering to the floor at our feet.

Her bare back greets me, flawless skin for me to run my hands along. The black lace of her panties serving as the worst sort of temptation, especially when I can smell her arousal like a tantalizing treat in the steam-filled bathroom.

With a coy look over her shoulder, she bends and removes those, too. The strip of fabric held between delicate fingers before she, too, lets those fall to the floor. Her quick steps carrying her into the shower stall and under the spray of the water before I can strip out of the rest of my clothing.

"Come on. You can wash me," she winks.

Yes ma'am.

Fourteen

ARI

The spray of the water runs down my back in a thick wave as I shut my eyes, fists balled into my chest. Anything to ignore the fact that Adrian is getting naked behind me, ready to join me in this shower because I invited him to. Because I want him here next to me. Because I crave those heavy palms on my bare skin.

Despite knowing it won't go any further than it has in the past, I miss him. Despite the distance I've put between us, I still want and need him. Against my better judgement, I'm okay with being weak today. Accepting of the fact that my bird desires him enough to force the woman to accept whatever he is willing to give.

My blood still roars with the events of this evening. I hate that it felt good to help murder that piece of shit, but it did. Paranormal or not. He wasn't worth inhabiting this earth any longer. Though I wasn't the one to tear that bastard apart with my bare hands, I watched. I reveled in his death. Enjoyed watching the light leave his wicked eyes. I was part of stealing his last breath, and that's enough for me.

Something snapped inside me when Adrian threatened his way into that room. I knew he would show. There was no keeping him away once Gomez texted him.

There's also no ignoring that the longer Adrian and I spend time together, the more attached we become, no matter how pissed I am at him. No matter how much my heart breaks at his continued rejections.

Us being pairs is the reason I can't walk away when he pulls that possessive male shit. My pussy soaking wet with my arousal the moment that growl rumbles deep in his chest. I nearly pinned him to the floor in the safe house kitchen when he had Mateo by the throat. The throb between my legs was so unbearable there wasn't a chance of me not letting him hold me after. Always so willing to envelop me in the essence of him.

Mom calling us into the office broke the spell. When she has that look of business in her eye, I can somehow turn off me and Adrian. It wasn't that I didn't want his touch anymore. I wanted to pay attention to whatever my mother deemed important enough to pull us into the privacy of the office. And sitting on his rock-hard cock would have been nothing but a distraction as I fought myself not to shamelessly grind into him. Begging him for the one thing he continues to deny me.

My mother asking what our issue was tore that cavern of emotions wide open. Those feelings of loneliness and being unworthy rushing back to the surface in a crashing wave. Those same notions I've carried since childhood thinking my parents didn't care enough to keep me. Feelings I'd locked away when I left Adrian.

Syriah has always been easy to spill every thought to. The words slipping past my lips with venom before I could stop them.

Watching him slaughter the werewolf that tried to murder my parents tonight gave us a blank slate. Adrian may not fuck me, but I am not willing to walk away just yet. No one has ever made me feel as understood and seen as he does.

I've been unfair, assuming because he grew up with his phoenix family, he was any more prepared to have a pair than I was. I never stopped to consider how this might affect him, too. That we'll both need to adjust and reformat our lives. Truths I didn't understand until Oliver explained Adrian's past a few days ago.

Truth be told, I don't think there's any chance I could choose someone other than Adrian, even if he renounces our pairing.

His arrival cuts my thoughts short. The heated skin of this torso, dick, and thighs pressed in tight against me, bringing my insides to life. My lashes flutter against my cheeks, having him so close to me again. My deep inhale pulling the scent that is so characteristically him inside me.

Callused hands run up my bare arms, goose bumps breaking out across the entirety of my flesh.

"Are you okay?" he whispers against the shell of my ear. His lips mold around the curve before lightly sucking. The slight pressure enough to drive the pulsing of my core.

"I enjoyed seeing you covered in his blood. I love that you were there to defend me and my parents." My fingers slip into his hair, my back arching as my ass grinds against him. "I wanted to fuck you right there on the floor in that traitor's pool of blood. I would have if you'd let me."

He chuckles behind me, spinning me to face him, my shoulder blades gently tapping the tiled wall. "Me too."

Our mouths meet. That same ferocity burning hot between us as our day in the gym when I was sure we'd have crossed that line.

His large hands grip beneath my thighs, hoisting me into the air, my legs wrapping around his middle. My arms wrap around his neck, the ache in my shoulder ignored for the hope that we can stop pussy-footing around our connection.

"Adrian, I have a lot I want to say to you, but right now —"

"Stop. Talking," he groans.

"Excuse me." Indignation thick in my tone.

"I'm trying very hard not to come all over your stomach like a teenage boy. We'll do this my way or not at all."

My pussy throbs in response to his words. His dominance enough to clamp my lips shut as his warm breath drifts over my heated, wet skin.

My pelvis shamelessly grinds into him, searching for relief. Wanting him buried so deep inside me, he fucks my shit up. I know I want him. It's no secret that I want him, but our connection makes resisting that overwhelming desire even more difficult.

He shifts my weight, so only one arm holds me. Sure fingers trail down between my breasts, taking one taut nipple and rolling before flicking it. The shock of pain shooting straight down to my underutilized pussy.

Those same fingers trail lower, my belly curving inward. Every nerve fiber comes alive under his touch. My Firebird seemingly looking through my eyes straight into his.

This is it. Our pivotal moment. Adrian will claim me as his tonight.

My teeth clamp down on my upper lip, anticipating the feel of him sliding into me for the first time. My moans loud with the press of his large thumb against my clit.

"Stop biting your lip." The bass in his voice vibrating through my body, only makes my pulse race. The muscles clenching, knowing what's coming next.

"Please." My fingers knot in his hair. "Please, Adrian. Please."

"Hush." His tone is harsh, but it only makes me that much more needy for him. I'm addicted to this man, and I've barely had him yet.

My head presses against the tiled wall as trained fingers slither through my folds, swirling water and my arousal around my clit.

Two long digits slipping inside my entrance moments later. A slow rhythmic pump driving the movement of my chest, rising and falling. My painfully hard nubs rubbing against his broad chest with every curl of his fingers along my inner walls.

"Fuck. Adrian. I can't…"

"Hush, or I won't give you what we both want."

"You're a bastard," I snarl.

"I know, but you're going to love me, anyway."

Too late.

The words shoot through my mind so quickly that I wonder if I imagined them, but I know I didn't. Nonetheless, I firmly push them away, refusing to recognize anything beyond our current physical connection. That's all I can handle. All I can focus on.

I'm not sure I'm emotionally ready for another relationship, but I hope to be in the future.

Adrian's fingers continue to expertly tease me. My release building to the point of a violent explosion when I roar his name, his fingers still working me hard. My forehead collides with his solid shoulder. A fresh wave of pain coursing through my head to war with the bolts shooting down my left arm.

Shit. A concussion is the last thing I need.

Slowly, he slides me down his body. Those large palms never leaving my skin.

"Turn." I do, confusion knitting my brow.

"Adrian?"

"Bend over. Far as you can."

My body bends at the waist. My hamstrings uncomfortably stretching. I've only just returned to actual activity since getting shot, and my body is happy to remind me.

My hands hit the wall, stopping my fall. The impact vibrating through my body uncomfortably. A little pain to mix with the pleasure sure to come.

A hand glides over my ass cheek, then along the small of my back. Soothing circles relax my rebelling muscles. The shift of my hips is more about my discomfort than enticing the male behind me.

"More."

With a groan, I walk my hands a little further down the wall. That continuous stretch tugging at my core now, too. A delicious reminder of what's coming.

"Good girl." The absence of his palm against my bare skin sends a chill up my spine until he swats my ass. "Don't move."

His palms find the curve of my cheeks again, his knees cracking as he kneels behind me. My eyes fluttering open only long enough to see him on his knees behind me.

So we're not going to fuck. Dammit.

That disappointment burrows in my chest. I'd thought for sure he'd take the plunge this time. That he'd sink into my heat and never want to pull himself free.

A gasp leaves me as his thumbs spread my cheeks. The soft brush of his breath over sensitive flesh making me squirm.

"Don't. Move."

It's a fight to hold still. My eyes press shut to ignore the rush of blood to my head and the shooting pain in my arm. The adrenaline still pumping through me from repeatedly stabbing Rolan mixes with the high of having Adrian touch me.

Images of Rolan's face play on repeat through my mind. His laughter gradually shifting to grimaces and howls of pain and pleas with each additional strike. *Beautiful.*

The moment he drags the flat of his tongue through my folds and up over my puckered hole, my entire body convulses. The threat of another orgasm coming so quickly after the first nearly drives me to my knees.

I have never experienced a man eating me from behind. The sensations so far removed from me lying on my back legs spread wide. From this position, Adrian does the work. Lapping up my arousal like a thirsty dog. His fingers painfully digging into my flesh, holding me open for him.

"Fuck. You taste like heaven," his words breathed against my wet and sensitive pussy. His tongue dips inside me, its twisting path making me grind against his face.

"Adrian." His name a tortured groan.

"Only once you give me what I want."

I move to stand, ready to impale myself on his rigid dick, but he pushes me back down. "Not yet."

His torture continues, his finger joining the fun as they drive into my cunt the moment his tongue probes at my asshole. All of me coming undone within seconds. A violent shake of my entire body that would send me hurtling to the wet tiles, face-first if not for Adrian holding me up.

"You're so good for me, Ari. So, so good." He swats my ass again, pulling me to standing. My vision blurring as I try to find my balance. The dizzy spell lasting longer than I'd like. "Let's get cleaned up. Then to bed."

Fuck. Not this again. He gets me off and then refuses to fuck me again.

That hope I'd let nestle in my chest fades away.

You're better than this, Ari. Don't cave.

Snatching my loofa from his fingers, I turn my back to him, lathering my body in soap. The suds barely clearing my feet before I stomp out of the shower.

Fuck, Adrian Alexander.

Fifteen

Ari

I've barely dried my body before climbing under the comforter with a huff. Never in my life have I had to work so damn hard to get laid. I get the stakes are higher this time. There's more that comes with sex with Adrian than just a dick into a hole, but come the fuck on.

The blankets are suddenly torn from me. The chill raking over my body, only to find Adrian towering over me. Water droplets glisten over his well-sculpted chest as it heaves up and down. His nostrils flared like an angry bull. His cock, a thick heavy rod standing at attention.

"What the fuck?"

"If you walk away from me one more fucking time, Ari..." His eyes press shut, neck rolling out as he fights to keep his temper in check. The muscles of his jaw and neck flex beneath his skin.

Why is he so pissed?

I'm the one he keeps rejecting.

I'm the one who has to hear "no" over and over again while he acts like some possessive asshole in front of everyone else.

Fuck him.

"You'll what? Ignore me some more?"

In an instant, his naked form hovers over me. My shoulder blades pressing into the mattress as much as it will allow. Anything to put space between us. I've seen Adrian brutally angry, but this is something else. This is other emotions mixed in rioting with the frustration I leave him with every time I stalk off.

Still, my ability to keep my mouth shut fails me. "Well?"

Our breaths sync for one, two, three beats of my heart before he nudges into me. No warning. No asking. Our bodies coming together in the exact way I've been craving for months.

A feeling I can only describe as laser strobes of light shoot through my body with every shift of his hips forward. My core working to open for him while he works to sheath himself in my heat. Our bodies quivering in unison when he finally burrows himself to the hilt.

I'm no stranger to sex. We know this. I've fucked plenty of men, but I can't describe what it feels like to be with Adrian. He hasn't even begun to really move yet, and my insides are unraveling. A feeling so similar to being reborn courses through me. The fibers that were just me coming apart to blend themselves with the pieces of him funneling into me. That thread we all talk about pulsing and thickening in my chest.

There's no catching my breath as I pull him close. Thread by thread, my body weaves itself together with each roll of his hips into me. I wonder if he feels what I'm feeling. If we're now connected internally.

Neon green orbs find mine as his eyelids flutter open. I'd seen them do this before, but never this bright. Never this vibrant.

"We match," he chuckles. "Our eyes. We match."

Mine must be glowing too. It must be why the colors of my bedroom all seem different. Every scent and sight uniquely transformed in minutes.

"Don't be scared."

"I'm not," I lie.

"You are. I can feel everything you're feeling now."

With a nod, my hands find the curve of his lower back, the ecstasy of us joined blurring my thoughts at the edges. We move together, pelvises meeting as his cock drives in and out of my wet depths. Each reentry knitting more of me back together.

Not just Ari anymore. Pieces of Adrian become part of me, too. Our souls and phoenixes merging in ways I can't understand.

"Adrian, you can make love to me later. I've been waiting months for this. Put in the work."

He chuckles against my throat, gripping under my thigh and stretching my leg high near my face. My muscles groan, pussy clenching around him. The shift in position opening me to him. Before I have a moment to breathe, I'm flipped to my stomach, the head of his dick rotating inside me. A breath barely inhaled before my face finds the pillow.

"Good arm against the wall."

I obey just before he slams into me from behind. One hand wraps around my long hair, yanking my head back. My throat stretched as much as my insides.

Thick fingers roughly rub against my clit in tight, hard circles. The added pressure hurling me toward the cliff edge faster than I would think possible.

"Is this what you wanted?" he grunts.

"Yes." The single word nothing more than a breathy moan.

The tightening of his fist in my hair amplifies the pain of him stretching me and the firecrackers in my arm and chest. But I ignore the pain, losing myself in the pleasure.

"Ahhh," I groan when he gives an extra yank, his thrust into me making our flesh crack like thunder.

"You'll take it, Ari. You'll take it because now you're mine."

"Always have been, you ass."

A burst of laughter sounds behind me, interrupting his punishing rhythm. Just enough for me to flip the script. Breaking away from him, an aching emptiness fills me as I free myself from him.

His thick length bobs between us. His length drenched in the remnants of me.

Hands to his chest, I mount him, immediately sinking down on his proud shaft.

"Do you think you're the only one who can play dom?"

My hips roll into him at a ferocious pace. His head falling back, exposing the column of his throat. My tongue rakes over his flesh, my body rising and sinking down onto his throbbing cock. Impaling myself in steel over and over has never felt so good.

"Ari, slow..." his voice trails to a groan as my teeth latch onto the flesh where his shoulder meets his neck. The need to mark him uncontrollable. A desire from deep in my belly mixing with a third raging storm.

"Mr. Alexander. You'll take what I give you because you're mine." My promise as I again bite the same spot. My teeth mark a deep indent in his pale skin.

Our pace quickens that burn so reminiscent of my flames. A reminder flashing through my mind that it's not a normal thing for phoenixes. My flames are the product of my dad's fire magic. Mom even made me get specialty bedding made, just in case.

The sheets may survive, but will Adrian if I burst into flames?

"You have two minutes to finish me." The words jumbled as I bounce in his lap.

He simply quirks a grin, pulling my release from me not even thirty seconds later. His name is a curse on my lips. His roar of my name only moments later the best music to my ears.

Our sweaty bodies collapse side by side, legs hanging over the edge of the mattress.

"What now?" I ask.

"Sleep." The single word a whisper as a sated smile pulls at the corners of his mouth, his body curling into mine.

Yes. Sleep sounds good.

Goodnight, my love. The words spoken in my head.

I think...

Sixteen

ADRIAN

After last night, there were a million things I should have explained to Ari, but I couldn't.

The bonding process stole my energy, the same as a rebirth would. Only sleep could cure the fatigue. I'd planned to have sex with my woman all night, but could barely keep my eyes open the moment we both came so violently our bond tugged and stars sparkled behind my eyes.

Still, I had the chance when I dropped her at work just hours ago. I tried to leave but couldn't.

I've been slacking, venturing into the office myself. Not that I need to work. I've got enough money to last me my immortal life, but I miss the routine.

Prior to Ari, my life was uncomplicated. My routine was solid. I spent my days parsing through numbers and my evenings and weekends serving the family who saved me. We trained, we planned, and I sat alone in my house, thanking the universe that I was free of my blood relatives.

Unfortunately, I've been sitting here in the lobby of her building since then, thanks to the bond. They warned me about the distance being a problem, but I figured we have strong bloodlines. We should be able to handle it.

It's one downside to the first year after bonding. Now that we're officially mated, things get tricky. The first year is a whirlwind of emotions, usually uncontrollable. Distance is a problem too. The farther you are, the more your heart feels like it's shattering and the physical pain increases. Not the typical levels we can ignore, but crippling agony that can manifest in so many unique ways. It's a side effect of the bond strengthening.

With time, a pair can slowly drift apart, much like a newborn growing more independent. Like that same infant, one day it will support itself, holding up its head or body weight. Initially, the bond behaves similarly. It needs to be nurtured and constantly tended to. Consistently supported and fed.

Raphael: You didn't!

The simple text flashing across my screen.

Fuck. Fuck. Fuck.

That can only mean Ari is struggling with even this much distance between us. With a sigh, I make my way up to her floor. The ding of the elevator announcing me.

The first guy I spot is Garrett, his desk two over from hers. Ari laughs at a joke he just cracked, her face pinched in discomfort. The closer I get that tension slowly eases away. My breathing slowing, too, as the pain in my gut fades.

My eyes press closed. That roll of my neck doing nothing to control the rage elevated by the bond just sinking into place.

"Adrian?" her voice small and questioning.

The strain that I expected to stay fades away as her hand finds my forearm.

Lowering my face close to hers, I keep my words just above a whisper. "Um, can we talk?"

She nods, leading me into a back office. One filled with all sorts of tech equipment that puts Talia's lair to shame.

The door is barely closed before her arms wrap around my middle. "How weird. I was feeling so ill before you walked in, then perfectly fine the moment I saw you."

I gently pry her away to meet my gaze, then lean in for a brief kiss on her lips. The brush so slight I can almost pretend it didn't happen. I'm careful not to linger. This moment isn't about that.

"Yeah, that's the new bond. We can't exactly be apart."

Although I am usually confident in speaking to people, fear weakens my voice. Nearly crippling me at the moment as I try to skirt around the blunt truth, unsure how Ari will respond. She said Talia told her what it meant to bond with me, but I never explicitly asked if they'd covered the side effects.

"Oh yeah, I figured something like that might happen. So, like, a week?"

She smiles up at me, teeth on display, as if she knew all along.

"Babe, no. A year. And it will be worse than you feeling sick to your stomach. It's mild because I've been sitting in the lobby all this time."

Those deep blue eyes search mine for several seconds before glancing away, only to narrow back on my face. The confirmation she needed must be there because she shoves me away. Her fingers tugging at her long ponytail as she paces.

"Adrian, you better be joking."

Pulling her back to my chest, she sneers, wriggling against my hold. "No, I'm not."

The fight drains from her. Her eyes darting back and forth as she works to piece together a solution.

"Okay. Well, we're going to just have to figure it out." Her fingers pull her high ponytail tighter. The long strands swaying behind her.

A quick knock sounds at the door. "Get out!" I bark at whoever is on the other side.

One of the other detectives pokes his head through the door, anyway. "Luxe, I'm sorry," his eyes drift to me. "Triple homicide. We gotta go."

Just as quickly as he came, the man slips back through the door, leaving us alone once more.

"Um, okay, well, I have to go. But can you follow us to the scene? Just until we figure out this distance thing."

I nod, pulling her back into me, crushing our mouths together.

"I needed that."

She winks at me. "You'll get much more than that later if you can avoid being an ass for the day."

"No promises."

Since PD is already on the scene, there are no lights and sirens. Their absence allowing me to speed along behind Ari's vehicle at a respectful distance without being noticed.

Somehow, I'm given a badge that allows me past that dreaded yellow tape you always see in movies or on the news outlets. Chicago is no stranger to crime and murder. Neither am I.

Seeing Ari in action is like watching a whole different person. The pair I thought I knew disappearing right before my eyes. Her mouth settled in a perpetual scowl and brow unnaturally straight. There's no forgiveness in her voice as she asks the cops every question under the sun. Her annoyance with their lack of being able to convey the information she needs effectively, clear.

If I wasn't already in love with this woman, I damn sure am now.

She commands everyone around her. Even Raphael and the other two homicide detectives — names unknown — who are with her. She's the point of the star leading the investigation. All eyes are on her as she makes her way through the brutal scene. Every detail stored in that beautiful mind of hers.

Much like her parent's house, there's blood everywhere. Except it isn't a private residence this time. The popular bakery just off North Michigan either hadn't opened yet, or the murderer locked it up tight.

I hadn't heard how they found the bodies, but even from the street, the male, thrown across a small circular table, and the young female, face down in a spreading pool of blood at the center of the floor, would be impossible to miss. Scenes like this always are. Whoever did this left behind their version of art for all to see.

That's the beauty of a storefront that's completely glass. It's a typical style here in Chicago. Anyone passing on the street could easily see inside. With the amount of bright and clotting blood on every surface, there would be no mistaking something horrible happened here.

It's clear whoever did this meant to make a statement. Let everyone know he took out this family.

A family I only now recognize as I find the woman propped up in the corner, her palm nailed to the tabletop. A piece of paper secured beneath it.

"Detective Luxembohrg," I call. An attempt at fulfilling the role of someone who is meant to be here. Ari narrows her eyes as she makes her way over to me. Those features of hers not softening in the slightest.

"Adrian, I'm working."

"Look," I point.

Her eyes track to the tiny sliver of paper beneath the nailed hand of the woman. "Ari, these are the Brambillas. They are one of the warlock families next to be tapped for the World Council. I thought they'd left the area ages ago."

The snap of gloves draws my attention to her hands, the blue latex snug against her thin fingers. Slowly she creeps forward, eyes trained on the floor, careful not to step in the streaks and pools of blood. With pinched fingers, she tugs at the slip. The clotting blood holding it stiff for a few moments before she gets the entire piece free.

Keep pushing. The next bullet won't be in your chest.

An audible gasp leaves her as she slides her arm to the side, allowing me to read it. It's not like I didn't already know this was Salvatore, but I can't help but be relieved. I'd rather his threat point anywhere but Ari. Her life means more than mine ever could. No, he'll do his best to ruin her in other ways.

"Does this have to go into evidence?"

"Yes," she whispers. "Michaels, bag."

The bald-headed detective who interrupted us earlier comes forward, tearing open a small plastic baggy and sealing it as soon as she releases the torn piece of paper inside.

"Michaels. Johnson. You guys head back, Gomez, and I will keep this one."

"The hell you will," her captain's voice booms through the space.

She turns to face him, her expression not shifting in the slightest. The same ruthless woman she's been since we arrived, staring her boss down.

"Luxembohrg, you just got back, and you have a stack the height of you to get through. You're not taking another case."

She squares her shoulders, chin notched just a fraction higher, making her taller than him. "With all due respect, sir, I believe this case is linked to several other unsolved murders, including the James couple from a few months ago. Gomez and I have been working them tirelessly, sir."

"Why?" The single word meant to challenge her. A test to see if she'll rise to the occasion and impress him with the knowledge only she seems to have.

My bird wants to tear his throat out. No one challenges Ari James.

"First, family murder. Seems to be the MO for at lease six cases we've worked. Carried out in personal spaces. Homes, places of business. The vicious and overkill stab wounds. Depth and length appear to match in the other cases. The condition the bodies are left in. I could go on, sir, with additional forensic evidence. Not to mention the note left here today."

She snatches the baggie from Michaels, shoving it into the man's hands. His tongue works over his upper teeth, cheeks hallowing for a few seconds while reading the two short sentences over and over. He keeps shifting his gaze from side to side. The back and forth repeated so many times it's as if he's confirming the message hadn't changed before his eyes.

"Fine, but I want this wrapped up, and fast. You get this serial killer off my streets."

"Yes, Captain."

Then he's gone, flagging Michaels and Johnson behind him.

"Ari," I whisper her name.

"Later. At home," she replies.

Ari doesn't linger, moving away from me to observe the scene further. Raphael, having watched the whole encounter, only sends me a pitying stare.

Me, I stand there like an idiot, watching my woman take in every detail, willing my dick to stay flaccid in my pants.

It's going to be a fucking long year.

Seventeen

ARI

"**M**om! Mom!" I yell as I stomp into our most-used safe house.

She's slow to turn the corner from the kitchen, the most delicious smells wafting in from behind her. While we usually order takeout for the group, Mom prefers to cook for all of us. It's in her nature to take care of those she loves. A trait that was evident from the day I met her.

Unfortunately, with every gut punch being thrown our way, time hasn't been on our side. Time she would need to prepare food for a hundred men and women, although there's usually no more than ten of us in attendance for dinner. Paranormals eat a hell of a lot of food.

But there's also always plenty left behind in containers for those that come and go. Our patrolmen, those looking for shelter, someone wanting a midnight snack. The safe houses are always fully stocked. *"You are all my babies. I'll make sure you eat if nothing else,"* she'd said to me when I questioned how much her grocery bill was.

"What's wrong, sweetheart?"

"Map. I need a map."

She nods. "Grab Bronson, he'll be able to craft what you need."

We find him downstairs in what I now call the War Room. Really, it's where the leaders and council members gather to meet behind closed doors. Adrian and I often included since I came into the fold. At first, I thought it was to keep an eye on me. They needed me to prove my allegiance to their cause. It was always there in their eyes and the way they spoke to me. That suspicion that I was nothing more than a liar and a spy for Sal hard to change.

A false notion I have worked tirelessly to reverse.

Then, I believe a morsel of trust developed, and they realized I had information that could help them. Details I was happy to give as my conscience took over and guilt filled my gut. I was ready to tell them everything if it meant keeping my found family safe.

"Bronson, I need a map covering the areas where I've carried out murders since working for Salvatore and then another with the recent murders since his disappearance."

Without a word, he saunters to the rear of the room. The blank wall standing tall before him as he just stares at it. The intensity behind his eyes so focused I would think he was looking straight through the drywall, concrete and structural beams. Back to us, his body stills. Then his hands move through the air, waves of matte black smog seeping from his fingers. Each pass is an arcing circle, a large map of the U.S. appearing on the wall.

Blue three-dimensional dots appear across the country, followed by red ones focused closer around Chicago. Every tiny dot making more bile crawl up my throat and my stomach knot.

"Done," he beams.

What the actual fuck.

I've seen a lot since joining the fight. But this was something otherworldly. Bronson literally just crafted a map on the wall by waving his hands.

"Um…"

I can't find the words to make sense of what I just watched.

Get it together, Ari. You literally turn into an oversized flaming bird.

His smirk grows. "It's a living map. With new information, a new pin will appear if Syriah, you, Adrian, or myself speak about a murder suspected or known by Salvatore. The blue is you, and the red is him. Sorry, first two colors I thought of," he shrugs.

I can only stare at the dots of colors marring the detailed map of the U.S. in front of me. "No. That's fine. Thank you, Bronson."

With a clap on Adrian's back, he retreats. "Also, congrats, you two."

Fuck. How does everyone know?

As if Adrian can read my thoughts, he bends, chuckling next to my ear. "It's our eyes. The glow never completely fades once the bond is in place. Not to mention, he can likely smell me on you."

"But I showered." My voice quirks a few octaves too high.

He chuckles again. "Yes, but when we had sex last night, I essentially marked you with my scent. No matter what, to other paranormals, my scent will linger on you. They'll know who you belong to."

Turning to face me, he slips his arms around my middle, pulling me close.

"And how do they know who you belong to?" With a grin, he presses his mouth to mine, sucking my bottom lip between his.

"They know."

Our kiss deepens. His dick hardening between us. A scent I'd noticed last night filling my nostrils. His arousal, I would imagine. Talia had mentioned things like this.

This is what it will be like for a year. Unable to stay apart from him. Wanting him to pound into my pussy every second of every day. Talia hadn't mentioned the distance thing, but she said we'd want to fuck like rabbits constantly. Truly, this feeling with Adrian hasn't changed in a long time, but the intensity has increased. A constant pull of wanting him buried inside me.

My hips roll into him, drawing out a long, strained groan. Instinct takes over as he lifts and then drops me onto the table. My giggle vibrating through the room, all too ready for what comes next. Without hesitation, he tears my blouse from my body. Exposing my heaving breasts to the man I'll never get enough of, the thin layer of lace barely keeping me contained.

Adrian's mouth clamps down on me through the thin fabric, his fangs sinking into the grooves of the pattern, tearing it to release my nipple. *Fuck*, I'll never get enough of this. Adrian is a craving that will never be satisfied. Even when this year is up, I know we'll always be like this.

"Dammit. Do I have to expect this every day now?" Tucker groans from behind me.

Instantly Adrian's body drapes over mine, hiding my exposed flesh from my brother.

"Seriously, Tuck. Why are you always walking in on us?" Adrian growls. He warned me about this. The possessive male that's always poised and ready to tear another man apart in my presence, even my brother.

"Mom said you were down here," he supplies.

Adrian's body shakes against mine, the movement so violent he could be convulsing. Drawing my hands out from between our bodies, I place my palms on his face, turning it so he's looking down at me. "Calm. The map, then sex," a wicked grin playing at my lips. "Tucker, give us a minute."

The door clicks shut behind us, Adrian finally releasing me. He's quick to remove his shirt, ordering me to lift my arms so he can put it on me.

"Well, at least it's black." He shrugs.

I place another kiss on his throat before hopping off the table. The thought is nice, but it won't keep anyone from noticing my headlights tonight.

"Tucker," I call.

He enters, his eyes quickly surveying the room for signs of decorum. His glare landing on Adrian's bare chest. That protective brotherly energy soaring to the surface.

"Oh, stop. It was either his nips or mine."

Tucker shivers, shaking his head before plopping into an open seat.

His gaze immediately shifts to the map on the wall. The trees swaying as if there's wind. The pitter-patter of rain droplets hovers over other patches of the map. It's truly remarkable. When Bronson said this was a live map, I didn't expect the weather was a feature included.

"So what's the theory?" Tucker asks, leaning back in his chair, hands clasped behind his head.

"I don't know yet. I needed a map so I could look at it all visually."

I stare at it for long minutes. The gears in my mind whirring, attempting to piece together any sort of pattern Sal has left behind for me. My focus on the murders since his disappearance.

"The major families. Those that are in leadership and next in line to be picked, do they normally live outside or within big cities?"

"It can go either way," Adrian's deep voice carries from behind me.

I try speaking to the map, uncertain how else to give it instructions. Maybe this is like programming software, and it will or won't carry out my command. An instruction manual would have been nice.

"Map…" I clear my throat. "Map. Place green pins where families in leadership live."

I jump back as the map blurs, then expands onto the next wall. The sheer size of it has turned it into a sprawling world, brimming with numerous intricacies, making it difficult for me to pinpoint where to direct my attention. Guessing Bronson intentionally only included the U.S. before, I now notice there are a few other blue pins in Europe. All correlations to the few times I traveled internationally at Sal's request.

Green dots speckle the world. My eyes analyzing each one. There are so many of us. Far more than I imagined.

"Map, add yellow dots to the locations of families next in line to sit on any council."

Worldwide, many more dots appear.

My last request. One I am not convinced I want to see. "Map for each that is dead, color half the dot in black."

The map blurs again. So many of the vibrant, glowing dots dull as the green and yellow dots go half-black. The red and blue don't change, knowing those were already long gone.

My eyes water. So many lost in this war I didn't even realize was raging. I played a far greater part than I initially realized. I hate myself for what I've done.

I swear Adrian and I have connected emotions now. A strength I know isn't coming from me, infiltrating my body. He slides up behind me, his front pressed firmly against my back. Those thick arms holding me close as if attempting to keep me in one piece. Likely the only thing keeping me from shattering apart.

"Ari, what are you thinking?" Tucker questions suddenly beside us. Adrian's rumbling growl vibrating through his chest into my back.

"Calm," I whisper again. His deep inhale serving as his attempt at releasing his irrational protectiveness.

"I'm thinking I need to know who each of these pins correlate to and every bit of information about them."

The door opens then. A sigh escaping behind us.

"You're so much like your father," my mother breathes. "We'll get everything set up that you need, but for now, dinner."

One by one, we follow her upstairs.

My mind refuses to slow. So many died, and so many will perish alongside them regardless of what side they choose. I despise that this has become our existence.

But we are phoenixes. We rule all. It's our responsibility to bring about peace between all paranormals again.

It's my job to be the leader my mother expects me to be.

Eighteen

ARI

Many will tell you certain things in life increase their appetite. Physical activity. Sex. Solving a murder. Typical things. Though I would never say it aloud, the prospect of taking a life turns me ravenous. My dinner barely chewed before I swallow each bite.

"Ari, slow down," my mother chides. Her mouth pressed into a straight line, eyes narrowed my way.

But I can't. There's too much to do. Too much to think about.

My thoughts center on a single topic. That map. Those families. Discovering a solution to eliminate devious individuals similar to Salvatore Danarius with minimal bloodshed.

I've barely swallowed my last bite before I launch myself from the table, darting back downstairs.

A bolt of pain bursts through my stomach just as I enter the War Room. My hand barely catches the edge of the table before my knees buckle, and I cry out.

Fuck, this is so much worse than I felt this morning. The repeated jabs leaving me doubled over, sucking in deep breaths that are doing nothing to help. Each pulse threatening to bring me to my knees.

It takes less than a minute for Adrian to appear in the doorway, panting breaths leaving him as his palms wrap around the door-frame molding.

"Please don't do that."

"Sorry," I snort. "I forget how big this house is."

He nods, shuffling inside the room. Each step allowing him to stand tall again. Several others enter at his heels. A shirt absently tossed into his hands.

"Thanks..." He only gets a grunt in response. The small sound is so nondescript I'm not sure who it came from.

Each new entrant has their hands full. Laptops, monitors, and other devices I can't identify. Each item is arranged on the table and connected and plugged in as required.

Two wolf-shifters who started training here last week carry a massive laser jet printer. Twins with the same black floppy hair and permanent wide grins. They're young. At just eighteen years old, my mother welcomed them when they arrived at our doorstep. Her promise to keep them as her own when they told her about their mother's death, a moment none of us will soon forget.

According to Tucker and Oliver, this isn't the first time my mother's kindness has been at the forefront of conversations. Syriah and Lanham unofficially adopted most of those that stay in our safe houses. The world needs more big hearts like them.

My parents gave them love, and in return, received undying loyalty. Loyalty they never asked for, no matter how much of themselves they gave.

They assembled the room quickly. Talia is already printing countless documents as the twins label and stuff them into folders with the family names on the tab. This feels so much like being at the station: digging through cases and solving murders. My heart leaps in my chest, finally feeling like home. This is who I am. This is what I truly enjoy.

Only now does it occur to me that though I was indifferent to killing for Sal, I had confused the thrill of living dangerously with the adrenaline rush of murder. The murders themselves aren't what excited me and made my heart race. I didn't enjoy watching the light fade from their eyes or smelling the scent of burning flesh as I left homes on fire. It was the danger of getting caught. The potential of dying and knowing my bird would bring me back to life. It was the chase of solving an issue.

The realization calms my belly. A small part of me feels better that I'm not just some ruthless murderer that enjoys it. In my search to embrace my phoenix, I may have gone about it wrong.

Emerson — twin one — hands me a folder. "Um, Miss Ari, I think you should look at this one." I take it from him, smiling.

"Emerson, stop calling me miss." He nods before directing his attention back to his task.

Slipping the folder open, there's no stopping my audible gasp. My fingers curling over the edges in so tight a grip I might tear the thing to shreds. Sweat beads across my upper lip, my pupils dilating as I take in the photo in front of me.

A woman stares back at me. Her face is a match for the one I'd watched get the nail removed from her hand, freeing her from that small circular top table this morning. "Adrian, Marty Brambilla had another daughter?" He nods as if it's nothing.

"Yeah, she died over a decade ago."

"If that's true, then why does it say she's living in Ohio?"

He snatches the folder from me, eyes roving over the text. "Ari, she's supposed to be dead. I know she's dead."

"How?"

He swallows next to me. His eyes focused on the tabletop beneath his palms. "My parents killed her."

The room goes silent. All of us seem unable to process what Adrian just said, except my mother. She's the only one with an unchanged expression and pity in her eyes. *She knew.*

"You said you haven't seen or heard from them in over a hundred years, correct?" Syriah questions. That calm demeanor once again on display. A composure I hope to emulate someday.

"I hadn't." Adrian's swallow is pronounced. His Adam's apple bobbing and eyes darting back and forth, attempting to build the courage to tell them about the visitor at his house. I'm still not sure of their relation, but there's no doubt their bloodlines run close. "Kenji showed up at my grandparent's house about two weeks ago. But that's not important right now. My family likes to leave a calling card. Our family crest burned between the shoulder blades of anyone they took out. I saw the body myself. I saw the brand."

Something isn't adding up. Also, why did Adrian never mention his family to me? All I know is they are the worst kinds of paranormals. Dangerous. Ruthless. Power hungry.

The information I received was always from others, never from him.

An issue for another time.

Right now, I need to get to Ohio. If we find this woman, it may only leave us with more questions, but at least we'll have one answer. One that might send Adrian over the deep end.

We can only hope this doesn't mean the Alexanders have dug their way out of hiding.

"I'm off for three days starting Tuesday. Who's road-tripping with me?"

Bronson quirks a grin. A yes.

The muted scrape of chair legs over the carpeted floors turns every head toward Adrian. His gigantic frame up and out of his chair before I can reach for him. Something like panic dancing in his bright green eyes. "Excuse me."

I'm on my feet seconds later, charging after him. His long legs taking the steps two at a time while I chase behind him. He doesn't stop until we reach his bedroom, only to slam the door in my face.

What the fuck just happened?

Nineteen

ADRIAN

My lungs won't inflate. My vision goes blurry at the edges as I hyperventilate. There have been too many coincidences surrounding my family as of late. Kenji showing up and now Viviana Brambilla, allegedly being alive and well.

I saw her dead body. Someone had flayed her torso open and slit her throat so deep I could see the cartilage. My position then was less senior. Just one of the guys sent to investigate the death of another paranormal. I've always been like Ari in that aspect. The one who needed to see the murder scenes. My initial curiosity centered on whether the deceased included family — a sibling, ideally a parent. It never was.

Viviana was one of a handful that bore the brand of my family crest. The flesh was still smoking and oozing tendrils of blood when we arrived at the scene. A fresh kill.

Panic seizes my chest. They are too close. Far too close for comfort. If they learn about Ari and me mating, they will come after her, and I cannot have that. I won't allow them to ruin the best thing that has ever happened to me. Because of them, I became an asshole bound to a life of loneliness. I did my best not to love. Not to care. The James family is the sole exception.

That was all Syriah, though. Her open arms are always willing to take us strays in because she has a heart of gold. That woman was every bit the mother I wish mine had been. And I will protect her and her daughter with my life.

My silence regarding Ari's question about companions for her road trip won't stop her from knowing I'll attend. The obvious reason: we can't be apart. The less obvious reason is that even if we hadn't bonded, I couldn't stay away from her.

For my personal well-being, I need to see for myself that Viviana is still alive. And if she is still breathing, that means she faked her death. Confirmation, she betrayed her family to side with mine.

The most probing question is what my family's angle is now. It's been a hundred and twelve years. *One. Hundred. And. Twelve.* They wanted power back then. They got it, sitting on the Australian council, despite us being from Prague. Not sure how they swung it, but that's how I left them. They held power, and I believed it would satisfy them.

A knee-buckling thought looms at the rear of my consciousness. One I stomp down. One I am not willing to consider. No matter how improbable this might be, I can't shake the feeling that it's all true. That there's a storm coming we aren't prepared for. Its path leaving everything in its wake as nothing more than a pile of rubble.

Overwhelming panic ricochets through me, tightening against my chest and rib cage. Worry that isn't mine.

My eyes are wide saucers in the bathroom mirror as I remember what an ass I'd just been. Treating Ari poorly by slamming the door in her face without explanation was the worst action I could take toward my pair. But I know she's out there, waiting just outside my door. I can feel her. Our shared thread wanting me to go pull her into my arms and just hold her.

Inhaling a deep breath, my nerves steady just the slightest. The twist of the handle swinging the door toward me quicker than expected. Ari falls in to my chest, causing the two of us to tumble to the floor in a mass of tangled limbs. Her back had been leaning against it. The yelp she releases so cute I nearly laugh.

She quickly stands to her feet, dusting off the back of her slacks. Her wince proceeding her quick reach for her bad arm, before dropping her hand.

"Talk to me."

There's no asking in her tone. My pair has every right to demand the truth from me. And if I care at all, which I do more than I can put into words, I'll tell her everything. It may not all be tonight, but one day she'll know it all. The good, the bad, the ugly and the regrets.

"You're going to need to sit and maybe have a drink, too."

She strolls to the loveseat at the far end of the room as if she's been in my space a million times. Our rooms are mirror images of one another, so of course she would.

I pull a bottle of Basil Hayden — her favorite — from a hidden cabinet within the dresser. Pouring us both tumblers full of the dark booze, I settle in next to her. Tentative fingers wrap around the glass, but she doesn't move to drink it.

I chug mine in three big gulps before pouring another healthy fill.

"So I need to tell you about my family. And I need you to not say a word until I'm done. But mostly, I need you to not look at me any different once I'm done."

"I can't promise that, Adrian." Her fingers brush my forearm. A touch so warm. One filled with bravery I wish I had right now. My gaze averts down to my glass. Shame washing over me for everything I've done.

"I know."

With another large gulp and a deep breath, I dive in.

"So my family is the worst kind. Power hungry. Murderous. They all hated me when I came along — except my eldest brother, Ezra. I don't think they expected to have another son. By that time, they were already killing anyone who got in the way. My parents made my brothers and I fall in line. Kill for them over and over. All of them were willing except me."

My words stall in my throat. The roof of my mouth bone dry, making my tongue mercilessly stick to it. With just my eyes shifting back and forth, I struggle to find an easier way to share my truth with Ari, avoiding the need to disclose all the heinous crimes I committed.

"I was the defiant one. The worthless one. The one my father and brothers beat to within an inch of my life so many times." A huffing laugh leaves me as I take another swig. "My dad is responsible for the first time I died. My second eldest brother for the second. And the brother right above me for five others. Kenji. He's the one that cornered you in my grandparent's house."

She slides in closer to me, hanging her thighs over the top of mine before climbing into my lap. Taking both our glasses and sitting them on the side table next to us, she pulls my head down to her chest, stroking through my hair.

"Go on," she encourages.

"Well, my mother killed my grandparents too, but I was young then. I only met them once. I was a hundred and sixty-two when I'd had enough. I just left in the dead of night and never looked back. The blood on my hands from them never fades." As if I can still see the blood there on my palms, my gaze locks on my trembling hands. "It never washes away." The words escaping in a choked half-sob.

Ari's warm fingers curl around my trembling hands as if that will stop me from feeling every negative emotion coursing through me. This is one of the many reasons I never wanted to have this discussion. Reliving those years stirs up far more shit than I'm often equipped to deal with on my own. I've had to bury it so many times, I'm exhausted. I just want to forget.

If I could carve that part of me out of my soul, I would.

Gripping my cheeks, she forces my gaze to hers. "Adrian, you're not like them." I nod, kissing her quickly.

"And you're not like him." Her hands drop from my face. The shame inside her felt so strongly that tears build behind my eyes.

"This isn't about me."

I nod, knowing she's deflecting. Hating herself as much as I do me. I can feel it. Her every emotion tumbling through me, and she can feel mine. The way the bond connects us is exhilarating. Terrifying and unimaginable. No one will know me the way she does. They can't.

"Anyway, I was already working with your parents when someone murdered Viviana. I was one of the few sent to observe and remove the body. They branded her right between her shoulder blades. It was still fresh."

A shiver runs through me, sharing my secrets with her. Things I wish I could keep buried. The darkest parts that will be the hardest to hear and understand. One day she'll know those too.

"Stop blaming yourself."

"Ari, don't. I've slaughtered hundreds in my lifetime for no other reason than my parents wanted them to cease breathing. I couldn't question it. I couldn't say no."

She opens her mouth, but my scowl has her quickly closing it.

"I killed children. Innocent kids that had nothing to do with this war."

My head drops to her chest, her fingers weaving through the strands of hair at the nape of my neck. Soft fingers massaging and soothing me. Her feelings for me sinking into my being with each passing moment.

A single word lingers just in the distance. Far enough away, we can both ignore it. It's too soon. Bond or not.

"Look, it's been a long night. Let's get some sleep. I'll tell Captain I won't be in the office tomorrow because I'm working some leads, and we'll figure this shit out." Her tone says it all. She's not going to take no for an answer. In Ari's world, her word is law, and I am meant to obey.

I may act the alpha, but I will bend to her will as long as it doesn't endanger her.

Tucking an arm under her thighs, I stand from the sofa.

"We can go to bed, but we're not sleeping. It's been too long since I've been inside you."

"See, that's my big birdy asshole."

A barking laugh escapes me as I throw her onto the bed. The both of us tearing at our clothes, only minutes passing before I sink into her.

Home.

That's what this is. Ari is home.

Twenty

Ari

The next three days pass in a blur. Visits to the office are only out of necessity. I spend most of my days in the War Room, shuffling through file folders of paranormals, or on the streets with Adrian.

With each file we review, they're categorized. Some, we're aware, have jumped to the dark side. Those traitors are currently our lower priorities. We need to identify surviving allies. At least we hope we can still call them as such.

I'd only expected one or two, including Adrian, to join me for this impulsive trip to Ohio. A group that doubled in size before I could blink. The original rental upgraded to accommodate the men and me. In other words, no one wanted to sit next to Adrian and I.

It's unclear if I should feel lucky to be the only female on this journey or not. A point Talia brought up several times while we prepared for our departure. But for me, it's the norm. I'm the only female homicide detective in my precinct. Just a typical day spent with the guys for me.

I'd wanted Mom to come, but I also know why she can't. To those outside our followers, my parents are both still dead. Rolan was the only outsider who heard otherwise. But the fucker's dead, so there's no one for him to tell.

It's been a week, and I'd almost forgotten about us killing him. The memory of Adrian sliding into me for the first time overshadowed the visions of that night. The sensation of my body reforming, merging with my other half, far outweighed a mere thought of Rolan.

Dealing with this new bond is a pain in the ass. The stronger it grows, the less we tolerate distance — the opposite of what Talia promised. Furthermore, every day comes with less time before we have to sneak off to fuck in a corner. Our birds scratching and clawing to get at each other. Our combined strength barely holds them at bay.

In the midst of our planning session last night, Adrian casually stretched his neck, then swiftly hoisted me over his shoulder before locking us into the half-bath next door to the War Room. There's no doubt they all heard us as he bent me over the countertop, driving into me with enough force I punched through the wall. There are bruises along my hip bones and the top of my pelvis from being slammed and held against the porcelain edge. Bruises I'd happily welcome again.

There was no stopping us, though. His thick length threatened to split me in two. An arm latched under my thigh, my one bare leg tingling against the heat of his skin as he dropped my foot in the sink. My pussy spread wide for him to drive into at an entirely new angle.

Hand braced against the mirror, my palm slammed into it repeatedly. Funny that it survived, but the drywall didn't until that final thrust. The heel of my hand shattering the glass with that last strike. The roar of Adrian's release rattling the walls around us.

Unable to catch my breath, I didn't move. My leg remained hitched high, my toes wiggling against the curve of the sink while our mixed cum leaked out of me onto the floor at our feet. Another mess to go with the glass and pieces of wall.

Yet, Mom hadn't even blinked when I whispered to her about it before bed. *"Your father and I did much worse."* She winked before disappearing upstairs, leaving me there both in awe and thoroughly disturbed.

"Please think about anything else," Cooper groans from the driver's seat.

My eyes go wide, not realizing he can smell my arousal. The twins snicker, shoving one another. "Told you," Elijah snorts.

Heat flares to my cheeks, my face burrowing into Adrian's chest. Sex and my enjoyment of it have never embarrassed me. I never cared about my promiscuity, and now that I'm in a "relationship", I blush. Damn this fucking bond.

It's unfortunate we had to bring Cooper along. The choice between him and Oliver was simple enough. To say that Adrian's aggression toward Oliver has grown substantially since we bonded would be an understatement. Accepting his generous offer guaranteed chaos. Drama, I am not equipped to deal with right now.

Oliver and I may be over that one brief kiss, but my guy isn't.

We now have an entire china set no longer usable because Adrian yanked the table cloth free when Oliver first announced he was tagging along. No one blinked an eye at Adrian's outburst. It's normal for new pairs to have no control over their emotions. Only the weight of my palm between his shoulder blades calmed him enough that he sat back in his seat, grumpily pulling out this phone and ordering a whole new spread of food.

We didn't stay to eat any. Instead, my pair chose to cuddle me to death in bed.

In addition, I needed Tucker to stay behind. He's never seen me in action on a crime scene and I can't have his protective brother routine getting in the way. Seeing as he and Cooper would rather gouge their own eyes out than be in the same house, choosing Cooper to come along made everyone's lives easier. Having both of them in the same car would likely end with the whole thing exploding on the side of the road.

"Cooper, turn on the radio."

He smacks the power button with enough force I'm surprised the thing didn't launch itself from the consul to poke him in the eye. Static, mixed with fuzzy words, comes through the speakers. Not surprising since we're in the middle of nowhere at the moment.

"Cord, please." Bronson twists back toward me, handing off the end of the USB cable I can plug into my phone.

I pick some random 2000s station, figuring it will have something for everyone.

Adrian continues to rub idle strokes along my upper back. His other hand cupped over my thigh, his thumb stroking so close to where I need him to be, I'm seconds from telling Cooper to pull over so I can fuck my mate on the side of the road. We managed our time well this morning before departing, but even three hours without Adrian moving inside me seems excessive.

His thumb trails higher, dancing over the seam along my crotch. A traced path over where my lips come together. Involuntarily, my hips shift upward, eager for his touch. His mouth brushing against the shell of my ear as he whispers to me.

"You'll have to stay calm so they don't know." I nod, still writhing beneath his devious fingers.

"What's the plan, Ari?" Bronson calls from the front seat.

I'm already lost in Adrian's touch. My teeth sinking into my lower lip, just as Adrian's broad palm cups me before pressing against my swollen bundle of nerves.

I'd heard Bronson's question, but didn't comprehend a single word. His head swiveling back in our direction just as a low hum drifts up my throat.

"Seriously, are you fingering her next to me?" Cooper snips.

"No, I'm not. We're sitting behind you, and her pants are still on. However, I would suggest we stop soon, or I might fuck her in front of you." The growl of Adrian's words nearly makes me combust, his assault on my clothed pussy driving me straight to a toe-curling orgasm.

The guys all groan. Each one annoyed with being stuck with us being a couple. A soft chuckle leaves me, tugging Adrian's hand away from my heated core. I can't afford for the guys to hate me before we even get to our destination.

"What did you ask me, Bronson?"

"The plan?"

"Show up at Viviana's listed address. Confirm if she's alive or dead. Find out what side she's fighting on. Kill or recruit." My shoulders shoot up before casually sinking back down. The calm in my tone is exactly the opposite of the emotions coursing through me.

Adrian's fingers weave through mine, a sign he's feeling everything I do just as intensely in this moment. His way of showing me he's here. That I don't have to carry the burden alone. I never will again.

"Great. Simple," Bronson quips.

Twenty-One

Ari

There are no side discussions for a while. Each minute ticking by as if we're not racing against a clock.

The music playing softly and the twins laughing at whatever they're watching on their phones distract me from what might need to be done when we arrive. I'd made promises to my mother and those who follow my family. I wouldn't kill our kind again unless it was necessary. A pledge I took before the paranormal leaders.

Only Mom had pulled me aside later that night. *"My sweet girl, you're going to have to loosen that rein a little. Those who openly denounce us are subject to death by decree."*

I'd sat with her words for some time that night. A meaning I couldn't understand then. Only Salvatore proved their meaning when he shot me. He continues to prove it with each new kill. Adrian's family, too, if they are part of this. A fear Adrian admitted to me while curled up in bed a few nights ago. The real reason this trip weighs so heavily on him.

We must consider those who previously pledged allegiance to Salvatore or the Alexanders as enemies. Their word alone isn't enough to earn our trust. Individuals like that will always drift to the winning side. Should the tides turn and it becomes clear my family is losing their grip on power, they will be the first to try to seize it.

"Looks like the security system was just activated," Emerson leans forward in his seat, his face lined up between me and Adrian's.

"Coming or going?" Cooper asks, his grip on the wheel tightening.

"Coming, per the code used."

"Good work, kiddo," Adrian reaches back, petting Emerson's head, the kid groaning the way a dog would with belly rubs. Yet, another side effect of being paranormal. Signs of affection such as those will please a shifter's wolf, strengthening their loyalty to the person who showed them that kindness.

A tense quiet once again falls over us. Only the tapping of the twin's fingers over their device screens filling the void. The beat of the music no longer there to drown out the pulsing thump of my heart.

It's another hour before Cooper pulls into a gas station. He exited the vehicle so rapidly, the car trembled from his abrupt departure and the forceful closing of the door.

Bronson moves almost as quick, jogging away from us as if we carry some rare disease that's sure to wipe out the population.

Is everyone always this bothered by being near us now?

"So…" Elijah stretches the word so long it only makes this that much more awkward.

"Out," Adrian barks, the seat he'd just been sitting in launching forward before the twins scamper out. The vehicle shaking one last time as Elijah tries to speed away from us, too.

Adrian rolls down the window, the purr of the engine still running.

"Cooper, you all need to get lost for fifteen minutes." Adrian's voice comes out strained and low. He's trying to hold back until we're alone. A new pair would never permit another to see his mate willingly.

The window has just returned to its original position before Adrian grips my chin, his jaw working hard. "Pants off."

There's zero hesitation on my part. The peel of the thin fabric down my thighs drawing out a moan. There's nothing sexy about the contortion of my body, but my skin is so damn sensitive every bit of anticipation leaves my panties soaked.

Like almost every encounter since we bonded, Adrian already has himself exposed by the time I'm ready to hook my leg over his hips. His large hand encircles his length, the soft pump making me lick, then bite my lip. If we had time, I'd swallow him down. Suck him off until he's shooting down my throat.

The corner of his mouth quirks. "Come here." Inching forward, he strokes himself once more, his knuckles brushing my pussy once. "Fuck me."

I don't wait, lifting my hips before impaling myself on his solid length. It's like breathing, having him inside me again. Like the world has settled, and all is right. A blanket of pleasure waiting to wrap around me every time we come together.

Adrian pumps up into me at a furious pace. His fingertips digging into the bruises he gave me last night. A mix of pain to weave with the pleasure. "Fuck. Yes, Adrian."

My head falls back, the column of my throat exposed to him. Those canines lengthening into pointed fangs. Each scrape sending a bolt of lightning straight to my core. "Mmm, you're going to make me want to bite you. Mark you as mine."

"Do it."

He only chuckles. His thrust forces me forward, our chests colliding and my fingers curling around the leather of the top edge of the seats to keep from hitting my head on the ceiling. Our mouths fall wide open. Breathing so heavily, we've heated the car to a sauna.

That familiar tingle swirls through my lower belly, only to lick up my spine. My only warning that my body is seconds from bursting into flames. A problem that would leave Adrian charred beneath me and the car exploding at this fine gas station.

"Adrian..." his name escaping as a hiss as he readjusts us. "Slow," I pant.

He understands, running a flat palm up my back, rolling his hips into mine at the most glacial pace before hooking an arm under my leg. He slips free, coaching me to switch directions. A loud groan escaping me as I sink back onto his throbbing cock.

His fingers lightly wrap around the curtain of my hair, pulling it back over my shoulder. "Ari, baby. You're squeezing me so tight. Is my pair ready to come?"

I can only nod, licking my lips once more. They seem so dry. Or maybe it's just that I can't catch my breath because I'm so full, and Adrian is relentless as he pounds into me like he'll never get to again.

"Adrian, please."

A plea for him to never stop.

A plea for him to make me shatter around him.

A need for him to never stop making me feel this way.

"You have sixty seconds," he growls in my ear. The lobe sucked between his lips as one hand slides up the center of my chest, before gently squeezing my throat.

"It'll take you that long," I retort.

A challenge.

So much between us is a challenge. A fight for dominance. A chance to one-up each other.

Shoving his forearm into my back, that grip on my neck tightens when my face collides with the center consul, he quickens his pace. So punishing, I'm blown apart in seconds. My walls clamp down hard, my orgasm rocking through me like a bulldozer.

"Fuck, Adrian. That was..."

He chuckles, his face against my heaving back. "Let's get you cleaned up real quick. You can remind me what that was later tonight."

Swiping my panties from inside my leggings, he wipes me clean. The both of us getting our lower halves back together within minutes.

The emptiness immediately has me craving more. But then again, I crave him twenty-four-seven. This fucking bond. I wouldn't change it, however inconvenient.

A wad of damp napkins sits balled up in Adrian's hand when I sit back in my seat. The only remnants from our fast food stop a few hours back. He wipes down every surface we may have touched. The sting of hand sanitizer thick in my nostrils.

"Get in the back," he places a kiss on my jaw. I'm quick to obey, climbing over the seat with a groan when a bolt of pain shoots through my left arm.

Most days, I'm proficient at ignoring it when Adrian is working to tear me in two, but then, in the aftermath, I'm always reminded I'm still not myself. I might never be. A reminder that continues to fuel my rage against Salvatore and everything he stands for.

My wince is unavoidable as I work to massage my shoulder and arm. Adrian hopping out of the backseat, disposing of the tissues and my panties as I whimper loudly. Whatever conversation he shares with the others muffled enough, I can't make out their words.

Cooper and Bronson are the first to climb back into the SUV. Adrian next, crawling in next to me.

"Not fair. Why do we have to sit in the sex seats?" Emerson whines.

"Get in or walk," Adrian grunts.

They do. All four of them rolling down their windows as we pull out of the lot. Anything to release the scent of how Adrian fucked me stupid. His cum still leaking out of me despite the quick clean up.

Thank goodness phoenixes usually only get pregnant once a year during their needing month — such a weird name. The thought mixes with the increasing hatred I let flow toward Salvatore and all power-hungry paranormals.

"You okay?" Adrian whispers, an arm draped around my shoulders.

My molars grind, letting the pain wash away every bit of pleasure Adrian just gave me. "I will be."

Twenty-Two
ADRIAN

After pretending not to massage the pain out of her arm for a half hour, Ari finally sleeps. I've noticed her working at it a lot these past few weeks. Each time telling me she's fine, but I know she's not. Her movements, strength, and daily apprehension reveal so much more than she thinks.

There's no doubt our non-stop fucking is aggravating it, too. The energy used to support the strengthening of the bond taking away from her healing from the gunshot wound. Every whimper she releases in her sleep shreds my heart just a little bit more.

Usually, I only catch her kneading at her shoulder and left arm, but I know she feels it in her chest and rib cage as well. I see it in every exercise I put her through. Every time we fuck, and she has to catch herself, she never uses her left, only her right. I've even caught her practicing firing solely with her right arm. Preparation to ensure she possesses the same strength on her right as her left once did. A plan B should her plan A fail.

On the outside, the wound has completely healed, but internally her body is still warring with the tiny remnants of metal that Dr. G couldn't completely remove. Throughout those first few weeks of healing, her body pushed out several chunks of shrapnel, but that doesn't mean it's all gone. Even the warlock we called in couldn't completely extract it, sensing microscopic pieces beneath the surface of her skin. Time alone might be our only savior.

There's no talking my girl out of anything if she's set on doing it. No matter how much I begged, she wouldn't relent. *"Adrian, this is something I need to do,"* she'd said. Her expression was so grim I knew in that moment she was blaming herself.

It was enough for me to back off. This is all part of her redemption. A small piece of her righting the world again.

My girl.

My future wife.

My pair.

This woman is mine. Only mine. There's no separating us now. Not even if we wanted to. A smile pulling at the corners of my mouth as the vehicle gradually slows.

Cooper stops at the curb. The cut of the engine is like marking a line in the sand. We all gaze up at the mansion beside us, realizing there's no turning back. Stucco, pillars, and fountains remind me of the drug lord homes down in Miami.

"Are you sure we're at the right address?" I question, dipping lower in my seat to catch more of the house through the smaller rear window.

Ari only mumbles incoherent words next to me, sleep still holding her under the blanket of dreamland. I wish I could leave her in the car while we investigate, but I can't bear to see her in pain. Nor could I take away whatever healing this will provide for her.

"This is the address in the file," Bronson supplies. Snatching the folder from the backpack at his feet, he runs his finger down the page, checking. "Yup. This is it."

"The file said it was a run-down apartment building. That's not what this is."

Unease creeps into my chest. This isn't right.

Thick, unrelenting tension fills the car. This time, the situation feels like stepping into a trap we might not escape. That boulder sitting at the base of my belly making me more nauseous with each passing second.

"Ari, baby. Wake up."

Her eyes pop open, those navy blue irises meeting mine before staring out the window. "Uh, are we making a pit stop?"

"Don't ask," Emerson shakes his head while opening his door.

We exit the car slowly, easing the doors closed quietly.

Ari sticks close to my side, her eyes focused and alert as if she hadn't just slept for three-plus hours. The front gate stands open.

There's a screen to the left with a keypad. A place like this would have a coded entrance. One that would have automation for closing the gate once someone passed it.

Stabbing at a few of the keys, there's no response on the screen. A sign this was a forceful entry instead of a welcomed visit.

Ari holds her gun low at her side. Cooper rolling out his neck as if ready to release his bird. Bronson's signature dark swirls dance around his palms. Those shadows he likes to call on to do his bidding are as helpful as they are terrifying.

The twins are who I worry about. We'd told them to only shift if they needed to. Only if they needed to run to stay safe. They've been shifting for the past decade but still don't possess complete control. It can be dangerous for young shifters in high-stress situations. One of us is likely to be the one to be clawed to death by accident, not their intended target.

Often, young shifters can't distinguish between those who are allies and those who are enemies. They can only differentiate between "like" and "other." Different earns your death.

"Emerson. Elijah. Stay close," I warn.

We creep up a flight and a half of sandstone steps leading to the front double doors. Large black slabs with intricate gold metal swirls adorning them. The front door, like the gate, remains open. The sliver of space barely wide enough to glance through.

"Everyone behind me," Ari whispers, the barrel of her gun wedged into the opening before pushing the door wide.

"Ari..." I warn. Most men cower before her scowl; I won't. This woman will be the end of me, either through non-stop fucking or during one of our outings.

Silence surrounds us as we enter the house. Destruction is all that greets us. Vases shattered. Tables overturned and couches shredded. It's as if a tornado tore through here and then doubled back to ensure nothing was salvageable.

"Bronson." My voice low. A signal for him to perform one of his many tricks. He whispers into his palms, hands clasped closely to his face as those black swirls lengthen. A ball of glowing light shoots out the moment he lowers them, darting through the space.

"What the hell was that?" Ari gulps.

"Locator. If anyone is here, we'll be alerted."

She nods but keeps the gun trained high, scanning.

We stay huddled by the front door, Cooper having pressed it shut behind us just in case there are any gawkers outside or the intruders are still here. We'll hear the door if they open it, giving us a chance to respond.

Everything about this is wrong. Viviana is dead. Her file says otherwise. Her residence was supposed to be an old seven-story building, not this. What the fuck is going on?

It's another five minutes of us breathing slowly before Bronson's swirling ball returns, now split into four, sinking back into his palms, becoming part of him again.

"Three dead bodies. No one alive inside the house."

Ari refuses to drop her gun as we move through the house. My fingers shifting into the deadly talons of my phoenix. I refuse to risk us. All it takes is one second of not being prepared for tragedy to strike. I've seen it. The one and only time I wasn't, Finlay died.

I rarely partially shift the way Tucker likes to, but today I'm making an exception. It's not something I spent hours honing or that came naturally to me. An energy suck I can't always afford or risk.

Despite the expansive layout of the first floor, it doesn't take long to clear it. There is nothing usable left.

"Ari, does this seem overkill to you?" I whisper as we stand in the middle of the office. Like the rest of the floor, someone had not only destroyed this room but also emptied it. No books, papers, or devices left behind. Someone planned this.

"Yes. Why destroy the whole house when clearly this room was a target?"

I only nod. I'd been thinking the same thing when we first walked in. It almost seems staged. A way to throw whoever found it off the tracks of the true intent.

A thought stirs deep at the base of my skull. If this was a planned event, someone tipped Viviana off. That is assuming she is actually still alive and someone else isn't using her identity as a cover.

Roots of doubt nestle in my gut. An inkling that tells me Viviana isn't dead. The databases don't lie. Their use of paranormal signatures leaves the chance of a wrong result exceedingly low.

My thoughts had occupied my focus enough I hadn't noticed I blindly followed the group to the grand staircase at the front of the home. Two curved flights shaping the massive foyer.

The light tap of our shoes on the stairs has my pulse bounding at my throat. Bronson's magic should be fool-proof, but what if it's not? What if it missed someone hiding here?

Cooper enters the first room on the right. The sight making my phoenix want to roar in protest. A man and woman lie naked on the bed. They'd either been sleeping or in the middle of having sex. Either way, there's no missing their flayed torsos. Their intestines spilling out onto the no longer white comforter beneath them. Their killer slashed their throats from ear to ear, matching Viviana's injuries from years ago.

Shouldering my way between the group, I stop as close to the bodies as the massive bed will allow. Shaking, I lift the man and woman by the back of their head, prompting them to sit up a bit to glance between their shoulder blades.

The contents of my stomach lurch up my throat. My gag barely keeping what's left inside me down.

The crest of my family stares back at me. That shield with the roaring phoenix dead center. "Sumus Custodes Tui" scrawled in an arc across the top, weaved into an array of feathers.

Bile rises up my throat. This can't be happening. They can't be here.

"We need to go."

I'm storming out of the house. Ignoring the pain radiating out from my belly as I rush away from my other half. This pales in comparison to what my family's reaction will be when they find out about Ari.

Fuck, thanks to Kenji, they likely already know.

I'm a hard man. An unforgiving man. I don't lose myself. I don't puke at the sign of death, but as I clear the bottom step at the front of the house, every bit of food rushes past my lips. Chunks and liquid flying onto the pristine green grass.

Ari's next to me moments later. The warmth of her palm at the back of my neck doing nothing to soothe the bile still burning my throat before splattering the ground beneath me. Moving her hand lower, she rubs circles into my mid-back as my hands brace on my knees. My chest heaves, tears burning the back of my eyes. I'd truly thought I was done with them. That I had cleansed my life of them forever.

Returning to full standing, I press my eyes closed. Every drawn breath is heavy with the pull of my chest. Not a single one settling the knots in my stomach.

"They're going to look for the third body and anything else they can find," Ari whispers, her face dipping into my line of sight. With a gentle push, she guides me to the steps, where my ass collides with an unforgiving thud.

Elbows braced on my knees, hands dropping between my legs, my head hangs low. Defeat stiffens my muscles. Fear paralyzes me.

I will do anything to protect Ari from them. To protect the James family.

"Talk to me." It's not that soothing voice she used moments ago when she found me puking my brains out. It's a command. That strength that she walks around with. Dominance that eventually earned her respect in her mother's ranks and must have propelled her to becoming a coveted detective.

"They were here. That was their brand. Their bodies were mutilated, the same as Viviana's was. I don't know why my family is here. I can't tell you what they want."

"Adrian, look at me." I don't. My head sinking lower. "Adrian Alexander. Look. At. Me."

Her tone makes me lift my gaze to meet hers.

"They only win if we let them. And we won't."

"Ari, you don't understand what they're like."

She scoffs, placing a quick kiss on the back of my head. "I do, Adrian. Salvatore was no better. I just chose to unknowingly side with the devil. They are one and the same, so yes, I do understand. I may not understand your childhood experiences, but we won't give up without a fight." Taking my cheeks between her palms, she forces my gaze to hers. "You're mine now. They can't have you."

Her words seep into me. The bravery alive inside her leaking into me. My gratitude sent to the gods above for making that a feature of the bond. "Just so you know, the devil works at the hospital." She only narrows her eyes at me, attempting to decide if I'm cracking a joke. I'm not, but that's a topic for another day. "Thank you, Ari."

I'm about to divulge more about my dark past when the others come jogging down the steps.

"We found the last body. Same condition," Cooper relays, his tone flat. "And this." He shoves a journal into my hands. Viviana Brambilla etched into the front. Etched on the inside cover, my family's crest stares back at me. The colored version where the phoenix glows cobalt blue is more vibrant in the natural light than I remembered it. Detailed feathers of each wing curving around "We are your guardians" in raised gold. The same gold outlining the shield.

I flip to the first entry, taking in the date, and my stomach drops.

We're so fucked.

Twenty-Three

Ari

Adrian was dead silent as we drove back from Ohio. He securely held the journal between his leg and the middle consul the whole way back, as if it might fly off.

A combination of stubbornness and anger put Adrian behind the wheel for our drive home. Our protests regarding his lack of focus ignored. It was clear he needed a chance to parse through his racing thoughts before clearing them.

I'd intended to ride home in the back so I could review things with the twins, but he refused to let me leave his side. *"Next to me,"* was all he said, his eyes pleading.

The tension Adrian carried was thick and palpable. It's a force that he let grow and fester for hours. With one hand on the wheel, his other remained wound with mine. The only time he broke contact was when we stopped, so I could pee.

Night had long since fallen, all of us exhausted from the quick turnaround. We'd planned to stay in a hotel for the night. Eight hours is quite the trek to do twice in one day. Yet none of us felt comfortable delaying our return to the safe house. Not after witnessing that horrid crime scene. Those people mutilated and left there as another display of the evil lurking in the shadows.

"Oh, sweetheart." Mom pulls me into a tight hug as we shuffle through the front door. "I'm so glad you made it home safely. All of you, she adds," placing her palm to each of their cheeks before pulling them into hugs as well. Her hold on the twins just a little tighter and a little longer. In my mother's eyes, they're still just babies. So am I.

The moment my mother released Adrian, he stormed past her without a word. His steps are just slow enough to snatch my hand, tugging me behind him. The heavy clap of his shoes seems to reverberate off the walls. Every bit of his mood swirling inside me the way it must be him.

He bypasses my room when I reach for the handle. A hard pull yanking me the few extra steps to his door. The hinges squealing loudly with the force of him yanking it open before slamming it.

"Adrian, you need to calm down."

He ignores me, heading straight into the bathroom, the shower screeching through the room. When he reemerges, he's only in his boxer brief, his shirt and jeans left behind. Glorious, chiseled muscle stares back at me. For as much time as we've spent wrapped up in each other this past week, I haven't stopped to appreciate his body. The cut lines and narrow waist. The curves of his thighs and indentations beneath his shoulders. Those lats standing tall at the side of his neck and that delicious V bordering his pelvis.

Everything about Adrian is perfection.

His emerald eyes bore into me as I kick off my sneakers one at a time. My fingers curling around the hem of my loose-fitting tee. His grip stopping me with my wince.

"Let me."

With grace, I wouldn't think he'd possess, he removes each article of my clothing. His fingers grazing across my skin. Leaving searing lines of heat behind each place he touches. His breath tickles the shell of my ear as he leans in close, breathing me in.

"Always so wet. Always so ready."

"Adrian," his name a whisper on my lips. "We should talk first, yeah?" A meek attempt at trying to help him control everything he's feeling.

Although I really want to have sex with him now, the incident at Viviana's mansion would be traumatic for anyone. Baggage he might have never unpacked or will need to unpack again.

His cheek presses to mine, body bent to bring them level. The feel of his smile spreading temporarily making me forget the protest I'd been trying to make. Without a thought, I tug his briefs down, leaving us both bare. Our bodies are naked, but something else passes between us. A sensation I can't place or describe. An understanding, maybe.

"Let's clean up." He only nods at my words, leading us into the shower. "Then I'll take care of you for once."

He doesn't argue as he washes us both. His fingertips soothe my scalp as he shampoos my hair and caresses my body. A tenderness to him I witnessed not too long ago as I healed. Only now the timid, shaking hands are absent.

Exhaustion hits me the moment we climb into bed. His body warmth blocking out the chill of what we found today.

I'm not sure how long I've slept. My legs and his are tangled, and my cheek rests on his chest. Cracking open my eyes, he's leaning against the headboard, the journal open across his lap. The words are unclear from this distance, but the tension in his body is unmistakable.

"Adrian." My fingers glide over his cheek, turning his focus to me. Those green eyes are so haunted. Past demons floating through his consciousness that I can't erase for him. "Go to sleep."

Immediately, he drops the journal to the nightstand. The soft thud somehow startling.

There's not a word on his lips as he slips under the comforter, the large blob of his body moving far enough to nestle between my legs.

Long, warm fingers run down my pulsing core, dipping inside me before his dick replaces them minutes later.

He moves slowly. A lulling rhythm that nearly puts me back to sleep. This orgasm, unlike usual, feels less like a raging storm, more like quenching fire with water. A calm washing over me as we finish together.

I'm nearly back to dreamland when he whispers a confession he thinks I can't hear.

"I will love you forever, Ari James. I wish times were different. I wish I didn't have to worry about your safety. Our only concern should be where we're going to live or how many kids we're going to have." His hand runs over the center of my stomach. "Or convincing you to quit your job so we never have to leave our bed." Tender lips press to my forehead. His deep inhale making me inwardly sigh. "I hope that one day my wishes come true."

Then he snuggles in closer, resting his chin atop my head. His breathing quick to even out while I lie awake, replaying his words.

The bond continues to prove to be a challenge.

Talia fabricated a false FBI background and credentials for Adrian, enabling him to join me at work daily. Captain Barlow scrutinized the intrusion with a spyglass, pissed no one told him the feds were coming in.

Adrian's response: we don't have to tell you a damn thing when you have such a prolific serial killer on the loose, one that's crossing state lines. Captain shut up after that.

Gomez joined the hunt for Salvatore and his accomplices. No one has seen the warlock. Only a few have heard from him. We've learned there have been sightings of Kenji near many of the crime sights, but otherwise, nothing unusual about him. Not a single whisper of the other members of the Alexander clan.

Every spare moment Adrian obsesses over that damn journal. His refusal to let anyone else but my mother view it, driving my frustrations high. I can't help him or us if he's not willing to share it.

Meetings at the safe house occupy my nights, disturbing my sleep as greatly as my time having sex with Adrian does. I swear I've seen the War Room more than I've been at the precinct or my apartment combined.

Lucky for us, the consultant from London had a delayed arrival. However, I don't think any of us are ready for the mess she'll walk into today. Our usual circle, including the twins, gathered in the war room to welcome her over an hour ago. The anticipation of what is coming leaving me twisted in knots.

I'm itching to meet this woman. To learn her identity and the World Council's motivation for directly involving her. In truth, they can do as they please, but it should have been in consult with my mother. Not behind her back.

Yes, we know the situation has become dire. The death toll climbs each day. Confirmation of who is on our side and Salvatore's becoming increasingly clear.

The biggest mystery, though, remains those three dead bodies. We still don't understand their connection, if any. The Alexander family's involvement is suspected, but the specifics remain unclear. It makes no sense that they've suddenly come out of the woodwork and here in the United States when they've always kept their business abroad.

The doorbell rings. Tucker's body immediately stiffening. An odd reaction, but we're all on edge.

Adrian keeps my hand knotted with his on his thigh, as if I need some sort of reassurance. I don't. This woman just better not get in our way.

Cheerful voices become clearer as they near the door. Syriah's laughter, followed by a thick British accent, making me sit up straighter. She'll know who I am and it's still pertinent I make a good impression. Maybe she'll see we've got it handled and leave. Or she'll despite me the way everyone else has, knowing what I did for years.

The door opens, and Tucker shoots from his seat. His back plasters to the wall against our living map. His chest is heaving, eyes bulging as a tall brown-skinned woman enters the room. Her perfectly styled curls fan out from her head in a well-shaped curly fro. My god, she's gorgeous.

"Get out!" Tucker yells. "Get the fuck out!"

She wears the same shocked expression he does. Her lips parting and chest pumping as if she suddenly can't breathe. I have no idea what's going on. But the room stands still. Not a single individual breathing other than my brother.

"Tuck, what is wrong with you?" I move to stand from my chair.

He rushes past, pushing aside the woman, exiting the room angrily. Each thunderous step resonates, creating the illusion of his presence in the room with us.

"What the hell was that?" Exasperation thick in my tone. Tucker's usual composure disappears if Adrian mistreats me. Those outbursts are ones we're all used to, but this wasn't that.

This was something eons beyond protecting his family member.

Talia stands from her seat, her head tucked low. "Isis here..." she points to the woman from London. "...is Tucker's pair."

Then she leaves the room too, much slower than he did and without another word.

I hope she goes to find the man she fell in love with, but wouldn't fault her for just wanting to disappear. The day everyone warned them about is here.

Who on earth could ever be ready for that?

Twenty-Four

Ari

The silence becomes so stifling I have to speak up. Anything to break up the awkward tension looming over us like a dark cloud. I couldn't tell you if my reaction was less intense around Adrian for the first time or if I simply didn't recognize it then. My mixed heritage limits my understanding of their feelings. Mine too, for that matter.

"Isis. It's a pleasure to meet you." I reach out a hand as I make my way to her. Her grip is firm as she shakes it.

"The pleasure's all mine."

I gesture her to the seat Tucker had just occupied. "Let's get started then. There's a lot to catch you up on."

A small nod is her answer. The acknowledgment enough to relax everyone's shoulders as we plow through everything from the beginning.

I'm the beginning.

Not once does judgment ever cloud her stare as we walk through each of my kills. Then the ones since Salvatore disappeared after the night he shot me. Seguing to the odd murders with the brands with Adrian's family.

It's then we turn to the map, drawing it all together with visual representation. Her fingers grazing over a yellow dot in Egypt.

"Someone you know?" I ask.

"Yes. That's where my family still lives. I left for London about seventy-five years ago and have never looked back. It was then I took a position as a policymaker, focusing specifically on paranormal crime. It's why the World Council and Gorman Board thought it necessary that I come."

I nod, our focus returning to the map.

"Well, it seems Salvatore has been quite busy. He will be brought to justice for what he has done." She turns slowly to Adrian. "As will your family, Mr. Alexander."

His grimace says it all. The prospect of them being punished is exactly what he wants. Actually, he would prefer them eradicated from this earth, but there's been enough death.

Isis clears her throat. "Reporting all this to the councils could result in both you and Ari being included."

I swallow loudly. I never imagined punishment for unwitting or coerced actions. It should have been a given.

I am a homicide detective. A law enforcer for the human world. How could I have ever thought we would never have to face the consequences, regardless of our intent?

"Understood," Adrian nods. "What's your plan while you're here?" His fingers steeple beneath his chin. A sign he's hoping her answer will be nothing more than observation.

"Until Salvatore and now your family are caught, Mr. Alexander —"

"Adrian, please," he interrupts.

"Yes, of course. You're stuck with me until we can apprehend whomever is leading this slaughter campaign." A nervous laugh leaves her as if we would be upset by it.

After this session, I can understand why they sent her. She possesses a sharp mind, noticing details others miss. My tolerance of Isis shifting to appreciation the longer we discuss our findings. Having another woman here who doesn't look at me as if I'm seconds from betraying us all is nice. To her, I was never an outsider.

"Well, it's been quite a night," Syriah interjects. "Food should be delivered soon. Let's get cleaned up, eat, and then start fresh tomorrow."

"Mrs. James, if you don't mind, I would like to continue reviewing the files."

"Of course, Isis." Syriah pulls her close, hugging her to her chest. A past there I know nothing about. "It's been great to see you again after all this time."

"You as well."

"Isis, Mom, I'll stay too. You might have questions I can help clarify."

"That would be lovely." Isis places a hand on my forearm with a small squeeze.

The room empties, leaving only Isis, Adrian, and me behind.

"I'll be in the gym," he whispers. A hard kiss smacked against my mouth. An even harder glare thrown at Isis.

I figure that's as far as he'll be able to tolerate being from me. This room occupies the west wing's edge, unlike the gym, which is almost central.

Isis settles into a seat across from me. A comfortable silence between us as we both shuffle through file folders. I look for the clues I missed while she reviews them for the first time. Details I'm hoping will now pop off the page at me.

I pull open a folder for one family tapped to be next in line for leadership. The address is familiar to me. Yet my brain can't seem to figure out why.

Rubbing my eyes, I fight to search for the answer. I wish for the memory to come back clearly. The minutes ticking by effortlessly.

The chant in my mind somehow summoning the requested memory. Clarity finding me as if by magic.

The digits, when rearranged, match Viviana's Ohio address. The letters of the street name also a match.

I memorized the faces of the people in that house, and they don't resemble the man and woman in this photo. The individuals I'm observing now have a residence on the eastern shore. It would make sense for Sirens. They are water-loving creatures. The ones from eons ago slowly evolved through time to become shifters and then land-dwelling inhabitants that resembled humans. Their gifts kept intact through the years.

David and Lilith Collymor seem as harmless as can be. Their smiling faces as inviting as a siren's call. It says here they have four children but none are pictured here. There are no known locations for them. No history on them at all except their names and ages.

"What have you found?" Isis's crisp, accented words cut through my thoughts.

"The address for this couple is the same as the one in Ohio we went to for Viviana, but in a different order. And there's nothing listed on their children."

Isis grabs the folder from me. Her brow scrunching low as her eyes rake over the page. Eyes that can only be described as pure gold.

"Ari…" My name drawn out before she sucks in a breath. "These people are known opposition to your family's rule. Their children are being held prisoner."

"Excuse me?" My eyes bulge, snatching the folder from her, flipping through the pages as if they will reveal that same truth. "This isn't Medieval Times."

Isis sighs, pity coating her gaze. "Ari, you have so much to learn. You're young. You haven't even hit your hundredth year yet. This war dates back far before your time, even before your mother's. You're new to this, and I sympathize with that, but this is how things are."

"Are the children guilty?" I press.

"You mean the way Adrian is?"

My blood runs cold. I'd never considered that their parents might have forced them to obey. Or maybe they are evil or good. Too many factors lie hidden for me to know the truth. The idea of Adrian's imprisonment knots my insides, though I understand its justification.

My shoulders sink, the folder dropping to the tabletop. My face falls to my open palms, a sob breaking free. The only morsel of weakness I'll allow to show.

Isis's hand on my shoulder makes me flinch before my gaze meets hers again.

"No, they are not guilty. They were never asked to act as Adrian did. More accurately, they are being held as a bargaining chip against their parents."

I'm not sure which is worse. The monsters we're forced to be to protect others or the ones we truly are.

Isis's meaning is clear. They will dangle those children like carrots and use them as bait if necessary to control their parents. Unlike the evil out there, remorse may sit in our hearts, but not regret.

"I want them released and brought here."

"Ari, you don't have —"

"Don't I? Do my parents not preside over all paranormals? I want them brought here immediately. They will be my responsibility."

Isis sighs, her fingers pinching her nose. "I'll see what can be done."

"See that you do."

I rise from the table, leaving her behind. I've barely opened the gym door, and Adrian is there, scooping me up into his arms.

"I could feel you. I think you need a distraction," he snickers.

"I do."

So we fuck. Right on that same bench I'd nearly given myself to him on weeks ago.

Twenty-Five

ADRIAN

Isis's presence has both Ari and Tuck on high alert.

It's been hell trying to get anything done. Tuck minimizes his time at the safe house to avoid Isis. Anything to limit spending time in the same room as her. I don't know if he's terrified of her or him and Talia ending. It doesn't matter. Every interaction is awkward as fuck and it's weighing on the rest of us.

Isis's failure to fulfill Ari's request quickly enough — a request Ari refused to share — has Ari trapped in a constant pissed off state.

Just five minutes ago, Ari marched up to Isis, snarling that same damn fucking question. *"Is it done?"*

Isis's response is always the same. *"It's being worked on."*

An answer that's deemed unacceptable to my pair.

Those additional issues aside, I'm thankful for the days Ari doesn't have to work. It allows us to rest and temporarily escape the burdens of the world. A much needed reprieve from the heavy weights constantly hanging over our heads. The rope holding it in place precariously unraveling day by day.

The time off has proven useful in getting Ari to open up a bit, too. After an hour of pounding into her last night, she finally admitted what she had asked of Isis.

An impossible request that she shouldn't have made.

Yet Syriah never reversed it. She claims it's her daughter's choice to make wrong or right. Ari must learn to differentiate between sound judgment and missteps. Hard lessons every leader must learn in time. Syriah refuses to make those choices for her.

I believe Ari acted appropriately, despite knowing many others will disagree. The sirens who follow us may show relief. The Collymor children have only experienced their captivity and each other, each taken within weeks of being born. Other than rumors, they know nothing of a life with their parents. That should count for something. There was no nasty environment to influence their behavior to align with the treasonous people who created them.

All we've really accomplished is crushing their hope by imprisoning them.

One might assume that losing their first child would have been sufficient for the couple to change their minds. To surrender their wayward agenda and fall in line, but no. They continued to voice their opposition fervently, as they sired offspring after offspring.

From the information I had gathered, it seemed they had completely disregarded the fact that they had children, convinced they would never reunite with them. They were nothing more than offspring repopulating their species. Those young mean absolutely nothing to them. A heartbreaking notion.

Now Ari wants them here for her to look after. It makes me wonder if she wants children of her own. A conversation we've never had, but something I can't stop thinking about. A merging of our bloodlines — both phoenix and warlock. What that child might become is unknown. All we could speculate is the power it will hold. Three strong, prominent bloodlines might make an unstoppable hybrid.

Though species mixing happens, it's not that common for the offspring to carry equal traits of both parents the way Ari does. Though Ari has yet to tap into her warlock abilities at all outside of the fire magic, the power she possesses is clear. I've watched her practice sessions with Bronson in awe. But for whatever reason, she identifies more with her phoenix. Perhaps because that's the parent she can still hold each day. The one she can rely on to help guide her.

"Hey, let me ask you something?"

Ari hums, closing another folder and sitting it next to her bare leg on the mattress with her fingers still hooked around the edge.

"Do you want kids?"

The question seems untimely given our current situation. A mundane inquiry. A simple ask that would come up in any human relationship. Something Ari and I never did.

"Yeah, eventually," her answer distracted. I snatch the folder from her hands, forcing her to look at me.

"I'm being serious."

"You're always serious. You don't even know how to crack a proper joke."

"Proper?" I laugh. "Are you becoming a Brit on me now?"

"Ha. Ha," she snorts. "Yes, I want children, Adrian. I always have, but expected it wouldn't happen. I didn't have a dating life. After a while, I stopped thinking I would find a good husband, but never stopped wanting little ones. Maybe because I grew up an only child."

"When?" The single word bursts free before I can stop it.

"I —" she pauses. "I don't know. We have a lot going on. And for me, so much of what I know is human life. Do phoenixes get married first? Or is it just agreed that when it happens, it happens because we're pairs and we're bonded for eternity? I know there's a specific month each year when phoenixes are most fertile, but Talia mentioned that the first year of the bond is mainly so you can knock me up. Does that change because I'm a half-witch, and their bodies tend to behave more like humans?"

I have to laugh at her rambling speech. She's adorable when she gets like this. Trying to make sense of the warring worlds she knows. Her mind working overtime to tie them together so all the puzzle pieces align.

"Plus," she continues. "We'll know when I'm in my needing time. I always thought they were just terrible periods, but now that I know it was something more, we'll know when to avoid having unprotected sex. Or maybe we won't. I don't know…" her voice trails off, eyes casting down to her hands in her lap.

"I'm never using a condom with you." Her eyes meet mine. "Yes, they are effective for paranormals, too… oddly enough. We're not human, and I refuse to act like one." She glares at me. "However, I do think we should ask Dr. G about the pregnancy thing. You're only half phoenix. Like you said, we don't know if pregnancy works the same."

She groans, throwing her head back against the headboard. "Would have been nice to think about that before you started pumping me full of cum every day."

Rolling over on top of her, she giggles, my fingers tucking her hair back from her face. "You love my cum."

"I love you," she whispers.

My heart stops. She just said that, right? Those three words are the same ones I never thought I'd hear someone say to me and mean them besides Syriah.

"What did you say?" My eyes search hers. Those deep navy blue and silver eyes staring back at me. Her shrug is one of nonchalance, tucking her lips into her mouth.

"You heard me."

My lips crash into hers. Tongues and teeth clashing as I devour this woman. I realize I should have said it back. Should have poured my heart out to her. How did we get here so fast? How did I fall head over heels for the one woman I thought would drive me absolutely insane?

A fall that had nothing to do with her being my pair. The bond doesn't make you love the person. Doesn't make you become addicted to them. The pair bond is based on primal need, not emotion.

A knock sounds at the front door. The double tap muted back here in the bedroom at the rear of the condo. Sounds so foreign they seem out of place, as no one has visited us here since the shooting.

"Whoever it is will go away," I breathe into her neck.

"Fat chance," she shoves at my chest. Fishing through the blankets for my black t-shirt before slipping on my boxer briefs underneath, she speed walks out of the bedroom.

Grabbing for pajama pants, I nearly topple over, hopping on a single leg to hurry after her.

"Coming," she calls, just ahead of me.

Laughter bubbles out of me as I stop short behind her, the door already open, revealing Talia and Isis, both with stark expressions. "What's up?"

"We're supposed to be at Tuck's in twenty minutes. Did you forget?" Talia rolls her eyes.

"I have no idea what you're talking about." I honestly don't. No one said a thing to me.

"For questioning?" Her nose scrunching in annoyance.

"Seriously, no idea what you're talking about."

"Give us five minutes," Ari snorts, ushering the two into the living room.

Tucking my lips inward, I march behind my woman, wondering what the hell I missed.

Ari rifles around the bathroom, freshening up before slipping into a pair of loose-fitting jeans. "Guess we should get you stuff to bring here." She places a kiss on the side of my throat before she fights to knot her longer-than-ever hair atop her head.

"Later," I agree, watching her saunter out of the bathroom the moment she's done looking at herself in the mirror.

It takes me two minutes to dress before I'm darting back toward the living room, slipping into my boots by the front door.

"Alright, let's go." I breathe.

We slip into Ari's 4Runner, with me speeding off toward Tuck's house. A route that suddenly feels unfamiliar to me. It only now occurs to me how long it's been since I was last here.

It had been even longer for Ari. She'd mentioned at some point, Tuck stopped having her over, but I couldn't tell her why. I promised to allow him to keep that aspect of himself private and disclose it to her only when he thought it was the right moment. It was never my secret to share.

I know it hurt her, though. She wanted to be close to him. Tuck's distance only succeeded in her believing he wanted to keep a barrier between them. Whether it was because of lack of trust or something else, she didn't know and I wouldn't say.

Tuck answers the door before we can even knock. Anger distorts his features. "What's she doing here?"

I immediately think he's talking about Isis. My mouth opening to come to her defense. "Tuck, she means no harm. She's not here to break you guys up —"

He growls in Ari's direction. "I meant you." His sister jerks back as if physically slapped. He's never spoken to her that way in front of me, and my phoenix roars in protest.

"Watch your tone." My voice low, the extra bass meant to intimidate.

"I told you not to bring her here."

"Man the fuck up! We need her, so either tell her the truth or destroy what little relationship you've built. I don't give a fuck, but you damn sure better watch how you speak to her."

Confusion mars their beautiful faces. Ari refuses to take her eyes off her brother, so much sadness building behind her eyes. The glassy sheen, one I wish I could wipe away.

"Tucker," she starts. "I'm not sure what I did or happened, but if I can help..."

We all watch his features soften. Gone is the monster that was prepared to make an appearance. I can only imagine he hadn't bothered hiding it from Isis because she would feel it in him anyhow. Sense it the way a pair senses everything.

He runs a hand through his hair. His breath puffing past his parted lips as he allows us to pass inside. A deep inhale of Isis as she walks by, not even remotely missed by our group. He clears his throat, leading everyone downstairs, stopping Ari as we clear the bottom step.

"Ari, I'm sorry. I need to warn you. You're going to see… something when we enter this room, and I need you to not hate me for it." I'm just around the corner listening. There's no predicting how this will go. My heart racing and the unease of her potential reaction spider-walking its way down my spine. Not because my mate isn't familiar with the dark, but because she already fears the punishments we may face enough. To think Tuck might join us would break her.

Her hand grazes his cheek. "You're my brother."

With a nod, he leads us down the hall and into the room the others disappeared into.

A woman sits bound to a metal chair in the center of the room. Crusted blood streaks down her throat and across her cheek, a contrast to her light brown skin. Her head was bowed until I entered.

When she raises it, an audible gasp escapes Ari.

She knows exactly who she is looking at, and so do I.

Twenty-Six

Ari

Salvatore's likeness is in that woman's face. A female replica right in front of me. There's no way she's not related to him. Hell, she could be his twin forty years removed.

Creeping closer, my eyes narrow on her, scrutinizing every similarity. "Who are you?"

A dark laugh escapes her. A wad of blood spat at my feet.

"Come on, Ari. You know who I am." A wolfish grin pulls at her wide, dry lips. "And I know who you are. My father's favorite pet."

I recoil at her words. My back colliding with Adrian's front. "What the fuck is she doing here, tied up?"

I turn to face Tucker. This is his house. He had to know she was down here. Is this what he was talking about? Is this the reason he won't allow me to come here? He takes hostages and beats them? Or does someone else?

The questions rattle through my brain, not a single person's expression concretely answering a single one.

Then he flips. Like a switch carelessly flicked before entering a dark room. A sinister grin stretches across his face. A mischievous gleam behind his eyes I've never seen before.

I don't understand what's going on here.

The man standing across from me isn't the brother I know.

"Ari, big sis, this is Salvatore's daughter, Lucia. She is my prisoner. I want to know where he is, and she will tell me. I've been breaking her slowly, and today she caved."

"Fuck. You," she spits.

In an instant, Tucker squats in front of her. His movements swift and catlike. So smooth it's as if he was built to move so effortlessly. A single long finger braces under her chin. Her body trembling under his touch. That digit shifts into a small claw. A trickle of blood dripping free once it punctures the skin.

"Tell them what you told me, sweetheart."

"Fuck. You," she growls again.

"Tell them," he warns. The tip digs in a little farther, her whimper shifting my insides.

The scene is too familiar. I've tortured answers out of a few of my targets. Then there were others I played with like this. Minutes or hours of toying with them while I watched the hope flicker from their eyes. That transitional moment of watching them realize they were about to die making my heart race.

But Adrian's hand on my lower back reminds me I'm not that person. Not anymore.

"Tucker, what the fuck are you doing?"

I attempt to charge forward, but Adrian holds me back. Talia and Isis watching with indifferent stares. Waiting.

Lucia whimpers again. Her body trembling before tears stream down her face.

"My father has more followers than you could ever imagine. Do you think your walls are safe? They're not. He's infiltrated you, too. So go find him where I told you, but you won't win. You won't."

"Who?" I roar.

Now I'm pissed. Will I never be able to escape him?

Tucker cackles a dark laugh. A nearly imperceptible smirk pulling at the corner of Isis's mouth.

Lucia's gaze drifts toward me. "Figure it out, you traitorous bitch."

Tuck roars in front of her. His entire hand now talons striking across her chest. I struggle to stop this. To keep this from happening. This isn't my brother. He's not like them. Then his eyes find mine, so dark you'd think the devil possessed him, and my fight dies.

This is what he'd been trying to tell me.

This is Tucker. My brother likes to torture. Maybe likes to kill, too.

A knife appears from the back of his pants. The metal of the blade glimmering with that dark sheen of the metal alloy that nearly killed me.

"Tucker," my voice a croak. No more words come, each lodged in my throat.

He waves the knife just in front of her face, the four-inch blade dangerously close to her skin. Each time I whine his name, only quickens his motions. An effortless glide of his weapon twirling around her pixie features.

The veins in his hand and forearm bulge with how tightly he has his fist clenched around the handle. His arm angling high above her heart before the groan of upstairs floorboards under considerable weight stops us all dead.

"Who else is here?" Isis demands.

"No one," Tucker growls, standing to his full height.

He charges upstairs as if he hadn't just been about to stab someone in the chest, each of us following on his heels.

Snarling growls grow louder as we near the basement door at the top of the stairs. A hoarse sing-song voice carrying over them.

"Arianya," it croons. "Arianya."

A chill steals down my spine. That name. So similar to mine. But it's as if I've heard it before. Something inside me knowing it belongs to me as much as the name Ari does.

"Arianya, come out, my dear."

That voice calls me forward, my hand reaching past Tucker toward the door handle. Adrian yanks me back, the both of us nearly tumbling down the stairs to fall to our death.

"Don't," he warns.

I fight against his hold, elbowing him in the gut, so he releases me. My hands shoving Tucker aside as I burst through the door. Two massive wolf heads greet me, glowing yellow eyes and streams of drool dripping past their yellowed canines to the floors.

My eyes scan the living room. Searching for where that voice came from. It's just the wolves here. Their paws beating the carpet, creating a thunderous sound. I feel the crew at my back. Each one ready to attack. Ready to defend.

"Arianya. You have something that belongs to us."

"Fuck you. Come out. Cowards hide behind werewolves."

Only their scent gives them away. The nuances just different enough from wolf-shifters to confirm that's not what they are.

No, someone forced these two into these forms. Not by the moon, but by some other influence. A witch or a serum. I'm not entirely sure.

Wolf-shifters choose when to take their forms. Their species sitting just a little higher on the food chain than their cousins snarling before me. Werewolves don't possess that kind of control over their beasts.

The shadows shift in a corner to the left. A hag of a woman breathing into view out of thin air. Her skin is so pale that it appears to have the grayish-blue sheen of the moon. Veins black as onyx instead of blue.

This is the witch from Adrian's house. The one that tried to kill him all those months ago. It has to be per the description he gave me.

Anger courses through my veins, my focus on the witch in front of me, grinning with sharp, jagged teeth. Keeping my eyes trained on her, I unholster the gun at my hip, leaving the one at my back hidden for now.

"Let's play."

I shoot.

As if she were a mirage, her body disappears into a cloud of gray smoke just as my bullet would have struck her skull. Her dark cackle filling the air only moments later.

"You'll have to do better than that, Arianya."

That fucking name. It shouldn't be on her tongue. It's not meant for her.

Two additional wolves spring out from behind the doorways, pausing briefly before launching their attack. Yellowed teeth glare at us as they leap through the air. Their massive paws stretched, extending their gnarled claws toward us.

The house isn't big enough for us to shift into our birds, but just the same, Tucker grows next to me. His arms half transformed into wings, his talons on full display. A beak distorts the shape of his mouth as he roars into the face of a werewolf mid-air, aiming for him.

His talons strike true. A screeching whimper escaping the gray beast as it writhes underneath Tuck's onslaught. Each strike and pluck of his beak shredding the werewolf before our eyes.

Aiming my gun, I fire as a second werewolf charges my brother. Adrian, suddenly dragging me backward with enough force, my arm jerks high. The bullet ricochets off the mantle before lodging itself in the wall. The wild howl from our furry enemies vibrating through the room.

"Get off!" I fight against his hold. My gun still gripped tightly in my dominant hand. That familiar pain, though less, tingling down its length.

"No! I need to get you out of here."

Elbowing him again, I break free, darting around the corner into the kitchen. I need to find that witch.

Temptation almost has me looking back for Adrian. If he gets hurt...

I glance back, revealing Talia swinging a jagged metal bat. Like a graceful ninja, Isis spins behind her, slashing through the chest of a werewolf with gold daggers. I don't know where the hell those came from, but they appear to be authentic. Ancient even. A visual representation of her culture. Her home.

Yet, there's no sign of Adrian. Ready to continue my search for the hag, my glance catches on movement out of the corner of my eye.

A werewolf stalks toward me, each step backward, drawing me further into the enclosed kitchen.

"Come on, you bastard," I growl before it launches itself at me.

I fire. My clip emptied into its chest, sending it crashing to the floor before skidding to my feet.

My chest heaves while I watch. While I wait. My backup gun pulled from my waistband just as it clumsily works its way back to its feet. Its legs wobble as it raises its massive head in my direction. Not wanting to waste another bullet on it, I shove the gun back into my waistband, diving for the drawers where I know Tucker keeps the knives.

Pulling a butcher knife and one the length of my forearm free, I spin back to face the limping beast. This time, I don't wait for it to attack. Charging forward, I drive one knife into its thick neck. Pain vibrates up my air, through my chest, and down my side. Our joint howls are both laced with immeasurable pain.

But I don't stop. I can't as I jerk the knife free before bringing both down on its head and shoulder. Every strike brings tears to my eyes. So much pain. So much death. When will it stop?

It collapses at my feet, shuttering breaths leaving it convulsing as a pool of blood forms under its head. "I'm sorry," the words whispered for only the dying creature to hear.

Sprinting back into the living room, I suck in several deep breaths. My pulse bounding at my throat so forcefully the vessels may rupture. Two werewolves remain alive in the room, their presence overshadowed by four carcasses sprawled across the floor. Where did the other two come from?

It's then I spot Adrian almost hidden behind the wall in the next room. He and a tall man go head to head.

The stranger's girth overshadows Adrian's size two times over. The man's long fangs, drape over his bottom lip. Skin ashen despite his olive complexion, not a hint of a flush creeping over his cheeks or neck. No sweat or signs of tiring.

Vampire.

Charging forward, I slip my forearm across his throat, yanking him back. Caught off guard, his legs tangle with mine, my back colliding with the floor as we both go down. A howl breaks free of me as the vampire arches. The new angle only aiding me in looping my legs around his waist. Thank goodness I'm tall or there's no way. He writhes atop me, shouting every derogatory curse my way, as Adrian stumbles back to his feet.

"Motherfucker, go to sleep," I groan, squeezing tighter. His fingernails shift into claws, their sharp points digging into my tender flesh. The bite of pain dull compared to the remnants of what my gunshot continues to do to me.

"Not her, Domingo." The witch chides. That voice booms from behind me. So close I could touch it.

Adrian's there in an instant, his knee pressed to the vampire's sternum. Hands pressing to either side of his head, Adrian takes a deep breath, roars, and then snaps the vamp's neck. His body goes limp atop mine, crushing me for several long moments before Adrian kicks his body aside.

"Light him up," he points.

At first I have no idea what he means. The fatigue and pain making my brain foggy. My ability to call to the flames at will momentarily forgotten. They overtake me quicker than they have in a long time. I can't recall the last time I'd called them to the surface, so determined to stamp them down so as not to fry my mate.

My clothes singe to ashes, my naked body left there as I place my palms on the vampire's back. The witch cackling somewhere nearby, but unseen as his body disintegrates beneath my palms. When he's nothing but ash, I remove my hands, knees pressing into the carpet beneath me.

Adrian's outstretched arm appears in my peripheral vision, his shirt in hand. I take it, sliding it on quickly. Its length hits just above mid-thigh. Something I would normally care about in front of my brother, but not today.

The losses suffered are too much to overlook.

The witch's cackle sounds behind me again, a lazy groan sounding near her. "Christoph, let's go. We have what we came for." Glancing to the right, that same cloud of smoke surrounds Lucia. Her body curling forward from the gash Tucker left her with. In an instant, they disappear into thin air. Not even the smoke cloud left behind.

Only one werewolf remains, its rear paw held high off the ground.

"Stop," I order Tucker and Isis as they tag team stalking toward their prey.

The room goes still.

Stepping right in front of the wolf's maw, I stare it in the eyes. A rich chocolate brown staring back at me. Eyes that seem eerily familiar.

With a sudden certainty, I know that when I command this werewolf to shift, it will do so. As if a voice in my head is guiding me, I take one more step closer.

Reaching a palm to the fur by its ear, Tucker lunges forward. My over-the-shoulder glare stopping him in his tracks.

"Christoph, is it?"

The wolf snarls, baring its teeth.

"Kneel."

Reluctantly, it settles on its haunches. Its rear right leg leans out to the side. Likely injured in the worthless battle.

"Ari, we should detain him," Isis says, her voice closer to me than I would expect.

Staring into those brown eyes, my chin cocks higher. "Shift."

In the blink of an eye, the fur recedes. The animal characteristics revert to its human form. One I know so well. *Johnny Christopher Nighlen.*

His eyes bore into mine. Fury and hatred burning behind his stare. Not a single trace of the cop I've known.

"Speak." My final order.

"This time, you'll die."

His last words before Tucker's talon drives straight through his throat.

Twenty-Seven

ADRIAN

Explaining the shit show that took place at Tuck's house was a nightmare.

Every leader filed into the War Room wearing grim looks. The head of the werewolves, Kenan Green, sneering at us as if ready to tear our heads from our necks.

I can't blame him. Though he is as against traitors as we are, they were still his kind. His to protect. His priority was to ensure they were on the right side of this war. A guarantee it seems we can no longer cling to. That look was as much about this own failure as what we took from him. Still, my gut twists. Kenan has always been unyielding in his loyalty to the structure of our world. We can only hope this incident doesn't change that.

Syriah brought the meeting to a start, only for it to turn ugly fairly quickly. Almost every grievance became a pointed attack on Ari. My temper hangs on by the thinnest of threads with every accusatory question slung her way.

But my pair handles it with grace. Her temper remains even keel. Yet the sadness and anger rages inside her. A warring twirl of tit for tat, keeping her on edge. Pride swelling in my chest that she's strong enough to hide it all. The only thing she's willing to show is the physical pain she still lives with. The leaders in the room carefully tallying every wince or hiss of pain.

"How the hell did you not know?" Cooper's tone laced with disbelief as he slings his words at Ari.

As if Tuck's clothing scorched her skin, Ari damn near tore them from her body as she raced up the stairs the moment we walked through the safe house front door. Her face scrunched in pain as she charged into our room — formerly mine — stealing a pair of my sweatpants that were entirely too large for her. For a moment, I couldn't stop thinking about the woman in my clothes, surrounded by men while wearing nothing underneath.

My eyes press close, attempting to stamp down my fantasies of fucking her on this table instead of the terror that wound its way through me while we fought our enemies. It's been a while since I last engaged in hand-to-hand combat or knife fights with a paranormal. Likely their reasoning for attacking inside Tuck's house. Not to mention they wanted Lucia back.

As many times as I've seen it, Tuck's partial shift is unnerving. It's never always the same, except the talons replacing his fingers. He shifts whatever parts of him will serve the best purpose for the moment. Not being in his full phoenix form likely nearly drove him to the brink of madness.

They attacked him in his home.

His safe haven, which held the three most important women at once. It's understandable he lost himself so quickly, wanting to protect his girlfriend, sister and pair. Their lives threatened for a prisoner he'd been holding captive downstairs.

I'll need to find some time to speak with him alone. I am familiar with how such guilt can slowly eat away at you, turning you into a mere shell of your former self, fixated only on seeking fiery revenge.

The instant Nerissa's voice pierced the silence, the pit in my stomach dropped. When that witch is involved, whatever happens will become your worst nightmare. She's only dispatched when our opposition needs to make a pointed move against us. Nerissa has no true allegiances to anyone. As long as her "employer" is against the James family, she'll do what needs to be done.

Despite slaughtering the werewolves and vampire, she escaped with Lucia. No doubt they had another witch or warlock warding the place from the outside. An invisible barrier against any who may have heard or seen our commotion.

Honestly, good riddance. Keeping Lucia tied up and tortured in Tuck's basement was just asking for a war we don't need on top of the one we're already wrapped up in.

Ari tenses next to me, our thighs pressed together, bringing me back to the present. "Oh, I don't know, Cooper? I'm new to this world. He always behaved normally. Sure, once I learned a werewolf's scent, I could tell he was one, but there was never anything remotely suspicious about him."

Cooper barks a laugh, launching from his seat, the legs skidding across the floorboards as he leans into Ari's space. "And you're supposed to lead us," he sneers.

"Enough!" My hand shoots out, wrapping around his throat. "Speak to her like that again, and we'll have another dead paranormal today."

Cooper swats my hand from him. My arm falling easily due to my loosened grip. My hold had only been tight enough to make my point clear. I'm not fucking around and he will not attack Ari when she did nothing but defend us.

"Adrian, sit down. I can fight my own battles."

Ari squares her shoulders at Cooper. "Apologies for not picking up on any signs, but our interactions were limited to occasional cases at work —"

"And the bar," I snort. My anger getting the best of me, allowing the words to spill free.

I can feel her eyes boring into my skull as I slouch in my chair. Words I shouldn't have let escape. A tone that makes me seem like I'm on Cooper's side and not my pair's. I will always pick her side, right or wrong. "Not now, Adrian. We can deal with your jealousy later."

The twins snicker, large hands covering their wide mouths.

"Instead of coming at me, maybe sit the fuck down, and let's figure out where to go from here? Or is that beneath you?" Cooper's eyes drift from Ari's face to her mother's, then mine, and back to my pair's.

Ari stands tall, eyes piercing into Cooper's until he lowers himself back into the seat Oliver put back in place for him. He knows this is a battle he can't win. At the end of the day, Ari will succeed Syriah and Lanham. It's how our world works. It would do us all well to give her the respect she deserves.

The bickering ceases immediately, Ari locking eyes with each of us one by one. A small nod coming from Syriah, a hint of a smile quirking at the corner of her mouth. Her pride over her daughter, commanding the situation, shines through for anyone who is paying enough attention to notice it.

"Lucia is not important. She gave us what we needed information-wise," Ari relays as she lowers herself back into her own chair. "We know that someone among us is not on our side. There's nothing I loathe more than a rat." She pauses. A pregnant silence that hangs heavy in the room. Scanning each face, I wonder if the traitor is staring back at us. "If it's you, now is your chance to come forward. You'll be allowed to live if you do."

No one moves. Only momentary glances at their neighbors reveal their skepticism. Not one look shared to give away the truth.

With a nod, she speaks again. "Very well. I will interview everyone who has access to the safe houses. That includes the inner circle, our armed force, and each leader."

Cooper shifts in his chair, his growl heard by the entire room.

"There's no one I trust more than Adrian right now, so he will either sit as my second in each interview or appoint whom he thinks would be best. Bronson," she turns to face the warlock. "Can you craft a truth serum?"

He nods.

A hoarse, deep voice carries from the doorway. There stands a man I never expected to see again, blocking the light. "I would like to join these interviews. I've clearly missed a lot while unconscious."

The room fills with gasps, Ari's hands flying to her mouth. "Dad," she whispers. The term of endearment given so much freer to him than it had been to Syriah.

"Everyone out," Syriah commands. "Adrian, Ari, you both stay."

I sink back into my seat, not ready for whatever this family reunion is about to become. I realize I'm only here because I can't be apart from Ari, but then why send Tuck away?

With the door closed, we remain silent while Syriah directs Lanham to the nearest chair, distancing him from where Ari and I are seated. Our fingers intertwine beneath the table as her body visibly shakes. Those big blue eyes, wide saucers, locked on her father's face.

At least ten minutes of this staring contest has ensued when Lanham finally clears his throat.

"I don't care that you're paired to my daughter, but so help me, Adrian, you better get your hands off of her."

His eyes narrow, his emotions burrowing into my skull. My body heating uncomfortably as I shake Ari's hand free, only for her to snatch my hand back, trapping it between the both of hers. The temperature of my insides only grows hotter.

"Lanham, please," I choke, Ari likely noticing the temperature change and releasing me once more. My body immediately cooling the moment she breaks contact.

It's been decades since Lanham tried to fry my insides.

"Better," he croons. "Now tell me what the hell has been going on here."

Twenty-Eight

Ari

I'm so shocked to see my father awake and speaking in this room with us I can't even focus on how hot Adrian's palm just became or that he forcefully released my hand at my father's order.

I'm on my feet before I can stop myself, slowly stalking for the man. Unsure if I am dreaming or hallucinating or what. The nights I've spent at his side while he remained suspended in time funnel to the forefront of my mind. I never expected to meet the man. To know him or hold him and have him hold me back. I never thought I would hear his voice.

"Dad," I whisper.

He smiles at me. A sad, closed-lipped tug at the corner of his mouth as I throw my arms around his neck. The bite of pain ignored for now. His chin digs into the top of my head, pulling me close.

As I take the seat beside him, only one question pops into my head. "Why are you awake?"

He chuckles. "That potion proved stronger than intended, but I heard every word. Even though I couldn't talk back, I loved getting to know you, my precious girl."

Tears sting the back of my eyes. The Luxembohrgs had been great parents. Always kind and loving, even now when I barely call them anymore. But hearing my birth father speak such heartfelt words breaks something inside me. A wall I constructed long ago when I didn't think I'd ever have a relationship with my real parents.

"There's a lot to cover, honey." Syriah slides a hand across his upper back and over his shoulder. "You should rest and eat something."

"I've been resting. I would like to talk to my daughter." My mother nods, turning his face toward hers before planting an indecent kiss on his lips. I know they've only been my parents for five minutes, but this is wildly uncomfortable to watch.

She whispers soft words into his ear before leaving the room.

"Now, let's talk." Lanham's voice booms through the room. The tenderness it just held, addressing me, draining away. "My daughter?" His eyes narrow on Adrian.

"Sir, you know pairing is not a choice."

He holds up a hand, halting Adrian from continuing. "I am well aware. Yet, I have a few qualms with how you've treated my daughter."

Emotions race through Adrian. Each one filling my chest as if they were my own. Time and distractions nearly erased the memories of how much I'd told my dad about Adrian and me butting heads from the beginning. I'm sure I recounted nearly every moment of wanting to ring his neck or knock him down several pegs. I'd never spoken about the positives until after we'd bonded.

"Dad." I place a hand on his forearm. "Wait, can I call you dad?"

He chuckles again, nodding. "Of course. That's who I am."

Right, of course, he is. I started calling him dad when I finally felt comfortable freely calling Syriah mom.

"Adrian has been so good to me since I was shot. Before that, technically, but…" I'm unsure how to describe the shift between us from when we initially visited his grandparent's house. "He's taken good care of me. Sure, he's still an overbearing asshole all the time, but he means well. Our family is important to him."

I hadn't expected to sing such high praises of Adrian, but it's the truth of how I see him now. My feelings for him bubbling to the surface.

"I love him, and I know he feels the same. You can give us the dad's speech later, but we have a lot bigger problems to worry about right now."

Lanham's eyes track between me and Adrian's approaching form. My pair stops right behind me, with both hands cupping my shoulders. His chest brushing the back of my head as be bends to brush his lips over my cheek. A flush creeps over my skin, arousal blooming between my thighs. This is so embarrassing to happen in front of my father.

Adrian simply pulls up a chair next to me, and we dive in. Recapping everything from the moment I started trailing Adrian to the events of this afternoon is exhausting. Lanham rarely interrupts, listening closely. The questions he asks point at specific details neither of us can believe we'd never considered.

Only when Adrian chimes in with the current updates on his family does my father choose to speak freely.

"It's been a long time since we've had two formidable enemies coming at us from both sides. Adrian, my boy —" Adrian's eyes softly press closed at the term of endearment, my fingers slipping through his in a show of support. He squeezes my hand gently, his lashes fluttering against the apples of his cheeks, before focusing back on my father. "— I hate to ask this, but I need to. Do you hold any allegiance to the Alexander family?"

"No." The barked answer is instant. A growl following it. The reaction to the question felt in my heart. Every bit of that truth nestled in my gut.

"He speaks the truth," I relay to my father. His nod of confirmation allowing my shoulders to uncoil.

"Well, then, we have a lot to prepare for. Ari, it'll be a few days before we can start practicing together, but I expect you and Adrian to help Oliver with making sure everyone is top-notch. You'll start interviews the day after tomorrow."

Adrian's jaw grinds, the sound unnaturally loud with him so close to me. "Is there a problem, Adrian?"

"Yes, sir. There is."

My father waits patiently for Adrian to reveal his jealousy. I can't blame him. He'd known what we were and found me making out with Oliver — happily. We've never talked about it, but Oliver and I formed a friendship I very much miss. Yet, I know it would be an unnecessary drama created to push it.

"Oliver touched my pair. I realize I should not hold on to that grudge as your daughter was unaware at the time and has clearly chosen me, but it's impossible to ignore the reaction he still has to her."

My father grunts. His hand coming up to swipe over his mouth before a small smile curves his lips.

"There was another phoenix that was holding your mother's attention when we met." Mother said as if he's referring to both Adrian and I. "I was desperate for her to return my affections. We'd already known we were mates, but it's rare for cross-species mating. Her grandfather was not happy about it." He chuckles, running the memory over in his mind. "He showed up when I came to pick her up for a date one night, so I set myself on fire, thinking it would impress her. Just left me butt-ass naked for everyone to see, but we were inseparable after that."

Adrian furrows his brow. My smile spreading remembering Mom telling me the story.

"My point is to ignore Oliver. She's yours. She's chosen you. Focus on making my daughter happy, so I don't have to tear out your organs and burn you alive."

With that, he stands, a small wobble to his legs as the door swings open, Syriah appearing. "Let's eat, sweetheart."

He throws an arm around her shoulder, following her from the room, hers wrapped across the middle of his back. A picture-perfect couple. An enviable love I hope Adrian and I find someday.

The pure joy that emanates from them is infectious. My bird all but purring inside as similar emotions course through my pair beside me.

"So, I love you, huh?"

Adrian curls behind me, his front pressed to my back, chin resting on the crown of my head.

"You're the one who said it," I snort.

"Yeah, I did because I do."

"Good. You can show me how much later." I turn in his arms, palms flat on his chest. "But maybe we need to go home for that. I don't think my dad wants to hear me screaming your name right now."

A burly laugh bursts out of him, his head thrown back with abandon. It's uncommon to see him so relaxed. That boyish side rarely takes center stage. Possibly because he never got to be one with his family. Had this been the man I knew from day one, I wouldn't have fought him so hard. I would have likely fallen into his charm and his laugh, despite my determination to just fuck random men instead of dating them.

"Let's skip dinner and go home then."

A mischievous glint shines in his eyes before he grabs my hand and we bolt from the house.

Food can wait.

Twenty-Nine

Ari

"How long is this agent going to be up our asses?" Garrett groans as Adrian settles into the seat at my desk.

Eyeing Adrian, I can only hope he doesn't respond. He's made it abundantly clear he would prefer to tear out Garrett's throat for eye fucking me every damn day.

As my eyes rake over his colossal frame, it's obvious how much he doesn't fit in here. His perfectly cut suit is much nicer than anything an FBI agent could afford. Unfortunately, it was also the only one he could find at one of the safe houses while his house was being rebuilt. We ordered more, but apparently, getting custom-tailored suits shipped takes forever. Adrian's reasoning for not buying them at a store lost on me.

Adrian's house was finally cleared for demolition last week; the rubble cleared only days ago to yield the new foundation we drove past to observe on the way here.

He'd held me to his chest as we stared at the carved-out cement this morning. *"I'd hoped we would live here,"* he'd said.

I'd wondered when that thought first crossed his mind. Too nervous to ask aloud, somehow fearful of what the answer might be, I kept quiet. After someone ransacked the place, he clearly wasn't thinking about a future with me. My need for him then wasn't enough for him to seal the bond. It wasn't enough to just want to be with him.

That same night, he took me to his grandparent's home for the first time. The night something shifted for us. For the better, I'd say.

"As long as it takes to solve that stack of murders," I shrug.

Garrett groans again, his palm clapping against my thigh as I sit on the edge of his desk. I tense under his palm. Garrett has never been secretive about his desire to take me out, yet he has always been respectful. Never once crossing the line of professionalism.

"Still on for drinks tonight?" he asks quietly, as if trying to keep it between us. I'm unsure why he's whispering. It's all the detectives going out together tonight. Of Course, Adrian will be there because we can't separate but we've already talked about him staying on the other end of the bar. He didn't like it, but it is what it is.

"Everyone better be at the bar tonight. The first two rounds are on me," I announce, slipping from beneath Garrett's palm.

All the guys cheer at my announcement. Garrett suddenly very interested in whatever is on his computer screen.

As I slip back over to my desk, Gomez and Adrian huddle together, whispering amongst themselves. The low scrunch of their brows alerting me to the gist of the situation — not good.

"What do you guys have?"

"Luxembohrg!" Captain bellows from the doorway of his office. "Gomez!"

We both jump at the roar of our names, bolting for the captain's office. My glance back at my pair meant to convey my need for him to stay put. If left alone behind a closed door without him, the sight of another man touching me might trigger him. His bird ready to take over and eliminate the man who dared.

"How can we help you, Captain?"

He glares at me, sliding into the creaking chair behind his desk. "You can help me by finding this murderer." He sighs loudly, rubbing a palm across his face. Dark smudges live beneath his eyes, the bags so large I'm convinced only draining them will make them disappear. I've never seen Cap look so haggard. So drained of everything within him. "You've heard about Officer Nighlen's death by now, I'm sure." *Yup. I was there, and my brother was the one who slaughtered him.* "But we have two other murders. Similar to the ones you have been investigating. Don't tell the team. Look into them and take that worthless agent with you."

I'm not one to growl, but it escapes me anyhow. Low in my chest the way Adrian often does. My fingers curling into fists at my sides. Flames licking just beneath the surface of my skin, eager to set the place ablaze. My bird fighting to break free.

I take a deep breath, fighting to calm my over-the-top emotions. That same possessiveness that lives with Adrian is also within me.

If I explode on my boss, it will expose us all. That's a mess I don't want to clean up. We all have enough on our plates as is.

"Yes, Captain," Gomez blurts out, snatching the folders from his waiting grip and shoving me out the door.

Anger still rolls through me. How dare someone speak about Adrian with such disdain. I tell myself it's just the bond making me react this way. Driving me to the edge of losing all control, but a part of me knows it's not. Deep down, it's how attached I've become to Adrian. How I've grown to depend on him and trust in him and what he's capable of.

Ultimately, how in love with him I am, bond or not.

"Alexander, let's go."

He's slow to rise from his seat. Buttoning his suit jacket, he saunters forward with the arrogance of a man who knows he can't be touched. It's part of the act. Part of the persona he operates under here. Although, deep down, I know it's partially him too. The man he became after enduring years of pain.

We pile into Gomez's car. Adrian slipping into the passenger seat after letting me into the back.

Adrian takes one of the file folders from my hands. The slide of paper across his palms has become a triggering noise. We've had to open too many of these lately. Create too many.

"Fuck!" he barks.

"Your crest." The words drifting into the open space of the car. I know without looking.

Gomez takes us toward Montrose Beach. Cop cars swarm the area, doing their best to keep the public from traipsing through the crime scene.

We flash our credentials, lips pressed into straight lines as we stomp through the sand. The two bodies are supine, just like all the others, the waves lapping at their thighs. The lack of breeze is a small favor if we're going to gather any usable evidence. This task is more about appearance than actually useful for the three of us.

Just like the others, the man's intestines lie slung to the side of his body. A portion of the length pinned beneath him confirming the brands are made after death. His torso bare of a shirt. Shifting him forward, that same crest sits between his shoulder blades. Adrian's rage boiling inside him.

"Adrian," a warning for him to keep it together. We can't lose ourselves out here in the open. Too much hangs in the balance.

The fury only burns deeper. His heat searing my insides the way my flames never have. Rivulets of sweat rolling down my back, causing my blouse to stick to my skin.

Adrian, I need you to calm down.

He suddenly whirls on me, grabbing me by the arm to face him. His venomous stare makes me flinch away from him. Something I would have never done before we bonded. Before Salvatore attempted to murder me. A reminder the fear planted in me by that bastard that night can resurface whenever it pleases.

"How did you do that?"

What is he talking about? "Talk to you?" I snatch my arm away. "I opened my mouth and spoke."

"No, you didn't. Your father..."

I have no idea what he's talking about. My patience has worn out. Adrian's bullshit will have to wait.

Snapping blue gloves into place, I crouch next to the bodies. Trying not to disturb the scene, I search for any additional evidence, as I usually do. CSI creeps around, still collecting their own from the swirling sand, their soft chatter ignored.

Just as I suspected, they're paranormal. They don't carry the scent of wolves when wet, nor could they likely be vampires. There's too much sun and most aren't day walkers — my unofficial term for vamps that can walk in sunlight.

"What are they?" I whisper as Gomez crouches low next to me. "Sirens. Specifically Dania and Sebastian Tover, regional leaders for the west coast. They shouldn't be here."

Standing tall, I snap my gloves off before marching back toward the car. My phone in my hands ringing seconds later as I wait for an answer on the other end.

My father's voice rasps into the phone. His breaths more like pants than an even pace.

"We're heading to the safe house. Gather up the inner circle."

"Consider it done."

Thirty

ARI

I don't wait for Gomez and Adrian to get back to the car, sliding into the driver's seat.

I'm tired of the death. So over this war I don't understand.

It makes no sense that Adrian's family is suddenly around, killing off those who also fall on Salvatore's list. According to Adrian, Salvatore and the Alexanders are sworn enemies. They've never gotten along. The Alexanders decimated Salvatore's clan centuries ago. The grudge never ended, apparently. When you live as long as we do, it must be that much easier to hang on to.

Sure, the Alexanders may try to beat Salvatore to the punch, but that sounds too simple. Too easy for a motive. Knowing what I know of kingpin murderers, their plots are not as simple as power. Money and power are strong motivators until they're not enough.

"Tell me what's going through your head," Adrian presses from the passenger seat. His palm rests on my thigh, only a single stroke of his thumb before I slap it away. Now is not the time to be sidetracked by my greedy cunt.

"I'm trying to make sense of this. We have two power-hungry men murdering the same list. Why?"

He places his palm on my thigh again, rubbing slow circles with his thumb. "Adrian, if you don't take your hand off me, I will cut the fucker off."

He leans closer, squeezing. "I still have a second one I can use to play with you."

Gomez lets out a groan from the back, his head hitting the window glass, resulting in a twitch at the corner of my mouth. As much as I try to limit how much everyone around us has to endure when it comes to Adrian and me, he simply doesn't give a fuck about their comfort.

"I have a theory," Adrian says, his thumb going still.

"Are you going to share it?" Gomez questions.

"No." The word delivered so low I wonder if Adrian meant to say it out loud.

It's okay. We'll figure it out.

"How are you doing that?" Adrian questions.

"What?"

That's twice now. I'm utterly confused about what he is talking about. Maybe he's the one losing his mind instead of me.

"That's the second time you've spoken to me in our heads."

An unhinged laugh leaves me. This man has completely lost it. "You're insane."

"No, I'm not. Your grandfather has the ability to infiltrate minds. Lanham's father."

The revelation hits me like a freight train. *Like telepathy*. He's saying I can telepathically communicate.

"I've never done it before."

"Actually, you have," Gomez chimes in from the back. "How do you think I always answer your questions?"

Fuck. How long has this been going on without me knowing? How many others have heard me in their heads? Can humans too? Or just our kind?

Questions swirl through my mind. My attempt at trying to make sense of everything going on failing. It's honestly too much. Too many things I don't know. Too many secrets still kept close.

Danger still lurks under my parent's roof. There's still someone against us, lurking within our ranks — assuming Lucia told the truth.

My gut tells me she can. She had nothing to lose, tied there to that chair, brutalized by my brother.

I still haven't talked to him about that. Adrian told me why he acted the way he did. He wished to keep that part of himself a secret from me as we became more familiar. I can understand it. If I could hide the ruthless hitwoman, I was — I am — from them, I would too.

That Ari had no fear. No remorse for what she did. Who she hurt in the process meant nothing. That Ari just wanted to feel alive. To prove that she was the baddest bitch on this godforsaken planet. I thought I knew until everything became clearer.

Realizing I was nothing more than a pawn for Salvatore to use to rid the paranormals supporting my parents changed me.

I picked my side. I chose them. Despite uncertainty about our morality, I'd pick them every damn day. Good or bad, there's no changing my mind.

I would choose him, too.

Adrian's fingers weave through mine as if he heard me. A small squeeze sends tingling pinpricks straight to my lower belly.

For the rest of the trip, we travel in silence. There's nothing to say.

We're in a shit ton of deep water with no foreseeable way out. When Gomez said who that couple was, I knew we needed my parents. We needed Bronson, Cooper, and Oliver. Tuck, Talia, and Isis, too. That little love triangle serving as its own headache.

Something else we need to talk about — just Tuck and me. I'd seen the turmoil in his eyes when it came time to protect both women. That moment's hesitation when he had to choose between the two. A raging battle that none of us can say he won or lost. The slight angling of his body to protect Isis was the dead giveaway of the strength of the pairing bond thickening between them.

I can't say if Talia saw it, too, but she knew. They both did when they started dating. They aren't a pair — there was one for both of them out there somewhere. A day would come when they would have to choose each other or walk away. Deep down,

I think Tuck always thought he would choose Talia. There was no doubt until it turned out to be false.

It's funny how often life will kick you in the teeth just to prove you know nothing.

Talia, I believe, has the strength to walk away. The ability to detach herself, knowing this was the inevitable end to come. She might be a step above pixie-sized, but she is as strong as they come. A woman valuing principle over desire.

I don't envy her. But I don't pity her either. Just the same, my softening heart wants me to wrap my arms around her and promise it'll all work out the way it should.

We pull into the drive, the monstrosity of the safe house looming over us.

Cars line the street along the front of the house. More tucked into the large paved area at the top of the drive. Eyeing the ones closest to the house, I recognize so many of them. Each vehicle tagged to its owner.

I'm guessing Dad already started lining people up for questioning. Adrian decided he would be present for the interviews, along with Lanham and Emerson — a neutral party, as he is too young to really understand the politics at play here.

We will record every session and keep it on an encrypted network accessible only to me and my parents. I'd insisted on Adrian having access as well, but for once he bowed out. *"My bloodline isn't one to be trusted. It's better to limit my reach this time,"* he said.

The house is full of bodies when we enter. The regional leaders for each species are nestled in the living room chairs and the surrounding couches. Each one staring between Adrian and me with indifference or sneers.

No one was thrilled about my call for interviews. The distrust they had of me when I first arrived now thrown back in their faces. My mother believes they'll eventually understand. They'll see everything we've done is done with purpose in their best interest. Maybe in time they will respect me again.

I would think they would be pleased for us to be the next in line to lead the paranormals. Two phoenixes the way it should be. Two of the most powerful and pure bloodlines united. Tradition once again locked into place. Their stares convincing me that our pasts are keeping them from that place of acceptance.

My indiscretions are public, as is Adrian's bloodline. I can only imagine information has leaked about his family's crest being branded into the backs of so many victims as of late. Each recent death serving as another reminder we are losing control.

My father comes stalking around the corner, pulling me into a tight hug, ignoring how Adrian keeps hold around my waist. The stroke of his palm down the back of my head as comforting as it is unfamiliar. I haven't had the opportunity to get to know Lanham as well as I did with my mother. Time, I hope we will still have. And as much as I want to let him in, it's been harder.

"You three, in the office."

Gomez, Adrian, and I funnel into the office. My mother, Tucker, and Isis already waiting.

"What the hell is going on?" My father barks the moment the door shuts.

"Lanham, sit down and hush," my mother chides. With an exaggerated groan, he does as she says. "Tell us what you saw."

We have explained the location of the bodies. Torsos mutilated. Throats slit and the crest between the shoulder blades. Duplicates of the other scenes we've reported back on. Leaders who are well-liked and poised to advance within the council ranks over the next few decades.

"The only reason my captain likely isn't jumping to gang or cult violence is because Dr. Maurin has been leaving certain details out of the ME report."

My parents nod, Isis, stepping forward. "I have not been completely truthful with you all."

Shit, what now?

Thirty-One

ADRIAN

My instinct has me blocking Ari's body with my own. A need to protect her is an overwhelming pull that I can never resist.

Nothing about Isis has led me to believe she is a danger to us, yet she stands tall, admitting she has a secret. That she has not been entirely truthful since her arrival.

I don't trust easily. My parents taught me that sort of vulnerability would be the death of me. If I gave that trust to the wrong individual, I couldn't keep our familial line alive, protected, and thriving.

Those hard lessons have stuck with me. It's why I never expect others to faithfully show their true selves. Why would they? It's easier to deceive when individuals think they are getting one thing instead of something else.

Shoving me aside, Ari angles around me. Her back centimeters from my front, a gun tugged from her back waistband and pointed at Isis. There's a slight tremble to her arm. Not from fear or anger, but from the remaining shreds of strength that have yet to come back.

"You have thirty seconds to explain before I unload this entire clip into you. Hint the bullets contain dermanium."

Thanks to the twins — our little chemists we didn't know we had — we have an entire arsenal of weapons in the works replicated and enhanced off of Ari's prior gun from Salvatore. Everything from guns to knives to explosives to throwing stars. It's insane.

Ari was the first to get her gun. Since that day, it has remained holstered at her hip. Even at work, she carries her service weapon and her savior.

"Arianya —" Isis breathes.

"What did you call me?" Ari's face contorts into one of disgust. Brows so low and scowl so pronounced my woman is scaring me a little. Maybe she's got a bit of Tuck in her, too. That wild spirit that lets loose when enraged.

"Your name." Isis glances toward Syriah and Lanham, both wearing expressions of a lost past coming to light.

Ari moves closer. The muzzle of her gun presses into Isis's chest. "My. Name. Is. Ari."

"It is not." A simple answer.

The gun presses harder, exposed skin dipping under the pressure. Tuck suddenly lunges forward, shoving Ari aside. Her body so unbalanced she's tumbling toward the floor, my hand grabbing hold of her bad arm just in time to keep her from flying into the coffee table.

Ari's howl reverberates through the room. My heart shattered knowing I caused her this pain.

Every fiber of my being wants to erase it. The gunshot, the pain, the healing. The past. Clean the slate so none of this is our reality.

"Point that gun at her again, and I will tear you apart," Tuck pants.

The room goes silent, every eye bouncing between Tuck and Isis. Even if he hadn't accepted her as his pair, he would have reacted the same. The more time they spend in each other's presence, the stronger that possessive streak will grow. I would know. I've lived it for months.

This is a fucking shit show.

We're in a room full of mates. Our actions driven by our need to protect. Every move controlled by that bond.

A growl works its way through my chest and up my throat as Tuck snarls at his sister. Yet, Ari doesn't back down. She only raises her gun arm again, pointing it at Tuck's chest, directly blocking his pairs.

"I love you, Tucker, but I will shoot. I've had too many people lie and endanger us."

Long, dagger-sharp teeth extend out of Tuck's mouth. His fingers beginning to shift when Isis puts a hand on his arm. As if by magic, he settles. His human form restored, face evening out to the Tuck we normally see. A gift of the golden phoenix bloodline.

"Please, let me just tell you what I know," Isis all but whispers.

Her gentle voice commands our attention. That crisp accent adding a captivating lilt to her words. Still, I keep my body between Ari and Tuck. Most of us are not familiar with her bloodline gift of emotion control, and I'm not taking chances.

Should Tuck snap at Ari again, I might kill him. That's how strong our pair compulsions are. We lose reason if we can't control it. With us being in the initial year, it's unlikely I'd be able to if so much as another negative word spews out of Tuck's mouth.

Syriah leans against the massive metal desk, a gift given to Lanham right after they bought this place. Its surface is not flammable should he burst into flames the way he often did with his anger when he was younger. As I stare at it now, I realize Tuck has never shown signs of fire magic at all, while Ari is proficient in it.

"They sent me here to help investigate all the paranormal deaths, but I also requested this assignment." Isis slowly moves closer to Tuck's side, but her hand doesn't leave his arm, a slight flex of her fingers against his bare skin before he releases a deep breath. *Interesting*. "We have encountered sightings of the Alexander crest for some time."

"What does some time mean?" My voice low as I lean forward just a hair.

Her sigh is heavy, her narrow shoulders rolling forward as if weighed down with shame. "Forty-three years."

My focus tracks back to her hand on Tuck's forearm. Her fingers never leave his skin, only sliding closer to his wrist as she takes a step forward. The grip light but enough to keep him in his current state.

Anger boils beneath the surface. My insides frying at the mention of that fucking crest. My family's legacy of death tormenting me.

As if Ari possesses the same gifts as Isis, she weaves her fingers through mine. The anger doesn't fade, but with her touch, I feel as though I can control it. Keep my beastly phoenix contained when all it wants to do is rid the world of the Alexander bloodline.

Ari squeezes my hand softly. Reassurance she is here for whatever I choose to do. If I want to lose my shit and strangle the woman, she'd let me, then take me in the next room and fuck me stupid.

I'd let her. She's it for me.

"Go on," Syriah encourages. Her hand circling through the air before recrossing her arms.

"Here they are attacking known supporters of Salvatore and those from prominent families. The ones likely to be next in line for leadership positions."

"We already knew that," I growl.

"If you'd stop talking for a minute, she can finish," Tuck barks. The voice that of his alter ego. A discrepancy against the calm of his face. Isis grips him tighter. "Please continue."

In the blink of an eye, the Tuck we know returns. His tone even and welcoming.

Talia shifts on the couch. Her mouth pressed into a thin line, eyes glued to where Isis continues to touch Tuck. The fibers of their binding thread thickening before our very eyes.

When Tuck's eyes finally find her alone in the corner, his body deflates. The bond may be strong enough to pull you to your pair, but it doesn't erase old feelings. It simply pushes them to a tiny dark corner, a place easy to forget.

I feel for him.

I vividly remember every long hour spent with Ari. The agony of it. Struggling internally to be near her while also trying to keep distance. That constant tug of war, worse than being torn apart by rebirth. Now, another woman has her hands on him, and the one he loves gazes at him with eyes filled with crippling sadness.

A triangle far more challenging than what Ari and I faced.

I haven't asked either about it, but we've all noticed the increasing space between him and Talia. The way she no longer calms him when he's in danger of revealing the other half of himself, especially when Isis is present. Or the aversion of their eyes becoming more frequent. The PDA they used to bombard us with, non-existent.

What I've noticed most, though, is the glint in Isis's eyes when he loses himself. I saw her face when they attacked his house that day. The way she enjoyed his maniacal laugh and the way she encouraged the torture of Lucia. She seemed keen to take part.

Isis has also avoided unnecessary interactions with Tuck. If they don't need to be in the same room, one makes a quick exit. That's the last of them we'll see for the night. It's so fucking awkward.

"As I was saying, this has been an issue much longer overseas. Officials deemed the victims deceased, gathered them as they would for afterlife rituals, and then they were just gone. Each one has disappeared without a trace."

"Disappeared?" Lanham chokes.

"Yes. We didn't focus on it much. Many families prefer to reclaim their loved ones following the actions of the Gorman Board."

Ari clears her throat. "What is a Gorman Board?"

"They investigate suspicious deaths and murders of paranormals in the UK. Something along the lines of a human FBI," I supply, glancing back at Isis. Her nod confirming I'd done an adequate job explaining.

They're an ancient entity but have held strong through the centuries.

Isis only nods before continuing, "Then a board member saw one of the dead. He was walking down a dark London alley as if he hadn't bled out in the middle of an abandoned flat several months prior."

"That's not possible." Lanham attempts to stand from his chair. Syriah's fingertips to his chest forcing him back down.

"That's what we thought, too. We consulted every ancient warlock, witch, and vampire we could find. Reanimation is uncommon amongst us. Quite rare, actually."

The room goes silent.

"So I am here for *your* help, Lanham. For help from all of you."

"You're telling me the Alexander family is murdering paranormals and then reanimating them or bringing them back to life? For what purpose?"

Syriah's skepticism isn't hard to mimic. Only vampires and phoenixes have what could be called immortality, except under certain circumstances. All other paranormal species can die as easily as a human. Only werewolves and wolf-shifters heal rapidly enough for treatment and survival. At times Vampires too, dependent on blood loss.

"Will you all help me?"

Tuck is the only one who steps toward her, his large palm draping over hers.

I can't do this.

Thirty-Two

ADRIAN

I'm speechless and angry and confused.

My parents are the embodiment of the most deranged paranormals alive. I've known that my whole life. If only that level of depravity ended with them.

But, no.

They went and groomed my brothers to be just like them. How I saved myself from becoming such an awful being still eludes me some days. Maybe I was born different. Maybe my heart holds a different composition. I don't know. It doesn't matter.

If what Isis says is true, we are in a much worse situation than we ever thought.

There's a reason for the law forbidding reanimation. The foundation we lean on justifying imprisoning warlocks and witches with the gift. Throughout the centuries, those with the most proficient talents have succumbed to death. Our only option was to uphold balance and guard against the temptation of using those powers.

The dead are meant to stay dead. Phoenixes are that exception. We're created to use our gift of rebirth. For us, what we do is natural. Reanimation is not.

The nature behind that sort of magic has darker roots. The talent needed to do it requires reaching between worlds. A soul wandering between the living and the deceased, seeking its former earthly inhabitant.

A user of that sort of dark power must be able to allow their spirit form to depart from their bodies. We, as paranormals, must not separate our souls from our human shells. They are the essence of our beings and the heart of our supernatural creatures. To separate from yours leaves a door open for another to enter your human form and inhabit it. Further, projecting spirits requires intense concentration to locate the target soul. To snatch the wrong one could mean devastation.

Decades may pass refining skills for this reanimation step alone. As far as I know, Russian dungeons hold those who mastered such skills. Every power muted by the dermanium-laced walls surrounding them.

The problem is what the reanimated paranormal becomes. A warped version of themselves that's near impossible to control without mind infiltration. If these bodies require healing, only a phoenix in my bloodline can repair them. The vivid image of the mutilated bodies we'd found in Ohio filters back into my mind. It would take a cup of tears to heal those wounds after death — a massive amount compared to the norm.

A supply my family would have no problem keeping up with.

"Fuck!" The roar of my voice shakes the walls of the office.

I hadn't meant to allow my outburst to audibly release, but I couldn't restrain myself for another second — clearly.

Everything the Alexander bloodline touches is evil.

My temples throb, attempting to further piece together what this all might mean. The walls of the room closing in on me, knowing it's my blood responsible for this destruction and then possible abominations.

I refuse to consider the legal ramifications. Yet another disaster that would have to be parsed through with a fine-toothed comb. My mind is in overdrive, and I'm spiraling into a panic. My tank is one more fucking revelation from overflowing.

I just can't take one more fucking thing.

Ari's arm snakes across my back, her finger squeezing my side. I'd been so lost in my head I hadn't noticed her release my hand. But this is better. Her body pressing into my torso grounds me before my insides spark at the warmth of her so close to me.

"Excuse us," I mumble, darting for the door, not even waiting for responses.

Rushing past the lurking bodies, pretending they haven't been trying to listen at the door, Ari only cackles behind me. They wouldn't have heard a thing. Lanham spelled the room. As is protocol for any classified meeting.

We've barely made our way through the crowd when I abruptly spin to face her. "I need you. Now," I grumble against the shell of her ear. The shudder that goes through her body only drawing a moan out of me.

Leading us down to the basement instead of up to one of our rooms, the sublevels seem abandoned.

She treks through the open area, then down a hidden hallway leading to one of the interrogation rooms at the rear of the house. An area only a handful of us have unlimited access to.

A long table sits in the middle. A single chair on either side of the extended edge. She hops up, her ass colliding with the surface. Any other time, I would want her slow movements. The tease of her placing her fingertips inside her knees, spreading her legs wide for me. But not today. Not right now when I need to lose myself in my pair. When I need her to erase my line of thought before I snap.

A single talon replaces my index finger, the tip dipping into the top of her blouse.

"Use me, Adrian. Whatever you need."

A sharp tear fills the room as my claw drags through her clothing, leaving her clad in nothing but a seamless thong and t-shirt bra. She's beautiful. Always has been.

The soft brown of her skin already showcases a rosy flush in anticipation of the havoc I'm going to wreck on her body. The pump in her chest pushing her cleavage high against the edge of her bra.

A hissed breath escapes her as my teeth clamp around the space between her shoulder and neck. Her hands blindly undoing my belt, button, and zipper, shoving my pants and briefs down my thighs. Warm hands wrap around my hardened length. Stroking my dick and teasing my swollen head, she spreads the pre-cum with her thumb.

My cock throbs in her fist. Her touch so soft I know she's waiting for me to take what I need. This is for me, not for her.

That same finger tears through her panties. The fabric nothing more than ribbons as it falls to the floor. "Lie back."

She does, her grip tightening around me. My body moves willingly, her shoulder shifting to notch me at her entrance. Those delicious muscles of her pussy already trying to clamp around me.

I roughly tear her hand away, my focus shifting to where we're about to be joined. I could stare at her for ages, but now is not the time. Now, I need to bury myself so deep inside her we become one. My only concern is to make her cry out my name in pleasure and beg for more. Even if we don't have long.

Sinking in the first inch, her walls flutter, then clench around me. That wicked grin spreading on her face, welcoming me inside.

My gaze drifts down to her flat belly as I pull back and sink in a little further, determined to take the first few strokes slowly. I'm not myself right now, and I would hate myself if I hurt her. Especially as my palm runs over her stomach, wishing there was already our offspring growing inside it.

The idea of impregnating her has been increasingly occupying my thoughts every second of every day. The image of her swollen with our baby only making me thrust faster. Harder. My body wanting to race to the finish line and fill her with my seed. Something inside me convinced if she's not pregnant already she will be today. Our baby will be the change our world needs.

I can only assume it's my bloodline resurfacing, driving my urge to have a family of my own. Pure and filled with love and maybe even laughter. Not death and abuse.

"Adrian. Let's go!" she scolds.

Her tone snaps back to the present, my talon retracting as I prop her still-booted foot on my shoulder. "You may want to hold on."

Before she can respond, I slam into her. The entirety of my length finding its home. Her back bows off the table, her moans vibrating through my body, straight down to my dick.

Her arms swing overhead, fingers curling around the opposite edge. The only thing for her to hold on to besides me. "Yes, Adrian," she moans, her teeth sinking into her bottom lip.

I'm lost in my fury. My worry. The bullshit surrounding us. I'm lost in her and Tuck's dilemma. The possibility of seeing my parents again. Of wanting Salvatore's head on a silver plate for harming the woman I intend to spend eternity with.

Letting go, I lose myself to it. The man I've become slaughtering the one I was.

My life has changed since pledging my loyalty to the Jameses, but I am not my best version. Not yet.

Get out of your head.

Ari's voice blares loud and clear in mine, drawing my gaze back to her face. Perspiration dots along the bridge of her nose and forehead. Mouth gaping open as she takes my punishment. Her tits are still in that simple bra, bouncing toward her chin as I drive into her. Only a pump or two from spilling out.

"You're mine," I growl.

"Shut up." Her smirk attempting to stay put as I grab hold of her other leg, dragging her naked body across the table so her ass nearly hangs off the end.

My pace never slows as I watch my dick sink into her stretched entrance over and over. The bulb of her clit is a delicious berry I want between my teeth, but later. We'll play later at her condo.

Leaning my weight on her, she fights against me. Her legs folded, and her knees pressed tight against her chest. That pussy squeezing me so tight I know she's on the verge of her release. So am I. My balls already drawing up, but I'm not done. I'm not ready to be done.

"Adrian," she breathes. Her hands reaching for me, settling for her shins.

"That's my girl. Take it." My lips suck at the exposed skin of her throat. The taste of salt from her sweat coating my tongue before I capture her mouth with mine. "You're mine to use. Mine to love. Mine to fuck. Ari, you are mine forever."

"Yes," she breathes.

There's no more holding back my orgasm as the first jet of cum shoots inside her. Her core clenching down on me, milking me dry while her release tears through her. Her blue eyes roll back as she tries to arch her body again. My weight pinning her beneath me.

"Adrian!" My name a growl on her lips before my teeth sink into the flesh of her thigh. The top row lengthens, becoming the sharpened points of my phoenix.

The skin breaks, the tang of her blood on my tongue.

"Fuck, Adrian. That hurts like a bitch." Pushing up as space allows, she attempts to look at the damage.

Yet, she doesn't understand what I've done.

"I told you, you're mine."

"So, you bit me?" She shoves at my chest, sitting up. Her legs keep me close to her, my semi-hard length still inside her. Those fluttering walls making me want to go again.

A tentative finger runs along the bite mark, her hiss only drawing out my grin.

"I marked you."

I hadn't intended to tell her. The bite of your phoenix pair will leave a mark. My tears will close the skin, but the scar will remain, a shimmer to it in the hue of my bloodline. My signature cobalt there, so everyone else will know she's mine.

"Well, why don't you just drop a bun in the oven while you're at." Her tone is sarcastic as she pulls me close, wiggling against me.

My dick not getting the memo that it wasn't an invitation to fuck her again. Yet, I can't help the flex of my hips into her. A low melodic rhythm forming as I move twice more.

"I'm working on it," I wink before pulling back and thrusting into her so hard the table legs groan.

Her smile is all I need to give her more of what she wants.

I guess we're making time for round two.

Fuck everyone else upstairs.

Thirty-Three

ARI

Adrian and I entered the War Room over an hour later. Though it is nothing to be ashamed of, it made me itch, knowing everyone could smell the sex on us. The way they treated us like mindless animals, looking down on us, affected me more than I thought it would. An emotion like shame or embarrassment flooding me.

Feelings I shouldn't have.

In a human relationship, this wouldn't happen. We wouldn't succumb to these uncontrollable urges at the most inopportune times.

Yet, it's normal in this world and still frowned upon. Which makes me believe it's not that we fucked down the hall, but yet another way they can hold Adrian and me at arm's length.

Shortly after, Lanham led me to the library. I'd perused through the old tomes while he did his fatherly duty of checking on me. Ensuring I'm alright. Giving me an opportunity to open up to him. I didn't have much to say. Rather, a million thoughts were flying through my mind.

Life had become so much more complicated since Salvatore handed me Adrian's profile and made him my next target. There are still so many things I don't know or understand. My mind constantly filled with questions and scenarios as I juggle my personal life, build relationships, and seek justice. An endless stream of *what ifs* partnered with every bit of new information.

"Has Adrian been good to you?"

The question startled me as my fingers roved over the tomes. So many titles with the history of our world right there at my fingertips. I need more time to read them all. Still, I couldn't find anything about reanimation, which was what I had been looking for.

I'd answered him truthfully. *"Dad, I know I said those things about Adrian before, but it's different now. He's a grump, but he's done nothing but protect me and try to help me figure all this out. We were a little... off until he was sure I understood what sealing the bond meant. Then, once we did, things changed. He does nothing but shower me with affection. So yeah, Dad, he's really good to me."*

My father's eyes had gone soft. Sadness coating them like I'd never seen. But he had to hear it all. *"With Adrian, I have hope for a family. Both the one I lost when I was separated from you and Mom, but also one of my own with a man who loves me."*

"We're not going anywhere," Dad said, placing a hand on my shoulder. Then he'd led me back out into the main house, Adrian and Mom joining him to walk us to the front door. Somehow it

seemed as though the tension he'd still held for Adrian had faded away. Like there was finally an acceptance of our pairing.

My father held me close, crushing me into a hug before we left for the night. His scent filling my nostrils now as I sit propped up in bed, flipping through the pages of dark spells.

Not ten minutes after climbing into bed, Adrian was fast asleep. Exhaustion wearing him down after an emotional day and those earth-shattering orgasms.

A heavy sigh escapes me, my neck rolling out. The ache building the longer I read through these pages. Adrian stirs. His arm draped over me, tightening. Head burrowing further into my belly as he releases a little snore.

To see him peaceful like this nearly destroys me.

There is no peace right now. Only war and destruction and betrayal.

There are too many against us. That's obvious. Still, there's a niggling at the nape of my neck. Pinpricks of uncertainty repeatedly poking me. I need to understand these links. A connection I don't want to consider because it truly is the worst-case scenario for us.

Isis's new information was enough for us to delay the interviews until tomorrow. I sense something isn't quite right with her. Should I find out she's hiding more from us, I don't care what Tucker tries to do to me. I will put a bullet through her skull.

I'll only act if I must. She's Tucker's pair. That much I'll respect.

"Why are you still awake?" Adrian grumbles into my stomach. The vibrations of the baritone of his voice tickling my skin.

"I'm trying to find more information about reanimation." A forced breath streams past my lips as my head falls back to the headboard.

"I'll tell you everything you want to know tomorrow. I'm an old man. Remember?" I can only chuckle, revisiting that moment in his kitchen and so many since when I've reminded him how much longer he's lived than I have.

He snatches the book from my grip, tossing it onto the nightstand. "Hey," I protest, "I'm pretty sure that book is old too, and it's not as durable as you."

"It's enforced with Lanham's magic. Nearly indestructible," he groans, yanking my body further under the covers alongside him.

See, that's what I mean. Books encased in magic are something new for me. I wonder if he does it for all his books or just the important ones needed for historical information.

Warm lips press against the bare skin of my lower belly. Just above the band of my panties. A wave of pleasure already rolling through me. It hasn't escaped my notice how often Adrian touches my stomach or runs his fingers along my lower belly. His secret hope plain as day. A gift I hope to give him someday.

He's barely touched me, but every single nerve sparks to life as the tip of his fingers sinks beneath the band. My body is ready for this man to do as he pleases.

I was always the dominant one in the bedroom. Telling men what I needed or wanted. They obliged, thinking they were getting a freak, but really, it was my need to control everything I could — or because they had no idea what they were doing with the rod between their legs.

With Adrian, it's different. He calls the play. He makes the rules. All I have to do is follow. The release on control easier to give than I would have thought.

"We should sleep," I moan.

His head firmly nestles between my thighs. The warmth of his breath makes me roll my pelvis up into his face. The flat of his tongue further dampening my panties. Those canines once again elongate, trailing up and down my seam before he moves down my thigh.

"I'm going to ask Tucker to teach me to shift the way he does."

That pulls Adrian up and over me, his face hovering inches over mine.

His teeth shrink back to their normal shape. All are perfectly even and white, except for two on the bottom row, slightly tilted. Resembling two leaning towers.

"No."

"No?" I sit up straighter, putting a little distance between us. I can't think straight when we're too close. Can't resist the pull of my body needing his.

"Yes. *No.* He's not teaching you."

"And that's your decision because?" My temper is rising. In bed, I have no problem with Adrian playing alpha, but in our everyday lives, I'm still me. Or rather getting back to the Ari I was. That fear that stifled me, knowing I wasn't completely invincible, slowly slipping away with time.

"I'll teach you." He places a wet kiss on my throat, my hand shoving him away.

"That's not what I asked you." Lips pressed into an unforgiving straight line. I keep my hand on his shoulder, holding him away from me. The muscles quivering with his soft pushback.

The pain is gone most days unless I really overexert myself in the gym, but my strength isn't quite what it used to be. Something I still need to work on.

"Tucker is not like…" He pauses, searching for the right words.

"Not like what?"

"You saw him in his basement. Ari, I'm sorry, but your brother can become a sadistic animal, and that's not you."

With a grunt, I shove him off me completely. Legs swinging over the edge of the bed, I'm stomping from the bedroom so quick he doesn't have a chance to stop me.

I need a minute. I need space.

He's not wrong about the man Tucker transformed into the day we were attacked. I suspected a hidden facet to his character. He couldn't possibly be sweet and innocent all the time. I'd seen that dark side flare behind his eyes at times. Watched him keep his control and remain the man we all see each day. The one that doesn't have to hide in a dermanium and cement basement.

No, it was what Adrian had called him and the way disgust flared behind his stare. The same intense gaze that many paranormals had fixed on me when I initially joined their ranks. Mistrust and hatred made obvious. Although Adrian loves Tucker like a brother, his disgust with that behavior lingers right below the surface.

If his sentiments toward Tucker haven't changed, it's safe to assume his feelings toward me haven't either. Stalking for the spare bedroom, I grab a pair of sweats from the closet before driving my bare feet into sneakers.

Snatching the keys off the kitchen island, I leave. Adrian howls my name down the hall behind me. I don't stop, and he doesn't run after me. Likely still butt-naked, so he can't.

It's been years since I've gone running. Years since I pounded the pavement to escape my own emotions. The bar and bourbon had long ago taken its spot, but now, past three a.m., the bars are closed.

I know my direction as my feet carry me toward the lake. Every step nearly cripples me. The pain starting in my chest and then knotting through my stomach, only to seep out into my lungs. Still, I press forward. I just need a few fucking minutes alone.

The scent of salt water wafts toward me the further I run. Every question spiraling at once. Their assault enough to distract me from my gasping breaths as I fight against the agony rolling through me, that tiny voice telling me I have to go back. I need to be near Adrian, or I might die from this.

What I need is to save everyone. A solution that continues to elude me.

The moment my feet hit the sand, I stop. I can barely stand. The urge to vomit or cry threatening to bring me to my knees, but I fight it. Tossing my sneakers aside, I allow my toes to sink into the sand.

My strength finally gives out, my knees colliding into the soft grains beneath me, my palms catching me before I face plant. Each panting breath only makes the daggers stab harder. *Fuck, how do people survive this?*

Pain lances at my side as I fall over, curling into a ball. The thrumming growing with each passing second. It's a searing burn, so intense I don't know there's someone behind me until a hand clasps over my mouth and around my waist, hauling me up from my position. I kick out, tossing back an elbow that collides with an eye socket. My attacker grunting but only tightening his hold on me as he tosses me into the back of an SUV.

The pain ricochets through me as I suck in breaths. I'm trying to compose myself when a voice I know well sounds next to me. His presence missed in the heat of it all.

"It's good to see you, my pet."

Thirty-Four

ADRIAN

Fury has me nearly tearing this place apart. I have no idea where Ari went. In the sixty seconds it took me to put on pants and shoes, she'd disappeared.

I checked the garage. Both cars were there, the doors locked and hoods cold.

She could only be on foot. With the pain already coursing through me, I was certain she hadn't gotten too far.

Yet when I reached the street, she was nowhere to be found.

Where are you?

The words sent out into the universe via my thoughts as if someone might answer.

Bolts of pain streak through me as I try to breathe. Few places operate this late. Locations I can't imagine Ari would run to, leaving me with an endless list of places she could be. I have no idea what set her off. Only that she felt betrayed by me. I might have been harsh regarding Tuck. However, I was honest. If anyone can handle the truth, it's Ari. My pair is never one to shy away from it. Rather, she embraces it. Craves it even.

My feet tangle as I weave for the garage. My SUV is entirely too far as I fight against the tearing of my insides. Ari must be miles away and getting further. Panting breaths fog my windshield as I rip out of the garage. At this rate, I'm likely to get myself killed or someone else.

"Please, please, please, Ari." My pleas heard by no one but the interior of my vehicle.

Ari has only used her telepathy a few times. Both instances unknowingly. And we were right next to each other. I'm not sure the extent of what she inherited. Harry — her grandfather — could communicate anywhere in the world with enough focus. His ability to home in on the single person he wanted to reach was unmatched. Addressing multiple listeners simultaneously required proximity. The only true limitation to his gift.

Another thought hits me. I've known Ari for almost a year. Yet her telepathy only just manifested with me. Why?

Shaking my spiraling thoughts free, I focus on the road ahead. The traffic is non-existent at this hour.

"Ari, where are you?" I growl to no one.

My knuckles are white and aching from my harsh grip on the steering wheel. But it's nothing compared to the pain writhing inside me.

Pain: I'm able to grit my teeth at it after years of torture at the hands of my family. I had to learn then that you breathe through the pain. You fight through it. You let it build you up instead of breaking you down.

I've been weaving through the streets, traveling further north for twenty minutes when a slight ebb allows me to breathe like normal. Hope draws my spine straighter. I'm getting closer.

"Baby, where are you?"

Instinct drives me forward. The turns and direction based on the pain lessening or increasing.

A whimper filters through my mind. One I know didn't come from me. Relief floods me. She's searching for me. For anyone who can help her.

I want to believe it's just her writhing in pain from the distance, but my emotions tell me something has happened to her. She's hurt or in trouble. We have so many enemies. Anyone could have found her in the dead of night, crippled by the pain. Hell, they probably watched her place, knowing mine was destroyed.

It'll be no secret to the paranormal world that their leader's daughter has bonded with her pair. It's worth celebrating and discussing, even though there hasn't been time for the expected bond-sealing ceremony.

It should take place within a month of locking in the bond. We are well past that mark. I've never asked or looked into it, but from what I know, it won't affect anything between us.

Lake Michigan churns to my right. The heavy waves crashing against the stones and rocks. She loves the water, so I believe she may have gone there on foot. Ari didn't even take her phone, so it's not like she called for a ride to come get her. Her wallet is still in her coat pocket, and Tuck's house is out of commission.

I follow the shoreline; the pain lessening with each passing moment.

Adrian.

My name a whisper in my head. Her voice. My pair calling out to me.

"I'm coming, baby."

Large homes tower around me as I continue north. The mansions are worth millions. The one Ari pointed out months ago when we drove this same path as her dream home, passing in a blur.

She'd told me how she loved her condo but loved space more, and when the time came, she'd buy herself a big house like this. It didn't matter that it would be just her. I already knew she was my pair and couldn't help but dive into her vision, imagining a life with her.

For her, it would be a place to bring her family together. A place to host guests should they ever decide to trust her.

That's when it hits me. The reason she ran. The way I spoke about Tuck and the disdain I'd carried in my tone. I bet that moment reminded her of when she joined us. How they'd all talked about her and to her the same. I spoke to her as if she were a bug to be squashed under my shoe.

I take a turn down a side street, and the pain suddenly stops. It just floats away as if it never existed.

Without even bothering to cut the engine, I jump out of the car. I'm spinning in every direction, trying to determine if there's any change. Searching for any sign of her. The street is quiet and dark, except for one house. A light shines toward the rear of the home. Shadows engulf every visible room from the front.

I creep along the side of the house, praying it doesn't have motion sensor lights. The grass is soft beneath my feet, allowing me to move in silence.

The rear of the house is nothing but windows. The soft glow I'd seen from the street coming from a large living room with a wall of French doors.

From behind the tree, the expansive lawn and much of the house are visible. Ari sits tall on the white sofa, a guard seated on either side of her. Likely werewolves judging from their size.

Her eyes are tracking someone I can't see. My position leaves me with a blind spot in the right corner. Creeping between the shadows, I'm able to gain the visual I need. My heart fucking stopping at the bastard stalking in front of her. Proud of my pair for not giving a single thing away with her expressions.

Ari doesn't move an inch. Her eyes tracking his pacing steps, giving nothing away.

She remains stoic. Nonplussed, as he gesticulates wildly with his hands. It's very unlike him, but I suppose he has heard of the shit going on outside of his killing spree.

Few cross my parents, and I would wager he won't either. Hell, I'm surprised those evil souls haven't teamed up *Pinky and the Brain* style to take over the world. I laugh the thought away. That would be the day.

A presence stalks up behind me. Their scent giving them away instead of their sound.

"My boss would like you inside." The deep voice vibrates through me. A voice I don't know. A face I've never seen as I turn toward the man behind me.

He grabs my biceps forcefully. I let him. If it gets me inside to the woman I can't live without, then fine.

He shoves me through a backdoor. The glass rattling as he slams it behind us. We don't enter the same room I'd been watching Ari sit in. However, the guard guides me there, taking us through the kitchen and then into a sitting room initially. Each decorated elegantly in white and gold.

"Ahh, Adrian. So nice of you to join us."

Ari's eyes go wide. Her fingers curling over the edge of the couch as she takes me in. Now she understands why the pain suddenly stopped. Why she could breathe again so easily. I'd watched how her breaths gradually came easier, all while her face remained unchanged.

I note her feet are bare. Her clothes rumpled. Something uncommon for her. Even when she dresses like a bum, she's put together.

"We were just discussing the terms of me returning your friend," Salvatore croons. Those long fingers steepled together as he continues to pace.

"What friend?" I growl, lurching forward. His guard still grips me tight, pulling me back. My body colliding with his hard chest.

"That traitorous consult the board sent here to dig into my business," he sneers. Spittle flies as anger morphs his features into something terrifying. "She was poking her nose into my business, and I couldn't have the little bitch learning my secrets."

I'm waiting for Ari to rage. But She doesn't. Her appearance unbothered as Salvatore goes off on his rant.

"You will release her." My tone stern.

Salvatore only throws his head back in hysterical laughter. His hands clapping together when his eyes find mine again.

"Your mate knows what needs to be done. You two may go."

The wolf-shifter shoves me forward, Ari immediately rising from her seat. She takes my hand, leading me through the house and out the front door. Angling straight for my SUV, still idling at the curb, she slips into the driver's seat, slamming the door.

"Are you going to tell me what the hell he was talking about?" I ask once I've settled into the passenger seat.

"Drop it." Icy bitterness coats her words as she swings the car in a tight arc, racing back toward the city.

I don't push. In time, I hope she'll let me in without having to pry, but there's no doubt she's rattled. It's there in the tremble of her hands as she grips the steering wheel at ten and two. The corners of her mouth twitching as if they can't decide to stay in a grim line or quirk down into a frown.

"Ari," I try again as she parks in the designated spot I bought for me.

"What, Adrian?" she snarls. "What do you want?"

I'm taken aback by her outburst. My body leaning away as if she'd physically struck me.

"I want to know what happened back there." The fight for my tone to remain under control is a losing battle.

"Right." She wipes a tear from under her eye. "You want me to recap how Salvatore wants his favorite assassin back and for me to deliver my parent's heads to him while I'm at it? Want me to go over how my sacrifice will save us all? Well, too bad. I'm not in the fucking mood."

Engine still running, the door slams as she stalks inside.

For the first time in a long time, I have absolutely no idea what to do.

Thirty-Five

Ari

Last night was an absolute shit show. The worst possible evening I could have asked for. Between the way Adrian looked at me — a representation of what he really thinks of me — and Salvatore popping up out of nowhere with his request, I'm drained.

It's been years since I last called out of work. This morning's alarm only annoyed me as I stared at the ceiling from the couch. Adrian insisted he sleep out here last night, but I simply plopped down, closed my eyes, and ignored him. His presence only lingered five minutes before he mumbled an apology.

He didn't sleep either. His large body heard tossing and turning in bed before pacing, then tossing and turning again. His every emotion coursing through me, battling with mine.

No, work wasn't a place I could be today. Surrounded by the failures of every unsolved case linked to Salvatore and the Alexanders. Forget the true human cases that still sat there, too. I wouldn't have been worth shit today.

Everything in my life is falling apart, and I feel helpless to stop it. There's nothing I can do to save the people I love, or the innocent, or even myself. I'm just the former assassin seeking revenge I don't know how to get without taking everyone down with me.

A deadly puzzle every part of me wants to solve. It's a matter of how to do that without endangering anyone else.

It took no convincing to get Adrian out of bed when I finally shoved my pity party aside at eight this morning. I've never been one to feel sorry for myself.

Lonely. Angry. Betrayed. Abandoned. Sure. But I have never felt a hint of pity for my life or circumstances. I wouldn't have survived this long had that been my mindset.

"I need to sweat," I'd told Adrian when he'd bolted upright, noticing me at the side of the bed.

That lust had burned in his emerald eyes. A flame that no doubt ignited in mine, too, but my mind wouldn't let him touch me. Not now. Not after last night. The bond can kiss my ass.

My body needed the grind of a ruthless workout. Blaring rap and hip hop music aiding in the pumping of blood through my veins with every rep. The immeasurable ache of my limbs quivering. Every muscle screaming for me to give up, only for me to push harder.

To push until the point of breaking.

The drive over to the safe house had been the initial reset I needed. Clarity finding me with answers to so much of this mess.

My plan fizzles and dies when I run head-on into Tucker the moment I turn into the basement.

"Have you seen Isis?"

He's running a hand through his short curls. The length longer than when I first met him. The texture gives him a more boyish appearance. A complete contrast to the demon I saw in the cell nestled at the lowest level of his home. I still wait for fear of my brother to come, but it never does.

Maybe it's because I know we're both monsters. There's no way to avoid the heinous things we have done and will do in the future. Whatever is needed to keep evil off our streets and our family safe. In that way, Tucker and I are the same. It was only me who had to follow a twisted path to get there.

Her name on his lips seizes my heart. My exhaled breath lodging in my throat. A cough bubbles free as my airflow cuts off. An invisible fist squeezing tight.

How do I tell him I know exactly where his pair is? That he won't find her until I commit the most unspeakable betrayal yet.

I know he has been fighting the inevitable between them. Fighting to hold tight to the relationship Talia has already told me she wishes he would let go of. He means the world to her; however, years of waiting for this moment prepared her. The preparation doesn't make it hurt any less, but the acceptance makes it easier to keep her distance.

They understood the probability of their relationship ending. It's just one of those things that catches you unprepared. An arrival that comes all too soon.

She wants him to let go, but not for her, for him. Because the longer he holds on, the more he will hurt himself.

"Tucker, I —"

The words won't come. How do I tell him one of our enemies has captured her? The very one I spent years serving with a smile on my face.

"Tell me," he growls, towering over me. My sweet brother disappears in the blink of an eye. The soft features of his face transforming into something dark and cruel.

"Tucker, I need you to listen to me."

In an instant, his hand latches around my throat. The strength of his grip forcing me backward into the wall. But I don't fight him. My heart breaks for the pain I've caused our family. The torment I am continuing to rain down on them for choices I made when I didn't know they still existed.

Adrian zooms into sight out of nowhere. His body colliding full force with Tucker's. My brother's grip not immediately loosening before falling, jerking my neck at an odd angle. A bolt of lightning shoots down the side of my neck into my left arm.

Dammit, will Salvatore's gunshot wound never stop haunting me?

My pair's colossal frame spears Tucker to the ground. Talons out, the two claw at each other. A frenzy of slashes and growls.

Two pairs defending their own. A battle that could turn deadly in the blink of an eye.

"Salvatore has her!" The words bellowed so loud I'm sure the entire house heard me.

My chest heaves up and down. Hands shoving Tucker off Adrian, examining my pair's cuts and the bruise forming on his cheek.

"I'm fine," he winces as he touches quivering fingers to a gash beneath his eye.

"What the fuck did you say?" Tucker's in my face again, fingers curled into fists at his sides. His entire body convulses. His gaze casting down to my neck where he'd held me before he takes half a step back.

"Put your hands on her again, and I will kill you." Adrian's tone is as flat as I've ever heard it. No inflection but a glare of death in his eye. I have no doubt he would tear Tucker limb from limb for hurting me, but he'll have to beat me to it.

This might be my fault, but I won't tolerate him constantly threatening me.

"Thanks, but I can speak up for myself."

Adrian only snarls my way, his upper lip twitching as it curls high. My focus returns to Tucker, chin angling upward to look him in the eye. "Salvatore took her. I don't know where she is, but I know how to get her back."

Hope shifts his features again. "Let's go then." He's already racing for the stairs, my hand gripping his shirt just before he's out of reach.

"It's not that simple. Go grab Mom and Dad. Meet us in the War Room."

He quickly departs, surprising me with how fast he is moving, his facial wounds already healing to appear days old.

Adrian's have too. Moisture coats his skin. His tears having transformed his face back to perfection in just the few seconds I've been looking at him.

"Ari."

"Adrian, stop. I need to figure this out. I'll give myself up, but not them."

Adrian steps into my space. Our chests brushing with our paced breaths. The warmth of his washing over my face when his thumb runs an arc over my cheek. "I can't let you do that."

"It's not your choice."

"Hey guys, what are you talking about?" Oliver's chipper tone cuts through our tension.

I hadn't noticed him approach.

His light gray cotton shirt sticks to the taut muscles of his chest and torso. I knew he liked to work out before dawn most days, but it's already almost ten. I figured I would have missed him by now.

"Nothing." Adrian's tone turns violent in Oliver's presence.

Dragging Adrian behind me, our fingers linked, I lead us toward the War Room. The last thing I need is him starting a second fight before I've even eaten today.

"Is there a meeting?" Oliver calls, following closely behind us.

Adrian quickly spins us in the opposite direction, Oliver barely stopping short of bulldozing us over. "No. I'm going to fuck my wife. You're not needed." I swear steam seeps from Adrian's ears and nostrils. Something I envision dragons doing, but from what I know, they don't exist.

Maybe I should ask about that later.

Oliver's hands shoot up. The defensive position meant to show he means no offense and doesn't want to intrude. Yet, I don't miss the quirk of his brow. The question soaring through his mind is likely the same as mine. When did I become Adrian's wife? Or is that term just synonymous with pair?

"My bad. I'll see you later, Ari." He throws me a wink before disappearing up the stairs just as Tucker and my parents shuffle down them.

Mom looks tired today. The large dark bags under her eyes are more pronounced than I have ever seen them. Her shoulders sag a little more forward instead of the tall posture she's always held since I met her.

I envision sole global governance having that effect. She'd gone months without my father there at her side. Maybe the wear and tear is just finally showing.

"Ari, sweetheart." She hugs me close.

"We need to talk. Now."

Dad leads the group into the War Room. Each of us settles into our usual seats, except Tucker. For the first time, he puts distance between us. The physical barrier of the seats and the glare in his eye confirms he may not forgive this.

"What's the meaning of this?" The husk of Lanham's voice is gravely. They must have still been asleep. My mom told me she and my dad had very different sleep schedules. One a night owl and the other a vibrant morning person. That saying "opposites attract" is so true for them.

"Salvatore took Isis," Tucker blurts. Our parents sit up ramrod straight in their chairs. Their glares narrowing at Tucker before shifting to me, then Adrian.

"And how do you know this?"

Tucker's eyes drift to mine, my swallow audible, shame washing over me.

"Because Salvatore took me last night and told me."

My father rises from his seat, ready to charge Adrian. "Where the hell were you?"

"Dad, please. I ran off. It's not Adrian's fault."

"It damn sure is if that bastard is the reason you went out on your own."

"Stop it. You will not speak about him that way." I'm surprised at the bite to my words speaking to my father the way I just did. Not once have I raised my voice to either of my parents since finding them again. For one, I haven't needed to, and second, they have given me nothing but respect and love since I found them. I expect them to do the same for Adrian.

Lanham's eyes go wide. His cut jaw working as he sneers at Adrian.

"You are my daughter," he growls. "I will talk to him however I see fit. It's his job to protect you. If he can't do that, he serves no purpose."

My father's eyes bore into mine as I, too, stand. "Dad, I will not repeat myself. You will show my pair respect. My actions are my own. I ran. Period."

The room remains silent as my father and I sink back into our chairs. Adrian's hand finding mine beneath the table.

This doesn't mean we're okay.

The words whispered in my mind. Words I know Adrian heard when he weaves his fingers through mine and squeezes.

"Where is she?" Mom asks. The stroke of her hand along my father's forearm is a reminder of their undying bond. Their love continuously grows. A reminder that love isn't always easy, but they support one another.

"I don't know," I admit. A deep breath forced out of me before I continue. "Salvatore has a price. Though I can only pay part of it."

The room goes silent again. A deafening, pregnant quiet that makes my insides churn. We all know the asking price without me having to voice it.

They all know I won't hesitate to sacrifice to save them.

I'd already spent all night awake, resigned to my acceptance that Salvatore had once again trapped me into being his puppet.

A single tear slips free.

I'm so sorry.

Thirty-Six

ADRIAN

I barely see Ari for a week. Well, as much as you can not see a mate that you can't physically stand to be more than a hundred feet from. We often returned to the safe house and then to her condo on the nights before her work shifts. The back and forth is proving to be more exhausting than I ever expected.

Though we were back to sleeping in the same bed, that was all there was between us. Sleep. A canyon's width of distance. We were practically back to our baseline from when we met. A time I won't go back to. I can't. Not when I'm in love with her and terrified she's going to go play the martyr.

The woman wouldn't even let me touch her. Forget that I'm aching for her. Our bodies calling to one another. The bond insists on the need to make love every moment of every day. But we've denied it. She'd denied me.

And suddenly I understand how she felt all those months I'd done the same to her. Only this is worse. This is agony. Torture for me and my bird in its purist form.

Despite my age, I surprisingly lacked understanding regarding pair bonding. With Syriah's help, I filled in the gaps in my knowledge. Things a mother would pass on to their children. Secrets of the universe meant to prepare you for your other half.

Each session reminds me that without Syriah and Lanham, I would not have had this.

Part of the strong desire for sex in the first year is to produce offspring. What I didn't know is that it's actually quite rare to get pregnant during that time. My hope that she already was crumbling to ash in my palms. Add in that Ari is only half phoenix, and we're at a loss. Half-species aren't super common, and since witches resemble humans in the functioning of their bodies, we don't know what to expect.

Not that it matters. Ari won't so much as let me kiss her. That beautiful mind wrapped up in turmoil. Her search for a solution evades her. It consumes her every breath.

I can't bear the thought of her sacrificing herself, because it's the only part of the equation she can solve. Over my dead body. There's no way I'm letting Salvatore get his hands on her again. He will have to slaughter me first.

The water cuts, signaling Ari's shower ending. I've been waiting out here in the hallway, pretending I can't feel her tears. She cries under the shower spray almost daily. Tears she thinks I don't know about.

Her steps falter as she catches me leaning against the doorframe. Legs crossed at the ankles and arms across my chest.

"Adrian, move."

"No."

"No?" Her head cocks back, brows high as if she's truly shocked I'm not doing as she told me to. The two of us barely listen to each other. Why would this be any different?

"Like I said," my face lowering so close to hers, my lips brush the soft skin of hers as I speak. "No."

Her hands move to shove at my chest, mine catching her around her wrists. My grip just solid enough that she can't break through it without a damn good fight.

"A few things are going to happen tonight."

She snarls. Her teeth bared as if I'm supposed to be threatened. I wish the woman would bite me. Mark me, the way I did her.

"First, you're going to let me feed you." I run my nose along her cheek. Her eyelids fluttering closed for the briefest of seconds. "Then you're going to let me fuck you until you forget everything but us." She sucks in a breath, inhaling my scent. "And then you'll let me help you come up with a plan that keeps you safe and the ones we love."

"Adrian," my name nothing more than a breath on her lips. The three syllables are like beautiful music to my ears. I don't think she's said it once all week.

"You're not arguing your way out of this." I tear the towel from around her, her naked body soft from the exfoliation scrub she insists on. "You'll do as I say for once."

Her pelvis curves into mine. Desire filling her stare for the first time in eight fucking days.

Gods, I've missed her.

I craved her like a drowning man sucking in that first precious inhale of air after surfacing.

"And what if I want your dick first?" Her hand clamps around the erection tenting my gray sweatpants. Her favorite ones I wore specifically for this moment.

"No."

"No?"

"No." I peck her cheek before striking the curve of her ass. "Food first. It'll be here in five."

Stripping out of my shirt, I signal for her to raise her arms before draping it over her.

"Adrian Alexander, you're a buzz kill."

"You'll get your buzz later. Don't I always make good on my promises?"

Ari throws me a withering look before stomping off to the living room and flinging herself onto the couch.

The moment she gets her hands on her food, she's back to ignoring me. Every moan of pleasure as she consumes her pad Thai and fried rice, another bolt of electricity straight to my dick. The fucker throbbing and ready to sink inside her heat.

Leaning forward in her seat, Ari points at my container. "Are you going to finish that?"

I only hand it over to her, knowing she's barely eaten in a week. I kept a catalog of it all. If only caffeine were a food group, she'd have been in business.

"Ugh, I'm so full," she groans, sinking into the couch cushions.

I climb over her, face hovering just above hers.

"Too full for this?" My pelvis rolls into her. My hardened length pressing against the naked flesh of her core. Her legs instinctually spread wide for me.

I should let her sleep. She needs the rest as much as me, but I need her too badly.

"Yes, but I want it anyway." She yanks my sweats down, taking me in her hand.

"Eager?"

"Very."

Without further pretense, she eases me into her. Back arching off the couch as I slip inside. The warmth of her has my eyes rolling back into my head.

There's no way to forget the feel of her, but I've missed it. Her noises and the way her walls squeeze me so tight. The press of her short nails into my lower back and the scrape of them along my scalp.

It's only been eight days without the feel of her, but it felt like ages. This right here, us, is perfection.

"Adrian, if you don't want me to fall asleep, perhaps you should get moving." Her body cranking up to mine, breath washing across my ear as she whispers to me. "Give me a reason not to give Salvatore what he wants."

His name on her lips while I'm inside her is enough to send me into a rage. My hips pump furiously as I slam into her. Her unbound tits shaking beneath my t-shirt. The nipples peaked for me to see.

Pressing both her knees into her chest, I drop my weight on her, our pace so hurried I know I won't last. Every bit of me destined to pour into her in minutes.

Gripping the back of her neck, I pull her closer to me.

"You're mine."

"Yes."

"You can't leave me." The words escaping as mumbled grunts as my thrusts become jerking movements.

A hiss escapes me with the clawing of her nails down my spine. Her walls clamping down around my cock, teeth biting into my forearm. The pressure is so great that she's close to breaking the skin. I hope she does. I want her to mark me the way I did her.

"Harder," I coach her. "Mark me."

And she does. Her teeth growing sharper, breaking the skin as her orgasm tears through her, milking mine from me in the next breath. The trickle of blood trailing down my skin, dripping onto my shirt, staining it.

My fingers trail over the spot on her thigh. The textured ridges of the imprint of my teeth forever part of her.

"Your reward for fucking me so good," a lazy grin spreads across her face as she comes down from the high of our joint orgasms. "Keep it up, and I'm yours forever."

"I'm serious, Arianya. You can't leave me. I... I won't —"

Her eyes shoot open at my use of her full name. One she didn't know she had until Nerissa. The explanation given by Syriah drew large tears from her as she realized she never got to live by it. Even now she flinches with its use as if I called her by another woman's name.

"You won't what?" she questions.

She waits for my answer. Scooting back so I slip free of her. The mixture of us dripping out onto the sofa and coating her inner thighs.

In my mind, Ari knows how I feel about her. I transformed from detesting everything about her except her face to being passionately in love with her, willing to go to any lengths for her.

"Move." She goes to shove me out of the way. Her annoyance distorting her features.

I hold her down, palm strategically placed against her sternum. "Ari, I'm —" Her brow furrows as she waits for me to finish. Her eyes search mine as if she can find the answers on her own. "Fuck." I look away before locking eyes with her again. "I am in love with you. Mine and my phoenix's hearts belong to you. Without you, we don't exist, so when I say you can't leave me, I mean it. Because without you, we don't have a reason to live."

Her breath hitches. The length of her frame going rigid beneath me, unsure how to respond.

Releasing her, I get up from the couch, ready to stalk away, when she catches my wrist.

"I love you too, Adrian, but that's what I need to do. It's what needs to be done."

Her subsequent words shatter the hope those four blessed ones had raised.

If I don't do something, my whole world is going to walk out that door.

And if she does, she may not make it home.

Thirty-Seven

ADRIAN

"Y ou're going to stop her, right?" Tuck's probing questions make me groan for the millionth time.

Since the day of our spat, we've made up. Our bromance restored for the sake of doing what's best for the family. He'd been the one who asked me to come train with him today. I really didn't want to do this sparring match at all.

Yet, it was a necessary evil. I needed alone time with him. Ari needed alone time with her parents.

Tuck has been an absolute mess since Isis was taken. Lashing out at us all. Starting fights if someone looks at him in a way he finds unacceptable. At the same time, he has tried his best to be caring toward Talia. Trying to reassure her they can still be close. Her eyes pleading with him to let her go.

We can all see it. He's the only one that seems to want to keep them together. No matter how he feels about her, she hasn't been spared his countless outbursts. The single time he shoved her brought him to his knees in regret. Except for the incident involving Ari and the captives, he has never harmed a woman.

So, his shoving away Talia's touch was how I knew we needed one-on-one time.

My best friend is cracking under the pressure of the cruelty he's facing. It's not something I can fix, but I can be there. Reciprocation for how he'd been there for me as I worked through the shit with Ari and Oliver.

"You need to let her go." My words a grunt as I block two rapid-fire punches thrown at my face.

Tuck dances away before throwing two more shots directed at my flank and temple. His quick shift to the side dividing my focus as he lowers himself as if ready to wrestle me to the ground.

"I can't."

"Then renounce the pairing. Break yourself away from Isis."

He deflates instantly. Hands dropping to his sides, chin to his chest. "I can't."

"Can't or won't?"

"Both." I think he's going to walk away. Tuck doesn't talk about feelings that way. He shuts down. "In truth. I want them both. Talia's held a special place in my heart for a long time. Even before we started dating, we had a connection. Remember that?" He huffs a sad laugh as I nod. "I can't imagine a life without her, but Isis... She literally sets my insides burning."

"Your sister did the same to me. You need to choose and quickly. Because as this war continues to rage, you're not going to help anyone if you haven't."

"But what if…" His words trail off, ass colliding with the grass. I sit next to him, legs extended in front of me. I'd much rather sit here and talk through this shit instead of sparring.

"What if?" The question is meant to encourage him to continue. He won't on his own if not pushed.

"What if she doesn't choose me?"

I don't have a good answer for that. I don't know what Isis feels for him. We've not had the time for personal conversations, nor has she willingly opened up to us about anything personal except her family's official status in Egypt.

"Well, brother," I clap a hand to his shoulder, "let's get her back, and then you two can talk about it. In the meantime, though, I think you should talk to Talia. Let her open up to you. But Tuck, you need to listen to what she's saying and respect it."

Sad eyes look back at me. So he has noticed the signals she's been giving off. My heart breaks a little for him. Ari and I aren't perfect, but we're perfect for each other. I hope everyone finds that even though I thought I never would.

I never thought I deserved it after everything I did under the direction of my parents. Maybe Tuck feels a bit of that, too, with the deeds he's done.

"Boys, inside," Lanham calls. The both of us jump up from our spots, dusting ourselves off as we jog back toward the house.

The crew gathers around the island, Oliver standing too close to Ari for my liking. I'm quick to slide up behind her, wrapping my arms around her middle. Our birds settling as I snuggle up close to her.

"Not in my presence," Lanham barks in my direction.

I swear the man loved me before I mated his daughter. I get it. He knew what I was like before she came back into the picture. He heard accounts from her, and I let her run off and get kidnapped. All of that is on me.

We'd only just made progress, and now that's evaporated away. All because I'm a fucking idiot. Because I couldn't see how expressing how truly bothered I was by Tuck's behavior might make her feel as though I felt the same way about her.

He may be her father, but I'm who she'll spend her life with. With that knowledge tucked away, the memory of her whispering "I love you" on my lips as I made love to her this morning radiates warmth through my chest.

I stay tucked in behind her. Her fingers flexing atop my forearms, as if daring her father to say something more. Lanham's eyes narrow on us, but he doesn't say another word. His nod is barely perceptible before his focus returns to the group.

Cornelius rounds the corner with several leaders on his heels. His white waist-length hair billowing out behind him as if he's some action hero moving in slow motion. Everything from his blue eyes to his chiseled form gives him the appearance of perfection.

A thick white brow rises as he passes me. His full lips pressing into a straighter line than they'd been in when he entered. The siren has been more and more scarce lately. A realization that hasn't been concerning. It's common to see less of their kind in the warmer months.

He unnerves the fuck out of me. Those of us who have practiced over the years can ignore the call of a siren's song, but few can resist his. Cornelius's power has always been exceptionally strong. Still, he refuses to advance up the paranormal hierarchy as long as I have been around. A quirk most brush aside, but one that sits like a boulder in the pit of my stomach.

He nods in my direction as he settles in next to Syriah. "They reanimated the Collymors. Our men spotted them entering an apartment building in Lake View two days ago. On appearance, they seemed completely normal. None of the usual characteristics the reanimated carry with them. Their neck wounds appeared healed as if they never existed."

Shuffles sound throughout the room. Fear and outrage ricochet through us all at the confirmation of exactly what we suspected. Isis's words were true. A truth none of us really wanted to believe or accept. Deep down, I knew.

I could feel it in my gut.

If my parents were part of it, there was no reason to question anything she said. The Alexanders disregard our laws. The governing bodies are more of a suggestion than mandatory if policy doesn't align with their vision. No desire to pretend as if they care what actually happens to the paranormal populations as long as the power they've stolen remains theirs.

I hate them. *No,* the word isn't strong enough to describe the disgust I feel for my family. If there wasn't an Ari, I would ensure my direct bloodline died with me. Their very existence makes my skin crawl. A mission rooted inside me to eradicate them from this earth.

Every emotion swirls through me. The tissues of my insides heating with my fury. Ari's squeeze against my forearms looped around her middle, pulling me back to the meeting at hand.

"So what do we do?" Emerson asks. The twins are now integral team members. Syriah's adopted boys, in a way.

Ari breaks my grasp, her mouth set in a firm line. Her breaths deep, swelling her chest before she speaks. Only she pauses, glancing over her shoulder at me. The apology in those midnight blue eyes confirmation I'd failed.

Every muscle tenses wanting to reach for her. My tongue moving in my mouth, wanting to form the words that will keep her away from sacrificing herself, but they won't come. I can't move.

There's no stopping that woman. If she hadn't heard me before, she won't hear me now.

Adrian, keep it together.

"I've kept this between myself, my parents, Tucker, and Adrian." Her palms flatten against the granite countertop. "Salvatore is still here locally. He has taken Isis and has given me his demands for her return."

"How does this relate to the reanimated corpses that bore the crest of Alexander?" Emile snivels. His expression is one of boredom. He has all the time in the world, yet this meeting seems to be a waste of it for him. His interest in our survival wanes with the low volume of vampire deaths. A curiosity we've noted.

Ari redirects her attention to his face. Her gaze narrowing at his interruption of her confession. "Isis not only came here at the direction of the Gorman Board but because there were rumors of reanimated paranormals in the UK. Each mutilated and marked in the same way. She came for our help."

Emile clicks his tongue, leaning forward from his spot against the wall. "It seems since you've arrived, there's been nothing but bloodshed and upheaval. Perhaps it is best you return to wherever you were hiding."

A deadly growl erupts up my chest. The tingle that accompanies my teeth elongating into that of my phoenix is more intense than I've ever felt. Ari's palm is firm against my stomach, the only reason I stay in place. The only reason my pulse slows enough the rest of my body doesn't shift into my massive bird.

"I would suggest you watch the accusations you decide to throw here, Emile." Lanham's voice low. He's an intimidating man with his barrel chest and deep voice on a normal day, but downright terrifying when you piss him off. Before Ari, I never feared him; Lanham respects those deserving. Emile truthfully never has.

"No, Lanham. Open your eyes. For all we know, we've put our blind trust in a daughter we haven't seen since near birth." His eyes shift to that icy blue. The hue they find with arousal and when they feed. "Have you forgotten how she strutted around for years, killing us without a second thought?"

"Emile, I will not warn you again."

Emile only stalks forward. His long, lanky limbs a stark contrast to the girth of Lanham. Their chests bumping when Emile stops. The two are nearly identical in height. Eye-to-eye, as a stream of flames stretches from Lanham's pointer finger at his side.

"Let me bite her. It will put all our minds at ease."

Syriah gasps. Her reactions are seldom so extreme, but he's asking for the unthinkable. Emile's request is unheard of. Leaders don't demand their superior's compliance with siphoning memories. We all have a method for it, but a bite could also turn lethal. Should Emile release his venom, Ari will die. Rebirth notwithstanding, that betrayal will cause more bloodshed.

My body moves on instinct. Our bond urging me to protect my pair, no matter the cost. Talons drawn, my arm draws back, ready to sever Emile's head from his shoulders.

"Adrian, stop," Ari commands, with such calm in her voice, I halt out of confusion. That same apology shines in her eyes before she turns her focus back to Emile. Chin rising a fraction higher, she swallows. "Do it."

Thirty-Eight

ARI

I'd watched Emile bite a traitor just months ago.

There had been defiance in his eyes. An unwillingness to show fear in the wake of his fate. He stood there stoically, accepting his fate of being useless after his secrets were extracted. Yet, he could hide the agony of those sharp points piercing his skin and those memories being sucked dry.

The last thing I need is someone else in my head, but if it earns their trust, it's a small price to pay. I hope none of them will follow me when I surrender to Salvatore. They can't. There's no way for me to protect them should they choose to play hero.

It's several hours sitting in pensive silence while Bronson calls in a witch he knows. Her nickname — Spoliare — is one of nightmares for our world. There aren't many in the U.S. like her anymore. A witch with the ability to temporarily strip paranormals of their gifts would be a threat. Many influential figures prioritize keeping control over gaining potential allies. Too many.

My parents insisted we bring her here to take away my fire. The pain that comes from the type of bite Emile will give me would likely have me combusting in seconds in an effort to protect my-self.

Despite our best efforts, my father and I have had little time to specifically work my fire magic. The tricks Bronson has taught me won't control it if I lose myself to pain, ecstasy, and the threat that comes with a siphoning vampire bite.

They already had weeks of having to tame it during my early stages of healing. Countless moments when I would burst into flames that either quickly simmered or burned for hours. From what Adrian told me, Bronson had to spell his room so I wouldn't burn the place down.

I've yet to tell my parents about the telepathy, nervous about what it might mean that I inherited his father's gift, but he didn't. The battle between deciding if it's a positive or a negative only ending in a frustrating headache. No matter how many times I've asked Adrian, he gives me nothing either.

Yet another tomorrow problem if we survive today.

"Where is she?" A raspy female voice carries from the foyer.

As if shocked, I shoot to my feet. As I smooth my hands down my thighs, the urge to make a positive impression on this woman fuels my actions. Spoliare can still decline despite my mother's influence.

Bronson leads an abnormally tall woman into the living room, where I've sat in silence with Adrian and the twins, waiting. The two having shifted into their wolf forms to sleep at my feet. Their warmth missed the moment I move away.

"Hi —" I pause, unsure what her real name is. Too nervous about using her nickname in case it's one only used behind her back.

"Take her to the room," she waves me off.

Adrian slips his fingers through mine just as my parents round the corner into the living area. Their voices hushed. Mom's brow furrowed.

Please don't let it be another murder.

"Come on," Bronson guides us out of the room. They lead me down to the basement, our trio weaving through the maze of hallways before stopping at a lone room in the northeast corner.

Only concrete lines the floors. The walls are nothing more than the wood framing you'd see during construction. There are no smells here. No warmth. Not even a speckle of dust.

Yet a solid plank of wood sits dead center in the room. Leather cuffs I can tell are flame retardant ready for my wrist, ankles and hips.

"Baby, you don't have to do this," Adrian whispers, swiping his thumb over my cheek.

Curling my fingers around his wrist, my eyelids press shut. The warmth of his breath across my face settling me somehow.

Yes, I do. How else will you finally trust me?

His lack of response confirms he understood. A message just for him. We never talked about the night I ran off. It wasn't worth tearing open those old wounds when we found ourselves again.

I know Adrian loves me more than life itself and part of me knows he doesn't truly feel disgust with me, though he might over the things I've done. So I let it go until now.

I'm strapped to a solid board. First my ankles and then my wrists. Each strap secured tight enough to bite into my skin, but I give nothing away. My focus stays straight ahead as the last buckle slips into place, crushing my ass against the flat surface. The pinch of the buckle against my bare skin ignored.

I refuse to give an inch more than relinquishing my memories to Emile.

Thick sweat drips down my temples, soaking into the thin cotton of my V-neck T-shirt.

Though my heart races, I fight to keep my breathing even. A controlled in and out to give the appearance of calm. Inside, my bird screams. My flames are as much of me as she is. They do not want to be parted.

Only Bronson and Adrian remain. Tension keeps me coiled tight against the restraints, waiting for what seems like a lifetime. The soft patter of Spoliare's steps as she enters the room, stealing my attention while my pulse bounds at my throat. Her expression is just as disinterested as the moment she met me. Lips so thin they nearly blend with her face. The two pits of hell serving as her eyes, alarmingly captivating. As if those black pools are pulling you in to their depths with the intent you never see light again.

Adrian moves into my field of view, palms pressing against my cheeks, his mouth brushing mine for a brief second. "If you want to stop, say the word. I will stop it all."

"No. I need them to trust me, so I'll do this. For my family. For us." The last bit whispered so low I hope he heard it. I hope he knows I meant it.

Hoping I don't lose my life for it, I call out to the witch. "Spoliare, I'm ready." She quirks the tiniest of grins. The corner of her mouth barely tipped as she steps forward.

That raspy quality of her voice washes over me. The words bleeding together as if they are one continuous stream of letters and sounds. "This will hurt."

My breaths go heavy as Spoliare raises her palms on either side of my face. Their movement slow before the press against my temples.

Thousands of burning serrated knives rip through me all at once. Back bowing off the slat, the leather of the cuffs dig into my bare skin. Warm rivulets of my blood already run over my fingers. My curling fists so tight my nails break the skin.

If it was possible to experience knee-buckling, blood-curdling agony worse than my last death, it's this. A million poison-dipped, curved claws stabbed through me, ripping my fire from within. The warmth I always feel drifting from me to her.

Willing my eyes open, my screams continue to thunder in my ears. Adrian's tears, bluer than I've seen them, stream down his face while my father cradles my mother at his side. Their mouths tremble, but they hold strong. Whether it's for me or to save face, it's exactly what I need to see.

Spoliare's expression remains unchanged since I first saw her. The only sign this is taxing on her is the slight squint of her right eye, where a single drop of sweat settles.

My body convulses as the endless pieces of me are forcefully torn away by invisible hands. My fire fighting to stay put. The tugs suddenly less harsh, my body no longer jerks.

There are only pulsing beats inside me now. My consciousness sensing the last bits of my fire magic leaving my body. A now cold and half-empty vessel. My bird screeches loudly within. Its protest only felt by Adrian and me.

Eyes drifting closed, I mourn the loss of that part of me. Those flames that I've always counted on no longer linger just below the surface. They're just gone as if they never were.

Just as the pain subsides, a new one strikes at my throat. Sharp fangs puncture my flesh as I cry out. The suctioning of my blood sucked out through those two little holes. Strong hands on my shoulders pin down my back. The pressure unforgiving as I'm forced to hold still against the board.

This experience is nothing but novel sensations. The sharp pain is there, but there's also this sense of weightlessness. As if releasing my every memory to this vampire is making me light as a feather. As if I'm nothing more than particles floating through space.

Then my bird roars again. Each pull sends bolts of lightning funneling back to the forefront of my mind. Every sharp crack harder to withstand than the previous.

Gritting my teeth, my eyes find Adrian's. His gaze hasn't left me once, those full lips moving the entire time. Perhaps in prayer, possibly with nerves.

"I'm okay," I mouth to him, the tension allowing him to breathe again.

Then it's over. Those sharp points retract from my flesh, my lungs filling with precious air.

When my eyes open again, they meet the stares of everyone who had been around the island alongside us upstairs. Each waiting for confirmation from Emile.

Had they all been here throughout my torment?

Emile strides out from behind me, hands clasping around my father's, with a nod. Then he holds my mother's, her eyes never leaving my face.

"My friends. My leaders, I am sorry for what I've said. Your daughter, though she has done wrong to our kind, operates with the purest of hearts. Her goal is the same as ours. We stand behind her. We stand with you."

As one, the room takes a knee. My parent's chins held high as their subjects bow before them. A sight I never expected to witness. Each individual rises moments later, turning to face me, just to sink to that same knee. A gesture I don't understand for me.

Fatigue works its way through me. My head lolling to the side.

"Give it back." My tongue sticks to the roof of my mouth. Its cavern suddenly dry with thick cotton.

"You need time to rest," Spoliare replies, turning her back to me.

"No. Don't you dare walk away from me." My groaned words hold no bite. I don't give a fuck if I offended her. I need my fire magic back right now.

A softer version of those black pits meet mine. "Ari, you can't do that again right now. Your heart could stop."

"I am a phoenix." My voice grows stronger. My determination, steadfast. I want my fire back, and I want it now.

"You are half a phoenix," Adrian's voice carries from behind Spoliare's rail-thin frame.

"I am a phoenix and I am your future leader. You will return my flames now."

"As you wish." Spoliare dips her head in a bow before her hands clap against my temples.

That same pain returns. Only worse this time as my body reforms into the composition it was before. Reintegrating the flames into my being.

Open-mouthed breaths leave me as she removes her palms.

"You may be half witch, half phoenix, but Arianya James, you are much, much more."

Spoliare's last words seem to echo through the room before she aims for the door once more.

"What is your name?" I croak.

"Giannetta." Then she's gone.

Generous gift.

How fitting that hers is to rob those of what's theirs.

Thirty-Nine

Ari

The deepest sleep pulled me under its soft caress the moment Adrian unstrapped me from that unforgiving slab of wood.

There's no recollection of him carrying me upstairs, bathing me, or dressing me in pajamas before tucking me into our bed.

I woke this morning to an empty bed, but the pain of distance wasn't there. My bird purring calmly as if he were right there.

Paced, huffing breaths sound from the floor, my torso leaning over the side to see Adrian drenched in sweat on his back. Arms out to the side, he crunches high, every individual block of his abs contracting before he slowly lowers himself back to the floor. Every rep more enticing than the last. The reason for my phoenix's happiness gloriously revealed.

Hands tucked under my chin, I can only watch. His eyes remain closed, but a smirk forms the moment I settle in.

"You could stand to work out more," he chuckles.

"Rude."

He suddenly sits up straight, perspiration coating his face and broad chest. "Ready to talk about it?" he asks.

"I don't think you really want to talk about this."

A conversation so far avoided thanks to my exhaustion yesterday. But today I'm out of excuses. There's no more stalling, and I hate keeping anything from my mate. Even if it's in all our best interests that I do.

Calling to my flames, I focus. A small tendril dances around my fingers. Working with various warlocks, I learned to control them enough to create a flicker at will. The stream floats between my fingers, staying close to the skin between each digit. Adrian's eyes tracking its continuous path.

"No. I don't want to talk about it." My eyes cast away before finding his again. He only continues speaking, unbothered. "But I need to know how many heart attacks you're going to give me with your recklessness, and how many dead bodies will be at my feet because of it."

I flinch away from his words, my focus lost, and the flames soaring high. It only takes seconds to bring them back under control. The stream longer, snaking around my wrist.

"I'm walking in there alone. None of you can come with me. I won't give him my parents."

"Ari, I can't let you sacrifice yourself."

Sadness swells in my chest. Juggling between the old and new versions of Ari has proven to be more difficult than I ever imagined. "It's not your choice."

"But isn't it? We don't exist without one another. Hell, we still can't be apart."

"I think I have a plan for that."

His eyes go dark, jaw working furiously. I can only imagine he knows what I'm thinking. What they will all be thinking once this plan comes to light. Or at least the portions I plan to tell them.

Salvatore has fucked with my family for too long. Has fucked with me. I'm done. I won't allow it anymore.

That warlock declared war with his ask. He asked for endless bloodshed when he took Isis. He brought in someone who isn't part of this. I can only assume he knows Isis and Tucker are pairs. Salvatore was aware of us, so why not them?

We never figured out who has been selling our secrets to Salvatore. Yet, there never seems to be enough time. The interviews produced few insights. The inability to find our mole is a luxury we can't afford.

Perhaps Emile should have interrogated them. Maybe I should have ordered him to drain every secret. An ask that's against our principles. We value trust here. Trust I've been trying so hard to build. Instituting a mandate like that would destroy it.

It only now occurs to me that Salvatore asked for me and my parents to die. He never mentioned Tucker.

"Adrian, why wouldn't Salvatore want Tucker too? Dead or captive?"

His eyes drill into mine, slightly widening before drifting shut. "Because as long as you're alive, you are the rightful replacement for your parents. With them dead, you are the leader of all the paranormals. For their position, it's a role inherited, not elected."

Fuck.

"But could Tucker be elected as our new leader should we die?"

Adrian only shakes his head. "No. The firstborn must inherit the leadership role, or a new bloodline takes over. That's how it has been since establishing the different councils."

Why hadn't I thought of this sooner?

I should have guessed that was the reason Salvatore came for me. Should have known his relief at seeing me alive and making his demands was because of my birthright. A responsibility I don't want.

So many shoulda, woulda, couldas, and not a single one helps us.

I've been in this world for almost a year now, and even though I haven't confessed to my family, I don't agree with our structure. Our methods for determining who is fit to lead seems outdated. It only brings about turmoil to have the phoenixes rule over all. We may all be paranormals, but the system no longer makes sense in the modern age. A single council, representing every species, should legislate and enforce laws.

It's as if we never left the stone age, with the ridiculous levels of separation and the power struggles they've caused.

Holding Salvatore and the Alexanders accountable remains a priority. But not like this. Not at the expense of innocent lives.

"What are you thinking about?"

"Hmm." I hadn't realized I had retreated so far into my head. "Nothing."

"Lie to me again."

"I will," I admit. "Let's go get a workout in."

He only nods, jumping up from the floor before yanking me from bed.

The gym downstairs is fortunately empty. Our inner circle either knows we're in here and chooses not to enter or staggers their times around not being here midday.

Although the pain from my gunshot wound has completely disappeared, my strength has not returned to what it was. My left upper body strength is no match for the right. No matter how I've worked it, it's as if my body refuses to go back to what it was. As if I need to repeatedly be tormented by Salvatore's actions. The sounds of his bullet flying down the barrel, through the air and into my flesh forever haunt my dreams.

Jumping for the pull-up bar, my muscles on the left side ache. My biceps and shoulders quivering with the strength needed just to hold myself there. Tears prickle behind my eyes. The strong woman I used to be fading away right before me.

With a grunt, I attempt to pull myself up. The quivering quickly turning to a violent shake. My teeth gritted so tightly that pain radiates through my jaw.

In an instant, Adrian steps in front of me, wiping away my single tear before launching himself onto the bar. I expect it to bow under both of our weights, but it holds firm.

"Wrap your legs around me."

I do as he says. Our bodies pressed together, core to torso. He quirks that dirty grin as if he knows where my thoughts are sure to drift off.

Readjusting his grip, his eyes find mine. "We pull up together." I nod. "On three," he grins. "One. Two. Three."

I pull.

My muscles protest, yet I finally clear the bar. A first since the incident. Adrian's peck to the tip of my nose the cutest thing I've ever witnessed.

"You'll get one of those for every pull-up you do."

We release and pull again. Over and over. His lips meeting the tip of my nose each time. His strength bleeding straight into me. I know it's nothing more than a figment of my imagination. I'm not suddenly stronger after fifteen pull-ups, but I feel a little more myself.

We drop in unison, Adrian chugging water. "That's how we'll work bar exercises until you can manage on your own."

I'm not the lovey type, but my arms go around his middle, pulling him close to me. All I desire is to strip him naked and fuck him on the foam mat beneath our feet. But more so, he should understand the depth with which his kind gesture touched me.

For that words won't cut it. Not when I'm about to break his heart.

Forty

ADRIAN

Time passes faster than the speed of light when all you want is for it to slow down.

By day, I'm a fake FBI agent at work with Ari. At night, we head to the safe house, typically after a stop at her condo, where I try to keep hold of the woman slipping away from me.

Where we once thrived on a primal fuck, I now make love to her. Maybe as a plea for her to stay, maybe because I want to take my time stretching out our moments together. Those few minutes alone with her, before she turns back into the badass woman who will do as she pleases, seem to pass too quickly.

Between the influx of paranormals we've allowed into the safe house and Tuck's ruthless anger and worry, it's a wonder the place is still standing. He does his best to pretend that not knowing where Isis is holds no significance beyond her role in our community, but those of us in relationships understand the pain of witnessing a loved one suffer repeatedly.

It's been almost a month. Too much time for Salvatore to have kept Isis alive, yet Tuck says he can feel her. He knows she's still living through their bond. A fact that gives him as much solace as it does inner turmoil. Just knowing she still breathes isn't enough to combat the horrid thoughts of imagining what torture she might be enduring. *"I'm a monster too, Adrian. That's how I know,"* he'd whispered to me nights ago.

No matter how much I wanted to assure him he wasn't, I couldn't. We're all monsters in our own way.

Bronson and Talia have become a ruthless pair. Their ability to plan for any and every scenario to ensure Ari's safety makes my head spin. Yet, nothing will help me accept that my other half is throwing herself to the wolves to protect us all.

Then there are the novel weapons the twins have continued developing. They're goofy little pups, but they are geniuses with chemistry and physics. We'll each be strapped to the nines for the rest of our lives. Tuck asked them to craft specialty daggers for Isis so that when she gets back, she'll have her own custom weapons. An ask he'd wanted to be kept quiet, but those two talked so damn loud the entire house heard them agree.

We pretend he isn't making plans for her return. We hope we get her back, but none of us can be so sure. Salvatore is as unpredictable as my parents are.

Ari is more grouchy than normal. Her interviews were a complete failure when it came to determining who might be our enemy. Nevertheless, she does not meet anyone's gaze with the same suspicion they directed at her.

My temper hasn't been great either. It was only days after I assisted Ari with her pull-ups that Oliver started showing up during our workout times. Or when we were outdoors working on her shifting control. Apparently, Lanham ordered it. I call bullshit, but I'm not questioning Lanham right now. He's wound so tight I fear he'll explode any minute. He nearly blew a gasket when Ari revealed the intricate details of her plan.

She's been working on her magical gifts as well. Apparently, she has a lot more than we thought. The flames. The telepathy. Not to mention regenerative abilities. A lesser version of reanimation. Ari has more power and versatility than a single paranormal should. Despite the bigger target on her back, she sees herself as the one who can end Salvatore and my family.

In Ari's mind, only she possesses that kind of power.

I say it's the guilt driving that flawed thinking.

We'd all known she would be powerful. Her bloodlines are a mind-blowing combination, but the regeneration abilities shook us to our cores. Streams of nervous butterflies soared through my insides as I watched her run her hand over the wing of a bird that was on its way to death. The bird had released two sad chirps while Ari whispered imperceptible words, its third chirp that of renewal, but its movements were off. Robotic and rigid. The eyes, previously full of life, turned into dark marbles. Little black pits of hell.

It broke her heart to do it, but she snapped its neck. The crack impossibly loud in the clearing's silence in the woods. Burying it with a tiny tombstone at the rear of one of the flower gardens brought out the soft side she rarely shows anyone. *"It was a bird, too,"* she'd whispered to me before standing tall. *"I'll never knowingly use that gift again. It's not right. We're not gods."*

We have one more night before the plan goes into motion. Just a couple of brief hours before Ari acts as our martyr, with all of us standing behind her.

Salvatore has reached out to her on several occasions, never venturing to actually kidnap her again. My guess is they didn't want to wage an actual war before they were ready. Likely, they don't want one at all. Their flawed thinking convincing them Ari will come quietly and Syriah and Lanham will hand themselves over to keep their daughter safe.

Smart move on their part because if they had taken her again, I don't care what the consequences would have been. I would have slaughtered every single human and paranormal that stands with Salvatore.

Hopefully, I get to do that anyway. All of us are champing at the bit when it comes to destroying the entity that's working so hard to destroy us. It's time to bring down those who move against paranormal structure and tradition. And when I'm done with Salvatore and his scum, my family will be next.

The Alexanders have been eerily quiet. No more visits from my brother. No more dead bodies with the family crest or mutilated torsos.

It's unnerving. An unsettling twisting of my gut with every passing moment while I wait for whatever their grand plan is or whatever shoe will drop because of them. My worst fear is having them on one side and Salvatore on the other. Their followers lined up in two semicircles, closing in as they surround us.

They'll leave us with no escape.

Though so many have pledged their allegiance to us, those pinpricks of doubt still creep in. Their proclaimed commitment to good and justice remains unproven. Only their future actions will validate those claims.

Should we seem to be losing, some will run away in fear. A choice of opportunity over loyalty. The need for survival will drive them to jump, and for that, they'll die alongside every traitor.

I can't blame them. A different life might have led me to a similar choice. Anything to ensure I was safe from my family's slaughter, but lucky for me, I would have run in the same direction. To Syriah and Lanham, who have done nothing but protect our kind.

Ari locked herself in the bathroom hours ago.

We'd ventured out to one of our more rural safe houses this morning. One we don't frequent often. But the closest to the meeting point for Ari and Salvatore. His request for her to come alone was pointless. He must understand that's impossible. Bond or not.

I'm so lost in thought I barely hear the door creak open as she exits, wrapped in a towel.

Nothing seems off about her as she perches on the edge of the bed. The midnight blue comforter darkening just a shade from the water droplets still coating her skin.

She's beautiful like this. Her hair is even longer, loose in wet waves. The heat from her shower flushing her skin as if we just fucked for hours. Yet there's an emptiness to her stare. One that has been growing these past few days. Her mind whirring as we draw nearer to the inevitable.

Our plan to free Isis is nearly ironclad. Of course, things could go wrong. This is war. Perfection doesn't exist; things either go according to plan or go awry.

Crawling across the bed, I slide up behind my pair. My hands roaming over the bare skin of her arms as I inhale the scent of her. The moment her head falls back to my shoulder, I release a heavy sigh.

"Am I going to have to ask for it?" A sly grin crests her lips. Her eyes pressed shut as my palm snakes around her throat, not bothering to squeeze before sliding down between her breasts. The towel falls open, revealing her damp skin to me. My insides tingling, recognizing her arousal. Reveling in the quickening of her breath as her shoulder blades push against my chest.

"Never."

A single fang sinks into the shell of her ear, a hiss slithering past her clenched teeth.

"Make it count."

The words give me pause. My mind immediately latching onto the feel of her pumping heart. Ari hasn't once expressed hesitation in what is coming. Not until those words. A cryptic statement most might think is just our usual banter, but reveals the fear she had kept hidden.

Her acceptance of the reality that she may never come back home to me.

Salvatore wants two things: power and the killing machine he thinks he made.

He wants her.

My love.

My heart.

My pair.

My life.

Pushing against her emotions, I flood her with mine. Lust and love.

Fireworks shoot off inside me as my fingertips part the lips between her legs. Two fingers sinking into her core, only to groan when her walls clamp down on me.

A purr radiates from her chest, hands reaching back to sink into my hair before grabbing hold.

"You. Are. Mine." My canines elongate further, nipping at her ear. The tip of her tongue darting out to wet her lips as her head of waves rolls against my shoulder, eyelids fluttering shut.

I won't waste this moment with tenderness or kind fondling.

I want to ravage my woman tonight. Abandon all we are to our last moments of peace.

Her hips rotate in tight, controlled circles as my fingers plunge in and out of her. Her arousal soaking them and my palm. "Adrian." My name on her lips, a plea. A finality to it, as if she doesn't expect to ever call out to me again.

She has to come back to me. I can't accept another outcome.

Snaking an arm around her waist, I pull her flush against me. Her bare ass cradled against the bulging hard-on between my legs. Pulling my fingers free of her nearly breaks me. My mind taunting me into believing I won't get another chance to.

Another sigh escapes me as I push my sweats just past my erection, feeling her skin against mine. The feel of her settling over me and riling me up all at once. A vortex of mixed emotions swirling through me, and I can no longer wait to have her.

Her nails dig into my thighs, my teeth raking up the side of her neck.

With another tug, I have her lined up so my thick head presses against her entrance. Those greedy depths ready to suck me into her. Her walls pulse as she sinks down onto my length, heels digging into the mattress with her first bounce.

"Adrian, I need you," she moans. Her words concealing deeper meanings.

But I say nothing. I can't because if I do, I might fall apart. So I take her. Hard and fast. Every punishing thrust and clap of flesh a bit more of my emotion unleashed. Hopes that she's allowing herself to feel them instead of blocking them out, only making my movements more uncontrolled.

We're caught in a frenzy. My growls shake the walls of the room, and her cries are loud enough I'm sure the dead in Timbuktu surely heard them. We're usually quiet at the safe houses. Mindful of those around us and her parents being within the same walls.

Ari has always kept herself reserved around them. That is until her bird rages to defend me when Lanham reminds me he wouldn't have picked me for his daughter. It's as if she reverts to being a teenager who knows she shouldn't be having sex under her parent's roof.

Taut nipples pebble further under my fingertips. My pinches harder than necessary. My loss of control is long gone as our flesh slaps loudly. Our skin dripping sweat as her back slides against my chest.

"Fuck, Adrian."

"Do it. Now."

Her orgasm rips through her at my command. My dick erupting only seconds after she does, filling her to the brim. Filling her with what might be the last chance for our future.

The perfect mix of us, just the way it should be.

She immediately starts moving again, my semi-rigid cock slowly swelling back into a stiff rod inside her.

"Baby, you're going to kill me," I groan just as knuckles crack against our door.

My temper instantly rages. These last moments with Ari are precious, and someone has the nerve to fucking interrupt it.

"What the fuck do you want?" I snarl. The grind of Ari's hips against me doing little to settle the sharp edge of my tone.

"We need her," Oliver practically whines, closing the door behind him.

I keep my back to him, my muscles aching from the exertion of controlling my anger. His voice grating on me. The motherfucker has some audacity walking in here like months ago he wasn't trying to steal Ari from me. As if until we sealed the bond, he still wasn't trying.

"Get the fuck out," I bark.

"Oh, sorry, didn't realize you were, yah know." He sounds so apologetic. As if he didn't just hear our releases moments ago. There's no way everyone on the property didn't hear it. The smell of sex is so potent in the air that even a congested human could detect it.

"I won't say it again," my voice low. The warning meant to be a threat rather than an ask.

"Ari, we need you downstairs."

"Uh-huh," she groans, her movements never stopping. The clap of our skin vibrating off the walls with her panting breaths and whimpers.

A heavy sigh releases before the door clicks open and then shuts again. The moment we're alone, she moves to face me, immediately impaling herself back on my dick. Her arms cradle around my neck, hands cupping the back of my head. Everything I've been feeling since she told us about her plan, shining in her eyes. Those navy blue pools are like a mirror to mine.

"They can wait ten more minutes," she smirks before crashing our mouths together.

They wait an hour, give or take.

Forty-One

Ari

It was impossible to sleep last night. Adrian's warmth curled around me, only put me further on edge. A continuous reminder of everything I have to lose that sent my head spinning. The inevitability of the hours to come keeping me awake.

We've all clung to as much optimism as we could muster.

Isis is alive. What shape she's in is unknown and will surely dictate Tucker's response. A response I'm not sure I am prepared to witness up close again.

I may have to play captive for some time to appease Salvatore. Embody a role to get him to believe I will stand beside him once more. Anything to save my family from death. A final life they won't rise from this time.

In truth, I don't believe it. It will take so much more than me pledging allegiance to Salvatore. He will demand blood. He will demand debts I'm not sure I can actually pay. Lives, I don't think I have the heart to take anymore.

Adrian is prepared to stay hidden in the shadows. He needs to believe I am keeping cognizant of the bond and our intolerance for distance.

A problem I've already solved on my own. That omission part of the reasons I've kept my distance. I hate lying to him. Hate lying to anyone here when I've worked so hard to earn their trust. Trust with finite limits I will push when they find out the whole truth.

Only Gia — Spoliare insisted I call her that — and Bronson know. I didn't even have the heart to tell my parents. My scheme risks causing as much harm as it could benefit us. It may not even work, but Gia is willing to try.

She'd heard my pleas. My dilemma brought about a softness to those sharp eyes of hers. A depth within them made me believe she once lost someone important and didn't want the same for me. Someone she'd devoted her life to.

Just this once, her loss allowed her to agree to tap into magic she should not be touching.

Darkness cloaks the pre-dawn sky outside my bedroom window. Idle strokes of my fingers through Adrian's lengthening hair, allowing me to lose myself to my every thought.

Finally, tired of stewing in my own head, I untangle my limbs from him, slipping into the adjoining bathroom. I've literally never seen so many homes that all have en suite bathrooms. It's insane but quite convenient, too.

The lights burn my eyes as I flick them on. The haunted stare I've been wearing for weeks once again greets me in the mirror. I almost don't recognize who I've become. Not just physically but internally, too. Emotionally and mentally, it's as if I am a completely different human being — phoenix-witch.

The long strands of my waves fall from my fingers as I lift them off my bare skin. Waves that used to never brush my shoulders now curl around the bottom of my last ribs. I don't know this woman anymore.

If I am going to do this, I can't be the woman staring back at me. To save everyone, I must find the Ari I once was. The one who couldn't find remorse if someone pointed it out to her. The one who wore a grimace and a stony glare. Along the way, I found my compassion when I found my family. I found the guilt and a softness I had thrown away a long time ago when I learned I truly was different. Back when I thought I was a unique creature in this world.

I yank open drawer after drawer, my movements measured and slow so as not to wake Adrian. My search for the one tool that will help me find the assassin I used to be is nowhere to be found. My frustration and resolve climbing to new heights, in unison, until I pull open the last drawer at the bottom of the Jack-and-Jill cabinets.

A large pair of onyx black scissors glare at me.

It's as if I am watching myself as I snatch them from the bottom drawer. The thick metal seems heavy in my hands. A conundrum I can't quite figure out.

Only when my gaze meets my reflection again do I gather my thick hair in my fist. The ponytail held at the center of the back of my head. It sways a few times before it settles still. Those long, luscious locks glare back, almost daring me to revert to the woman I worked hard to prove I wasn't.

Then I cut.

Three sharp snips right against the big donut of my hand, one following the next.

Every strand floats to the floor at my feet. So similar to the dark cloud that has been chasing us.

Ari Luxembohrg stares back at me and grins. The corner of my mouth twitches high before I glance down at months and months worth of growth. The long strands reminding me of how helpless I had become after Salvatore attempted to take my life. That woman is gone.

The angles of my face instantly sharpen. That dark gleam I hadn't seen in a year falling back into place.

"There you are," I croon to the woman staring back at me.

It's only after that I confidently return to the bedroom, prepared to do what needs to be done.

It's hours of me staring out at the fields beyond the rear of the house. It seems to be an endless wash of land and trees. Vast enough, it will hopefully hide the battle that may ensue tonight should anything go wrong. Eradicating the evil we are up against is both uncertain and inevitable.

Adrian groans behind me, followed by that long sigh he does when he wakes. "You cut your hair?"

A lump forms in my throat as he slides up behind me, his arms wrapping around my middle. *I'm sorry, Adrian.*

"I cut away my weakness."

It's my truth. One I'm sure he'll come to understand in time. One I hope he forgives me for when I do what needs to be done tonight. When I risk it all for us.

"Get dressed," I say, attempting to pull out of his grasp.

I need to meet with Bronson.

Adrian's kiss on my cheek is tentative. Something unheard of for him. He can sense it. The shift in the air. The shift in me. A storm that's brewing. A plan he's not been aware of is moments from coming to fruition, and he didn't know.

Thankfully, he doesn't ask, quickly dressing before following me down to the cellar. Gia and Bronson are already sitting at the card table in the center of the room. Both with their hands folded atop the surface in front of them. Bronson's expression is as bleak as they come, while Gia only wears her blank stare.

"Adrian." My hand to his chest, eyes boring into his. "Go check on Tucker, why don't you? I saw him out back." His brow furrows. "You'll be close enough."

Driving to my tiptoes in my bare feet, I place a quick kiss on his mouth. Reassuring enough to send him stomping up the cellar steps, throwing open the doors before snapping them shut.

"Okay, let's do this. I don't think he'll stay away long."

Gia nods, holding out her hand. "Did you bring it?" I hand her the chain locket. The one my father gave me, claiming its ability to harness magic for some time, made it special.

She takes it, handling it gently, as she twists it up to the light, examining it for herself.

The chain instantly lengthens. The links thickening under the invisible spell Gia has cast. "There. That should be better suited to fit around his neck."

I nod, following her and Bronson into a hidden room at the rear of the cellar. The slab of cement only moving aside when Bronson's palm settles against the center. A groan of rocks dislodging echoing through the space.

That same slab of wood rests at the center of the room. The straps waiting to be clasped around me. My spine shudders as memories from last time flash through my mind. It's like reliving the agony and pain all over again.

They are quick to buckle me in. The leather biting into my bare flesh.

"Are you sure about this? It will be much worse than losing your fire, and there's no guarantee it will work."

"Do it." I grit my teeth, leaning my head back against the hard surface.

You don't have a choice, Ari.

The world goes completely still. Utter quiet suffocating me before shooting pain barrels into my chest. My eyes bolt open to be sure Gia wasn't our betrayer puncturing my heart with another of Salvatore's bullets.

But no, this sensation is unique.

That bullet burned while eating away at my flesh. This is like having my heart and soul ripped from me. Stripping away each tissue layer in tiny chunks. Each one separating all at once. A torturous prolonging of the pain while it crescendos to new heights.

Cries of agony shoot up my throat, the tissues going raw from my screams. I feel him there. His presence. His being. Our birds bound and then forcefully torn apart seconds later.

The locket glows in Gia's hands before she steps away from me. A stunning violet nearly blinding in its vibrancy.

I'm so lost in the beauty of that neon glow before me I'm not ready when the pain ricochets higher. This is much worse. The pain doesn't stop. It doesn't fade. It only intensifies.

"Did it work?" Bronson breathes, unbuckling the straps, catching me as I slump into his arms.

"I'm afraid it did," Gia frowns, handing me the locket. "As long as he wears it, he won't know."

I nod, fighting to catch my breath while my body mourns the loss.

I'm so sorry, Adrian.

Forty-Two

Ari

Night arrives too soon. The signal to put our plans into motion. Our caravan of cars headed toward the location Salvatore gave me.

Only Adrian will enter the property alongside me. I made it clear I wanted everyone else to stay back. It didn't matter how strong or what type of soldier you were; I wanted minimal casualties tonight.

Adrian won't enter the house. His promise to keep to the shadows of the exterior was a compromise I barely got him to agree to. For him, we still can't be apart. My deception glinting in the moonlight against his skin.

That same confusion marred his face when I handed it to him earlier. His large fingers held the chain delicately as if one sudden movement would destroy it.

I'd held his hands in mine, waiting for his gaze to find my face. *"This is my promise to you. I will make it back home to you tonight. Just please wear this for me."*

The shudder of his breath told me he wanted to believe my words as he slipped the chain over his head. But his eyes told a different story. Those emerald green diamonds dulled by his overwhelming worry and sadness. Emotions I could no longer feel.

Where I'm dressed for a battle straight out of a fantasy novel — black leather pants, heeled booties, a fitted tank, and a leather jacket — he's clad in everyday jeans, a henley, and sneakers. Funny, I run faster in heels than I do in a pair of comfortable shoes. *Figures.*

We don't speak as I pull onto the long gravel drive of the farmhouse Salvatore instructed me to meet him at. The all white siding glints in the moonlight the same as Adrian's necklace. Lights shine bright in every window and the full wrap-around porch of the lower level. Their glow cutting through the blanket of darkness that comes with rural properties like this.

A howl sounds in the distance. The wolf-shifters are ready for whatever fight this night might bring. Their posts scattered throughout the woods along the edge of the property.

I can only hope it's not one of the twins. No matter how much I begged, they refused to stay back in the city.

For me, they're just another two people I love to worry about.

"If we're old enough to design your weapons that kill, then we're old enough to fight with you." Normally, Elijah is the logical one, but those words came from Emerson. The goofy wolf cub I've grown rather fond of.

It may have been my mother who took them in as her own, but somehow, they became mine, too. I have to keep them safe. Protecting those boys and parents with their own children at home is my priority.

Gomez is out there too. He and his wife are ready to defend their peace. I didn't even bother trying to convince him to stay behind. It wasn't going to happen. If anyone is more stubborn than Raphael and me, it's his wife, Imora. I don't want to be around when she turns into a wolf and tears out an opponent's throat. A shiver runs down my spine just envisioning it.

"Let me go in with you. It's okay to be scared. Just let me —"

"Adrian, no. Risking me is enough."

His mouth presses into a hard line, eyes darkening as he stares me down. Please let this charm work, otherwise he'll know I managed this situation without talking to him.

One day I'll tell him the truth, but today isn't that day.

Large palms grip the sides of my face, turning me to face him. His mouth on mine seconds later, hungry and needy. A kiss that says see you soon. Conveying all fears and love we share.

"I love you, Ariyana James... soon to be Arianya Alexander." Only he could make me laugh at a time like this.

Just before they took Isis, we had discussed the meaning of being a pair. The expectations. Our desires for what we want outside of the relationship beyond our bond obligations. Unlike many paranormals and humans, marriage isn't a necessity for phoenixes. He thought it was important to blend the human life

I grew up in with the one we live in now. Not to mention, it helps us blend better if we adopt human practices.

His real reasoning, he wanted me bound to him in every way. Doing so through a human marriage is yet another thread bonding us. *"I hope you know this isn't my actual proposal,"* he'd chuckled, tucking me into his broad chest.

It was a good enough one for me if it was. I spent years believing I'd never find a partner like Adrian. Convinced myself that type of happiness wasn't meant for someone like me.

"Go. I'll see you soon." Words I don't believe but force from my lips just the same. He slips from the car, blending in with the shadows. My eyes trailing his movements before I exit onto the dirt drive myself.

The dirt is hard beneath my boots. Each small rock kicked, interrupting the hushed sway of the treetops. That eerie feeling from horror movies washing over me.

It's too calm.

Too quiet.

Too empty.

The wooden steps creak under my weight as I make my way to the front door. Still, the trees provide the only sounds and movement. Inside, quiet reigns. My breath held deep in my lungs until I'm sure. Inhaling one more deep breath, I call Salvatore. Just the old Ari following orders, as expected.

He answers after a single ring. "Let yourself in." Then the line goes dead.

The hinges groan as I ease the door open. An immaculate mix of farm style with a modern twist makes the space more inviting. Salvatore's influence is evident in the decor, furniture placement, and lighting. There's not a part of this place he hasn't touched. A confirmation he owns our rendezvous point.

Home advantage. Let's play.

There's not a single sound coming from anywhere in the house, only the soft click of my heels on the wooden floorboards.

"Hello," I call. A waste. I know in my gut Salvatore isn't here. A scenario we planned for.

But I also know the place isn't empty. My bird can sense someone else here with us. Not Adrian. Not the others. So who?

Fear coils in my gut. Maybe he asked me here as a distraction while he makes his move against my family. Against every other paranormal who supports and loves us. Only he'll lose his shit when he doesn't find them where he expects them to be.

Unless he does.

Lucia said there was a traitor amongst us. Yet she never told us who. Our interviews failed to reveal the answer. Our lack of answers led us to believe Lucia was only trying to rustle our feathers, and maybe Johnny was the only betrayer I knew.

Still, a tickle niggled at the nape of my neck. My gaze raked over every person as if under a microscope. Adrian was the only one free of my scrutiny. Yet no one else, not even my parents, was free of my watchful eye. Every reaction, daily routine, and interaction was analyzed over and over.

There were a few I suspected, but convinced myself I was wrong. My instincts failed me, or maybe I was too sex-drunk to make that accusation. It made no difference. My concerns extended beyond potential leaks. We were past the point of containing our secrets. Another reason for keeping so many of my own.

It's empty.

The words thrown out into the ether, hoping they reach Adrian.

I'm safe.

I make my way through the rooms, one by one. Each is immaculately clean. The lack of dust indicates recent cleaning or recent inhabitation. Upon entering the sunroom at the back, I find someone. A back ramrod straight against the cushions of the couch, his rear facing me.

A head of hair I could identify in my sleep staring back at me.

"What are you doing here?" Panic swells in my chest. I'd looked for Oliver among those in our caravan. He was nowhere to be found. No one had seen him all day.

I'd ignored it. Told myself there was so much movement today. With so many coming and going everywhere, we simply hadn't been paying attention.

His head rolls on his shoulders as I round the sofa. His hands and ankles bound, dark bruising surrounding his right eye. *Shit.*

"Oliver. Hey! Can you hear me?" My words are sharp as I shake him at his shoulder. His eyes flutter open. The swollen one, unfocused. "I'm going to get you out of here."

In seconds, I pull the knife from inside my boot, cutting free the ropes at his ankles and wrists. The sawing noises mingling with my ragged breaths. Why would Salvatore take Oliver? Sure, he's an officer, but not the highest ranking. His position doesn't compare to Isis.

There are dozens of others easier to snatch and worth more. Unless...

I push the thoughts away as I dip under his arm to help him stand. "Come on," I grunt, struggling to support his weight. Oliver isn't nearly the size of Adrian, but damn is he heavy when he's nothing more than dead weight.

"You should have picked me." The words whispered before I'm thrown to the ground.

He towers over me, menace in his stare. Those thick brows rising with his growing grin.

"What the fuck?" I roar, scooting back, the chair keeping me from jumping to my feet.

"Ari, you are too trusting. You were so blinded by fucking Adrian you never saw me. The moment he told you that you had a pair, you forgot about me. Our friendship and bond meant nothing to you."

"Oliver..."

"I'm not done." He's leaning close to me. Our noses only inches apart. "Then you were shot, and I took my hurt and used it in a different way. I chose the winning side."

Anger rages inside me, my flames itching to break free from my fingertips.

He's the one. He betrayed us all. For what? Promises Salvatore likely made him.

I died. The daughter of our leaders proved to not be invincible. His cue to switch sides.

How had I not seen it? His constant lurking since I'd recovered. Sudden appearances in places I was, even if it seemed odd. How he'd weaseled himself into our covert groups time and time again.

I'd ignored it all. Thought it was nothing more than him trying to be part of the team. To make use of his training. I thought his snarky remarks to Adrian, intended to provoke him, were merely the actions of a jealous man.

It's what we all thought. It's why Tucker finally stepped in and warned him away if it had nothing to do with business. We all feared Adrian would do something he couldn't take back otherwise. Actions no one with a mate of their own would ever fault him for.

Let my pair tear him to shreds while I watch. I don't give a fuck about a traitor.

Oliver straightens to his full height, extending a hand to me. I take it hesitantly, jumping back to my feet. "We need to go."

"Fuck you. I'm not going anywhere with you."

"You will if you want Isis back... alive," he smirks.

Instinct takes over, my movements smooth as my fist drives into his throat. Oliver rears back, clutching his windpipe that's surely damaged now. Each gasp for air only drawing out my own wolfish grin.

Wide eyes meet mine. As he stumbles away from me, his long fingers curl around his throat, before stalking my way once more. I let him tackle me to the ground, allowing him to believe he has the upper hand. His uncontrolled anger and mortification driving his actions instead of logic.

Enough time for me to claw my gun from my hip, pressing the muzzle to the center of his forehead.

"Take me to her or I'll put a bullet through your skull."

"Oh, Ari. You've discovered compassion now. You won't shoot. Not me."

"Try me, asshole."

He's unaware of who stands in front of him now. Assassin Ari mixed with the new, more violent version set on defending her family. The moment I'd chopped my hair off, the ruthless assassin came rushing back to the surface. This time, she was determined to protect those she cherished, no matter the cost.

Oliver has no idea what type of monster I am now.

The worst kind. The kind with everything to lose, but doesn't give a fuck if she loses herself in the process. A version that lives for others will risk it all, including themselves.

He presses his forehead into the gun. "Do it."

A challenge.

A dare.

He's not ready as I move the gun at the last minute. His mouth shifting from a grin to a wide groan as the bullet rips through his side. Not a regular bullet, but an upgraded version of what Salvatore had designed. The twins are genius.

Black veins immediately start creeping up his throat as liquid dermanium courses through his body. He leaps back from me, clutching his side. Eyes wide.

"You bitch."

"The worst kind," I smirk before I pull the trigger for a second time.

This one dead center of his forehead, his eyes rolling back the second it drives through his flesh and bone. His body stiff as a board as it falls backward.

I'm not even remotely sorry.

Forty-Three

ADRIAN

My phone buzzes in my back pocket. The incessant vibration pulling me out of my focus.

Hordes of our men and women stretch around the perimeter of the property. Tuck serving as one of the leaders tonight. Their positions taken just before sunset. Only a handful of us, including Ari and me, had orders to leave after dark.

Tuck and his crew assigned themselves to the northeast of the property. One of the most likely exit points should someone actually be here and attempt an escape. No way we were letting anyone get away. Not with Isis and Ari's lives on the line.

Tucker: How's our favorite assassin?

Me: Alive.

Me: Quiet out there?

Tucker: Could hear a pin drop.

I only snort to myself, tucking my phone back in my pocket. Normally, we wouldn't be worried about constant communication, but Syriah insisted on it tonight. There's too much on the line.

My mind wanders to the conversation I'd had with Tuck this morning. Turns out he'd been as surprised to see me as I was that Ari sent me out to talk to him. We knew it was some sort of setup. Our fearless detective enacting a portion of her plan that only she would know the details of until it was too late.

Tuck whispered to me while we sat in the grass at the back of the safe house, *"She's so much more like me than I would have expected. Too similar for me to ignore."*

"There's nothing wrong with either of you." Words I meant and that I'd hoped he would believe.

"She told me what you said."

"Tuck—" I was prepared to plead my case. The kid had become the best friend I'd ever had. A brother I wish the gods had given me instead of my own.

"No, Adrian. It's okay. I'm glad we have that cold-hearted side of us. We're going to need it to win this."

My fingers toy with the necklace she'd insisted I wore. An heirloom from Lanham's line. One I hadn't expected him to release to Ari. The metal has been warm since she handed it to me. A soft violet glow to it, as if working hard to contain whatever magic lives inside.

Absently running my fingers over the chain. My gaze drifts back up to the house. I'd gotten a glimpse of Ari about twenty minutes ago as she crept through the space. Although I heard her say it was empty, she has not come out yet.

Hugging the edge of the house, I make my way toward the back. There are more windows there. A chance to get a glimpse of what might be holding her up. If the place is empty, we need to get the hell out of here before we're ambushed. What other reason would Salvatore have her come to an empty residence?

It's something I wouldn't put past Salvatore to have set her up. He must have known I would be here. We can't be apart. He knows the laws of bonding to a pair.

A pit settles at the base of my stomach. Sweat breaking out across my brow when I still don't see Ari through the rear windows.

Where the hell are you?

The words sent out through my mind as if her telepathy works both ways. It doesn't. Hell, it's a miracle we found out she had the ability at all. Had she been in my head before, and I chalked it up to fantasies, not realizing I was actually hearing her voice?

No. That's not possible, I tell myself.

Keeping low, I'm about to peer through the next window when the soft thud of paws over grass sounds behind me. Spinning, gun in hand, before I face my visitor, a wolf-shifter charges toward me. One of ours, I realize, lowering my gun but not returning it to the band of my jeans.

In an instant, she shifts. Her naked form standing tall before me. One of our younger soldiers. A girl who lost her family in a hostile territory takeover. Her thick Louisiana accent cuts through the silence and her panting breaths.

"There's an attack. Emerson told me to run and tell you."

"Casualties?"

"I don't know. I ran as soon as the werewolves appeared."

"You're sure they're werewolves?"

She nods, sucking in a sharp breath.

"Is Tuck safe?"

"I don't know. He was shifting when I ran."

"You did good." I place a hand on her shoulder, waiting for her to look up at me. "I need you to go check the other posts. Stay hidden. Come back as soon as you've got a good look."

"Sir, what if..."

"You don't have time to think like that. Go."

She only nods before stepping back from me, her bone snapping and popping as she morphs back into her wolf form. A large solid black creature with piercing crystal blue eyes.

Fear clenches around my heart. That didn't sound as if we encountered escapees. We were set up, and I am going to kill that motherfucker.

I've waited long enough for Ari to come out. As I move back towards the front of the house, a distinct gunshot pierces the stillness of the night. The crack sending my pulse skyrocketing.

My heart hammers in my chest. I wait to hear someone cry out. But there's nothing before a second shot booms from inside the house, and I take off running.

My arms and legs pump as I round the side of the house, halting as I hit the corner.

Sucking in a deep breath, I keep to the shadows. My back remains pressed against the cool siding. My gaze darting right then left before listening for any sounds that aren't me. If Ari wasn't the one who discharged that gun, I don't know who the fuck did.

The same guard I'd first encountered still lies limp on the ground. I'm not above killing our enemies. If it's between murdering someone else and keeping Ari and our people alive, I won't hesitate. Still, there will be enough bloodshed in this war, so if I can avoid it, I will. Regardless, he cannot escape those special cuffs designed by the twins. The pulsing metal laced with dermanium weakening his beastly strength and ability to heal. Cleanup crews will find him where I left him later tonight.

It's been at least a half hour of silence since those gunshots. No one has come or gone. No movement that I've seen within the house.

Every passing minute ratchets my heart higher. I can still feel Ari, so I know she is alive. There's no pain or overwhelming emotions, so she should be okay. *Please let her be okay.*

Then there's the wolf-shifter. She hasn't returned either.

Fuck tonight.

Fuck Salvatore.

My fingers curl around the locket. The tighter I hold it, the closer Ari feels. As if her heartbeat is right here in my palm. Each thump a pulse against my trembling hand.

A series of clicks sounds in the distance. A signal from the vampires hovering nearby. With one last glance back at the house, I jog off into the trees. Willow, a young vampire, steps out from the shadows.

"We have movement. Several SUVs moving away from here. They drove out of an underground tunnel at the edge of the treeline. The windows are tinted, so we couldn't see who was in the vehicles."

I nod, that same panic creeping up into my chest.

"Did a wolf-shifter come through here?"

"No... who?"

"Nevermind. Good work," I nod again, willing my breathing to slow.

Only then do I realize how far I've traveled from the house.

Too far to feel no pain. There's nothing at all. Just that same warm metal against my chest.

Yet, it still feels as though Ari is right next to me. As if I have her cradled in my arms.

Something isn't right.

A growl rumbles up through my body, vibrating the tissues in my throat. "Follow them." She nods, signaling to the several wolf-shifters who had been lurking in the shadows. Racing ahead, she leads the wolves on a chase into the night. Vampire speed is seriously no joke.

Testing the theory that just ran through my head, I remove the locket.

My knees instantly buckle, crashing into the dirt at my feet. A pain so intense shooting through me I can barely breathe. My fist burrowing into the dirt barely keeps me from face-planting. Every gasping breath driving me closer to blacking out.

I struggle to replace the locket. My hand shaking as I drop it over my head.

The moment it touches my skin, the calm finds me again. Gulping down air, I climb back to my feet. A fresh source of anger and fear rushing through me.

"Dammit, Ari, what have you done?"

Forty-Four

ADRIAN

I can't run back fast enough. My legs won't move at the speed I wish them to.

There's no way I can shift. The density of the trees is too thick to accommodate my size or allow me to take flight.

The closer I get to the house, the more the scent of smoke fills my nostrils. The pungent odor only making me push that much harder, that much faster. Knowing the locket somehow made me believe I could feel Ari, I can't be sure she's fine at all.

Just as I clear the treeline the house comes back into view. Despite the distance, there's no denying the place will burn to the ground. Angry flames licking at the roof and out of each window heating the night.

Even from this distance, I see her. But I keep running toward her, while I watch her form stalk through the flames as if it's nothing. As if she feels nothing. Her palms turned upward, either supplying an ongoing source or relishing in the feel of the whipping flames on her skin.

Her grimace holds. That slightly pointed chin high as she stalks down the steps, flames licking up her arms. Her clothes remain completely intact. *Motherfucker the twins did it.* They'd promised her flame-retardant clothing, and they did it.

She doesn't notice me running toward her. Doesn't stop as she touches her hand to the hood of the car, the one we'd driven here. In seconds, it explodes in a thunderous roar, drawing me back.

A trail of flames follows her down the drive.

It's as if she's in a trance. Her focus remains trained ahead, that expression on her face refusing to falter.

Though I'm still running, somehow, her stalking walk keeps us apart. And suddenly, all her time with Gia made sense. It hits me. Ari never thought she was coming home to me. Not ever.

"Come out. Come out," she calls into the dark.

I have no idea who she is calling out to. Who she thinks is here watching and waiting.

"Don't be shy now," she taunts, flames now covering the strands of her hair. Those waves I love so much dancing with hues of orange and yellow.

Then she stops. Her flames retreating. The structure of the home behind her crumbling chunk by chunk. The car still blazing bright.

"That was expensive, you know." That voice. Salvatore's voice. His tall frame steps out of the shadows of a grove of trees. An immaculate suit draped over his lithe body as if we're not on a fucking farm.

"If I allow you to live, you can build another."

"Allow me. My dear, I own you," he snickers, adjusting his lapels.

I watch her step closer. My focus immediately shifting to other shadows crowding at his back. Hundreds of them. Their shapes are those of humans, but no faces or true forms to them. It's too dark to see who they are from here.

> **Me: Front of the house. Halfway down the drive.**

The text sent out to everyone hiding through the woods. My beacon for reinforcements.

Only when our supporters surround us do I move forward again, stopping only a few feet behind Ari. The warmth of the flames now trapped beneath her skin only boosting my temperature higher.

Slowly, those faces hidden by the shadows step forward, too. Their features coming into focus.

The battle in the woods has left many bruised and bloodied. These faces belong to the survivors. The traitors who took lives from us.

The urge to tear them all to shreds has my hands shaking at my sides.

Then the faces I haven't seen in over a hundred years come into view. My breath stolen as my mother and father step up to Salvatore's right and my brothers to his left. Kenji, a wolfish grin on his face, is last to join the line, his hands in his designer slacks.

His eyes rove over my torn shirt and elongating talons. "I warned you, brother."

"Ah yes, Mr. Alexander, it's been some time since you've seen your family, hasn't it?" Salvatore mocks.

Ari only takes a step closer, smacking her tongue against her teeth. "You don't talk to him. You talk to me."

My mother steps forward, Ari's arm rising with her gun in hand. Months ago, she could barely hold her arm steady, and now it's unmovable.

My little assassin.

"Stay where you are."

"Oh, well, this is a surprise," my mother's raspy voice coos. The lilt of her voice, a sound I thought I had long forgotten. Maybe my mind did, but my body didn't. My limbs wanting to curl in on themselves against it. "My son has a pair. An important one too. I'm so happy I could confirm this for myself."

She takes several steps forward, Ari erupting into flames instantly. Their heat forcing me back several steps. She might be immune, but I'm not.

"Oh, this is delightful." My mother claps her hands together as a vicious grin splits her face. "That baby will serve us well."

"Ba — Baby?" I stutter. I'm confused. What is this woman talking about?

I move to charge her. It's my chance to end this. Tonight. Right now.

My birth around Ari is wide enough that her flames won't hit me. Tonight the Alexander line dies. Once and for all, I will rid the world of them.

"Tsk. Tsk. Adrian. It would be a shame for your little one to never meet his or her father, don't you think?" My mother's words stop me in my tracks.

Every ounce of my blood runs cold, Ari's flames dying as she stares at me in terror.

She's pregnant?

A single tear slips free of Ari's eye. The apology there in her galaxies of midnight blue and silver.

Then my pair turns away from me and fires.

THANK YOU FOR
READING!
YOUR NEXT READ IS
JUST A PAGE AWAY...

Also by Britton Brinkley

<u>Misfits Trilogy (with L.A. Scott)</u>

Misunderstood

Misfortune

Accepted

<u>Night Life Duology</u>

Night Life

Night Life 2: Will to Fight

<u>The Company Series</u>

The Tournament

The Target (COMING 2025)

<u>Disavowed Birthright Trilogy</u>

Rise of the Grisym

Dimmer of the Light (COMING 2025)

Fall of the Phoenix Trilogy

Feathers of Truth

Feathers of Destruction

Feathers of Change (COMING 2025)

Standalones

Scarlet Hearts (COMING 2-14-25)

About the Author

Britton Brinkley was born in New Jersey and now lives in Northern Virginia.

Growing up an avid reader, the sciences and ancient civilizations mesmerized her. She has always loved immersing herself in new worlds. Britton now enjoys creating her own with her writing buddies Jay Gatsby and the little psycho Artemis Prime (the cats).

When she isn't writing, she's likely either reading, watching Criminal Minds, or some other true crime show on Investigation Discovery.

Learn More at BrittonBrinkley.com